NH CS RC Mr

Gravity Girl

Everybody gets what
they deserve. Amen.

A novel by
Tarin Elbert

Copyright © 2022 Tarin Elbert

All rights reserved

Published by Blue Alien Books

Second Edition

ISBN 9798444506783

Cover design and concept by JP Govay

AUTHOR'S NOTES

This work is dedicated to
everyone seeking answers
as to why we are here,
and where we are going.

My thanks to Jim Reyno, Tina Costanza and
Evan Gogou for their contributions to this work.

I love hearing from readers.
Drop me a line at:
gravitygirlauthor@gmail.com

Check out my other sci-fi thriller,
Day of the Bluebirds:
Everybody wants to rule the world

Dedicated to my Three Pillars:
Maria, Chantelle and Sylvee

"The only reason for time is so that everything doesn't happen at once."

Ray Cummings,
The Girl in the Golden Atom,
first published in 1919

Somewhere in time …

"The reports indicate this species not only kills its own kind, they also eat the flesh," said Salvatore Five.

"Cannibals," the other five Salvatores cried out.

"As the Guardians of sentient life, we must intervene."

"Yet, these life forms believe they are *intelligent* beings," said Salvatore One. "All the more reason to be vigilant."

"Which brings us to the purpose of this assembly," said Salvatore Six. "We have been informed that Mother, who created the species she carelessly christened the 'wise ones,' had ulterior motives."

"Yes, we know Mother's work," said Salvatore Three. "She has been successful in seeding the Cosmos with sentient life. Clearly, this project ranks as Mother's most egregious failure.

"What are these 'ulterior motives' you speak of?"

Salvatore Five and Salvatore Six merged voices to explain: "In our capacity as members of the Imperitus Council, we have spoken in secret with Mother's partner, Xeno. He showed us proof Mother has developed an unsettling affection for these creatures."

"I want to know more about Mother's ulterior motives," said Salvatore Four. "Why should we be concerned?"

"Xeno insists Mother's judgement has been compromised," said Salvatore Six. "She refuses to admit failure.

"He also told us Mother has broken our Prime Directives in her attempts to rectify her failed experiment. Most ominous, is Xeno's assertion that Mother's true intention is to create a life form that will challenge our authority."

The words "preposterous!" and "absurd!" echoed throughout the spatial void separating the six Salvatores.

"Salvatores, constrain your skepticism," said Salvatore Six. "We have confirmed that advancing the wise ones' development is indeed Mother's objective. Xeno found Mother's secret notes on her experiment and shared them with us. According to those notes, Mother intentionally designed the wise ones' faculties to advance with every generation. Currently, they use 10 percent of their brain's ability. Mother plans to help them evolve, to develop the other 90 percent, believing this will bring them to the Cosmic realm as our equals."

"Equals, or *rivals*?" said Salvatore Three. "Given their genetically entrenched predisposition for violence, I believe they will see themselves as a rival race. Do the rest of you not recall reports from the Angelus which predict the wise ones will behave like conquerors when they venture beyond their solar system?"

"It's the same mentality that propels the wise ones to loot, destroy and vanquish when there are conflicts on their planet," said Salvatore One.

Salvatore Five added that the wise ones' leaders have been "brainwashing the masses for decades with horrifying tales of 'evil aliens coming to ravage their world,' disseminated throughout their media, to feed fear and justify the need for making space weapons.

"Can you imagine conquering hordes of heavily armed spaceships invading our peaceful worlds?"

"I have read the reports detailing how much the wise ones worship their machines of death," said Salvatore Six. "Their leaders train armies numbering in the millions for the sole purpose of extermination and ruin. If they evolve as Mother plans, there may be no way to stop them."

"If they are *allowed* to evolve," said Salvatore One. "We can negate that chilling prospect. This species must be contained. We *will* uphold our pledge to safeguard our worlds from such calamity. The Universe is counting on us."

"But can we do this without violating our Prime Directives?" Salvatore Four wanted to know. "The Imperitus Council will be quick to condemn this."

"Of course they will, because the Council does not have our superior foresight," said Salvatore Six. "We are the Overlords. We always will be.

"On the surface, our plan will simply allow the wise ones to annihilate themselves. Just as the Martians did.

"At the start of our session, you all received the blueprint for the extermination of these barbarians. No one on the Imperitus Council is to know of our plan," said Salvatore Six.

"When reports come to us of their extinction, we will endorse the known facts, and confirm their demise was self-inflicted," said Salvatore One.

"There is a weak link in the plan," said Salvatore Three. "Hear me, Salvatores: Given his relationship with Mother, can we be certain Xeno will betray her?"

"Yes," said Salvatore Six. "Xeno's only condition is that Mother never learn of his betrayal."

"Xeno fears their looming arrival on the interstellar landscape will be catastrophic," added Salvatore Five. "He supports their demise. As should the rest of us."

Five of the six Salvatores chimed in agreement. Salvatore Two asked the others to consider his thoughts.

"If we proceed with this plan, are we not becoming the 'evil aliens out to destroy their race,' as their leaders are foretelling? Can we then belittle them for preparations to defend themselves?"

The words "preposterous!" and "absurd!" echoed throughout the void again, followed by the Salvatores' version of laughter.

"While I am in agreement with the plan in principle, I am disturbed by the plot to undermine Mother," Salvatore Two continued.

"If you recall, there was a time when we considered asking her to join the Salvatores. She is as advanced in abilities as we are. Of that I am convinced."

"If she is indeed as advanced as we are," said Salvatore One, "she would have reached out to us. She would not wait to be asked. It is clear she is not even aware of our existence."

Salvatore Three warned they should not let their egos get the better of their wisdom. They must also concede, he insisted, that it's perfectly rational to suppose there might be others with their powers.

"Perhaps they are not interested in joining us," he said. "Furthermore, it seems Mother has developed abilities that are extraneous to us, as a result of her interactions with the barbarians she created. They are cunning and conniving creatures; two alien traits Xeno's testimony leads me to believe Mother has assimilated."

"Are you suggesting Mother could be eavesdropping on our meetings and is able to conceal her presence?" said Salvatore Five. "That is not possible, we would detect a foreign entity."

"This is true," agreed Salvatore Two, "but who among us has been monitoring the celestial heavens for a foreign presence?"

"We must do a rollcall," said Salvatore One.

"Salvatores, reveal yourselves."

Mother immediately disconnected from the meeting.

CHAPTER 1
Rolling in the deep

Three men had eyes on a woman playing roulette in a Las Vegas casino. Her shoulder-length hair was fiery red and her long legs balanced on gunmetal heels. A flashy blue dress hugged her curves like skin. She was sex in a bottle … but that's not why they were watching her.

The first man kept count of the redhead's winnings. The second man wanted to steal her away for a fat reward. The third man wanted to put a bullet between her blazing blue eyes.

Jimi James was the man adding up chips as he watched the redhead score win after win. He worked off the books for the casino and had no official title, although in casino talk, he was known as a "cooler." Jimi was paid in cash and given a luxurious suite on the 43rd floor to call home. Never spent a dime for meals, drinks, or condoms.

Over the last four years, he kept tabs on high-rollers that made winning look easy. Casino owners don't mind losing a $100,000 here and there, it's good publicity and part of the cost of doing business. But when a gambler piled up chips until they were towering stacks, Jimi's job was to lame their luck.

When he got the nod from the casino's security chief, Jimi swooped in to serve the high-rollers a mickey. His favorite tactic was to become a drunken pest, forcing the distracted gambler to call it a night. Or start losing. Jimi did not have to fake the falling-down-drunk part all that much.

On slow nights, Jimi passed the time drinking bourbon and making nice with the ladies on the casino floor. Most were already cocktail-primed by the time Jimi cajoled them with the "What happens in Vegas, stays in Vegas" line.

"It may be the biggest cliché in the biz, but it *still* works," he loved to tell his buddies at the casino.

Buddies like Hugo Alazar, one of the casino's hardcore security personnel, who just sidled up to Jimi.

"Hey there, Hugo. Damn busy for a Monday night, any trouble?"

"Trouble usually comes around after midnight, when the drunks start seeing double. You checking out the redhead with the legs that don't quit? She keeps winning, Cross-eyed Mary will be calling you."

"The redhead's high-voltage, that's for sure. Eyes on her already. Whether Mary calls, or not," said Jimi, winking at Hugo then adding, "Another night at the Palace, another notch in my bedframe."

"Get that mud out of your mouth, Jimi. You know what happens to *dudes* like you? Believe me, you don't want to end up like one of those drunken old guys we keep throwing outta here for pressing the flesh with flesh that don't want pressing."

"What's it to you, Hugo? Stay out of my circle, man. Nobody invited you in."

"Look, buddy, don't get me wrong. I like you. You're smart, young and good-looking. You should be doing big things, Jimi. … I hate to see you throwing your life away in a place like this."

Jimi paused, looked the casino floor up and down, then threw back the bourbon and asked a passing waitress for another.

"Truth is, I like my life just the way it is, Hugo."

"Yeah, sure you do, Jimi. … You know, I remember when you first came to work here, a shy kid, kept yourself busy refilling the glassware behind the bar. Good-looking women would scare you into a corner. Whatever happened to that kid?"

"He learned fast, Hugo. Only way to survive in this town."

Jimi looked at Hugo, making his smile as big as possible.

"Something tells me you're in for one helluva night, slick," said Hugo.

He gave Jimi a friendly slap on the shoulder and carried on with his rounds, shaking his head as he left.

Jimi got back to work. He moved about the casino like he owned the place, riding a six-foot-two frame that was rugged but lean, with bulges in all the best places. He wore his ash-brown locks close-cropped on the sides but kept his bangs long in the front, sweeping them back from his squinty brown eyes like the movie stars of the golden years.

Jimi watched as the redhead piled up chip after chip. She never lost. A crowd had long since gathered, in awe of the damsel with flaming red hair who was working Roulette Table 3. They were mostly men, some in thousand-dollar suits, others in thousand-dollar shoes.

The hangers on erupted in cheers, hands high in the air, every time the redhead won another jackpot. Martinis and gin tonics spilled to the floor like a tremor had rattled the casino.

A waitress handed Jimi his bourbon with a smile. He gave her a wink and a nod, then turned in the redhead's direction again. The hand raising his glass froze on its way to his lips. The redhead was staring at him. Her eyes locked with his. He could feel his head starting to get warm.

Jimi's phone went off.

"Get your little butt up to the monitoring center—now," said the voice of his boss, Cross-eyed Mary.

Jimi put his phone back in his pocket and looked for the redhead again.

She was gone.

CHAPTER 2
Money for nothing

Deon "Jellybean" Carter was the man looking to snag the redhead, without pinching a fold on her chalk-white skin. He stuck to the outer edges of the crowd as he spied her, casually standing behind pillars and other obstructions like a shadow, never staying in one place for too long.

He was easy to spot, six-foot-nine and built like a fridge. He wore a dark blue suit that wrapped his bulging frame like a giant sock.

Carter was once a Secret Service agent who, after more than 20 years in the ranks, figured there was more money to be made playing bodyguard for the one percent than putting his nuts on the line for hackneyed politicians. Besides, he was tired of the greasy burgers and fried chicken he was forced to suck back during 48-hour duty calls, while the politicos he was safeguarding dined deluxe at posh establishments.

He was putting on weight—tipped the scales at 389 pounds last time he dared check—and knew it was just a matter of time before the Service put him out to pasture. Carter took great pride in his work and was lauded by his bosses as a superior sleuth. But that was window dressing for what Carter really excelled at: Finding the wayfaring daughters, wives and girlfriends of Washington's political elite, and bringing them back home to 'poppa.'

Like most everything that happens in the shielded residences of D.C., these cases were never reported. Discretion was Carter's calling card, a trait most appreciated by male politicians who staked their public personas on being devoted husbands and family men.

Carter's services were in high demand, yet, the feeling that his time in the field was nearing an end nagged at him. He knew that when agents get long in the tooth, most are transferred, forcibly retired or given desk jobs. Carter dreaded the thought of desk duty, told his friends it would be "like putting on your mother's underwear."

He always dreamed of being his own boss. Time to leverage some of the secrets he'd been keeping.

After coaxing a generous early retirement package from the Secret Service—in one lump sum—Carter made his home in Los Angeles, using the cash to establish a personal security agency. At a time when fear of kidnapping was at an all-time high among the well-heeled, Carter reckoned he would sit back and count the money. After two years, he realized the competition was brutal, and new clients were as sporadic as rain in Southern California.

The famed and flush in frantic El-Lay preferred security they were familiar with. Most of Carter's clients were one-timers, jet-hopping out-of-towners who were here one hour, gone with the next text. He was not earning enough to pay his office rent, let alone everything else. His buyout money was quickly depleted. The debts piled up. For the last four months, he paid his bills with credit-card advances.

Two days ago, everything changed. Carter got a call from a woman who insisted their meeting take place away from his office. An hour later, he watched as a silver Rolls Royce Shadow pulled up in front of his building. A woman rolled down the back window and said, "Mr. Carter, please get in."

She was vaguely familiar, but Carter struggled to pin a name on her. Oversized sunglasses sheltered half her face. She was wearing a dark grey blazer with matching zip skirt and spike-heeled pumps, sat with her heavy legs crossed in the generous back seat. She got right to the point.

"Mr. Carter, I am here on behalf of a dear friend who requires your specialized services. Your assignment is simple. There is a young woman we want you to locate, secure and hold. We will come and retrieve her—*promptly*—once you have her."

"Thank you for the offer, mam. I don't know who told you about me, but that is not something I do any more …"

"You will be paid $2 million," the woman jumped in. "I have $1 million in cash as a retainer, will give it to you right this minute."

Carter's eyes lit up as the woman opened a shiny black briefcase filled with neatly wrapped stacks showing Benjamin Franklin's face.

"It's all yours, Mr. Carter," she said, after placing the briefcase on his lap. "The remainder upon delivery."

This was too good to be true, the answer to his financial woes, Carter thought. But, it's too easy, there has to be a catch. What this woman was really asking him to do was kidnap someone, a grim federal offence, now that he did not have the Secret Service backing him up. He may be getting caught up in something seriously messy. Was it worth risking his reputation and his livelihood, he wondered?

But not for long. He remembered the stack of overdue bills sitting on his desk. Incentive came calling like a brick through a glass door.

Carter snapped the briefcase shut, looked the gift horse lady straight in the eye and said: "So, all I have to do is find this woman and hold her until your people come fetch her?"

"Correct. In this envelope, you will find some photos of her, along with her last known location and other information, should you require it."

"Why hire me? I suspect you have your own people that can …"

"We need someone with your particular skill set," said the woman, cutting him off in mid-sentence again.

"Our people are largely intellectuals and scientists. There may be some complications they are ill-equipped to manage. We checked you out, Mr. Carter. This assignment is tailor-made for you."

Carter's radar was still sending him a warning, something about this just felt off. But hell, he was broke and desperate, this woman must know that, too. She sounded as if she had indeed done a background check on him. The flush-with-cash folks were not accustomed to taking chances with their cherished coin, he figured. Unless the payoff made the investment well worth the risk.

Carter took the envelope, made a quick scan of the contents. Images of a good-looking redhead, taken from a distance. Last known location, Las Vegas. There was also a credit-card-sized cellphone in the envelope, and instructions on how to contact the client. No names.

"When I find this redhead, whom do I call?"

"Call me. It's the only number listed on the phone in the envelope. I will forward your call to the one who provided your fee."

Carter looked the woman up and down.

"You look familiar. Where do I know you from?"

"You can call me Oprah."

Carter almost lost it. Still, if this assignment pans out it will be the easiest dough he ever made. Carter thanked the woman and prepared to step out of the Rolls, his beefy right arm like a clamp over the briefcase.

"One last thing, Mr. Carter," said the woman, clasping his left wrist with a grip that defied her gentle appearance.

"When you find her, don't do anything to alarm her. Make very certain she understands you are working for people who are concerned about her. Whatever she needs, we can provide."

"Of course, you have my word on that."

"Mr. Carter, if the woman is harmed, in any way, there will be serious consequences … for you."

The car door slammed shut behind him.

CHAPTER 3

Killing you softly

Christo Sanchez was the man hired to kill the redhead. Most of his contracts were with the American military, who dubbed him "Crisco," like the vegetable shortening, after an agent misspelled his name at the point of first contact, courtesy of Sanchez's broken English. When Sanchez also turned out to be the slipperiest executioner on their roster, the nickname stuck.

At 13, Sanchez began honing his craft as a henchman for "Los Reyes," a drug cartel in Colombia. His stone-cold kills were the stuff of local legend and said to number in the hundreds. He never left a witness alive, preferred working by moonlight. Most of his victims were discovered with a bullet hole clean through the forehead, still laying in their beds.

His work for the American military began six years ago, when he was offered immunity and a free pass to the U.S., thereby escaping the wrath of drug lords he had fallen out of favor with over the years.

All Sanchez had to do in return was eliminate a certain up-and-coming politician in Bogotá for them. He agreed, but demanded one million U.S. greenbacks to boot, or he would make eunuchs of the two agents sent to broker the offer. Only one of those agents was able to father children after the deal was cut. Sanchez potted another million after agreeing to spare the second agent's manhood. To this day, $2 million remains his standard fee, give or take. His employers always pay for his services, promptly.

Sanchez is a large physical specimen, even though he's all of five-foot-six with his combat boots on. He's wide at the shoulders and narrow at the waist, powered by legs like you see at the Olympics.

He spends his free time perfecting his marksmanship and refining his hand-to-hand combat skills with martial arts masters at his favorite gym in San Diego, after hours of sweaty weight training. When a client specified no weapon be used, Sanchez would snap the target's neck with one twist of his wrists, like a ninja assassin does in those Japanese movies with sub-titles.

For the last two years, Sanchez also took private lessons from a black ops hacker, who trained him in the art of electronic surveillance, disabling complex alarm systems and getting around firewalls. Lately, too many of his assignments involved taking out individuals whose residences were virtual electronic fortresses. Sanchez knew he had to adapt. He also paid an American-born Latina big cash to help him improve his English. He wanted to lose his accent something fierce.

Although he was able to learn some basic hacking skills, Sanchez just couldn't get the hang of coding. All those rows of numbers and symbols made his head spin. He needed a different advantage.

Most recently, Sanchez purchased a half-dozen miniature drones on the Dark Web, devious little flying machines that would send back audio and video to their controller. Roughly the size and shape of a house fly, the drones could penetrate the narrowest of gaps in a building's infrastructure and had a transmission range of 2,000 feet. Even the most air-tight structures had ventilation pipes, an easy in for the assassin's tiny mechanical spies.

Sanchez was rarely seen without a month's-worth of wiry stubble on his big, square face, and hated it when people said he looked like Fidel Castro. The last fool who said that to him now shaves with a prosthetic arm.

Every Sunday, Sanchez took in mass at a Catholic church. He always wore his dark blue suit; his version of a successful businessman's uniform. He partook of Holy Communion, tucking the starchy wafer against his cheeks with his tongue and secretly spitting it out later, but never saw a priest for confession. He always dropped a fat envelope in the collection basket. It gave a slayer like him the peace of mind he needed to close his eyes at night.

The redhead was his latest assignment from the U.S. military. It didn't take him long to track her to a casino in Las Vegas, where he set up surveillance from inside a van in the underground parking lot.

He determined where every security camera was located. There were few so-called blind spots, and he parked his van in one of them, near a dead-end corridor. The halogen lighting was bright as sunshine, so he'd already knocked out a few in his vicinity, knowing security was more focused on what was going down on the casino floor, than it was on the underground parking lot. He knew it would be hours before security noticed a dimmed camera there and bothered to investigate.

Sanchez's phone vibrated.

"Crisco?"

"Who else, *stoopid*."

"Can we confirm the hen is in the henhouse?"

"Yes … but she won't be laying eggs much longer," Sanchez cackled.

"Very good. Confirmation in the usual manner. Get it done as soon as possible, absolutely no delays," said the commanding voice.

Sanchez seemed annoyed, held the phone from his ear for a few seconds before responding.

"How many jobs I do for you already, uniform boy? Never did I miss, and you talk to me like I'm Chico, delivering your tacos?"

"Just get it done."

"You know, I was thinking," Sanchez said. "You really want this to happen so quickly, makes it much more risky for me if I can't do it on my own time. I need to double my usual fee."

"Not this time, Crisco, you've only been on the job for a few days. Usual fee, or no more assignments."

"That's what the last shithead like you told me. Look, I am here now, she will disappear on you again, fly the coop, you know this will happen. Double, or I leave, now."

Sanchez could hear muffled voices laced with profanity as he waited for confirmation.

"Another million, that's as far as we'll go," came the reply.

"Double. And you transfer it to my account before I move another muscle."

"You are a slimy sumbitch, Crisco. Hell … OK. Done."

Sanchez hung up, then tucked a fresh coca leaf into his grinning mouth, a habit he picked up while guarding illicit coca plantations in his youth for Los Reyes. Chewing coca leaf helped his lungs breathe better in the thin atmosphere, kept him alert, and staved off hunger during the long shifts. He continues to chew the coca leaf, believing it calms his nerves and allows him to breathe without making a sound, handy when he creeps up close enough to a victim to place the barrel of his gun inches from their head.

He went back to watching the redhead on his laptop. She was still winning, up at least a million by his count. Kill the girl, take her money. A big smile cracked his surly face as he realized this was going to be a much bigger payday than he previously thought.

Sanchez picked up his Glock and brought the cold handle to his lips, kissing it three times, as he always did before a kill.

CHAPTER 4

Mirror, mirror

General Isadore Pope clicked "end call," then exited the Roosevelt Room and rushed down the hall to the Oval Office. His two guards followed in lock step.

"Sir, the President is in a meeting," warned one of the two Secret Service agents guarding the entrance.

General Pope's eyelids tightened as he looked at his soldiers, then back at the agents.

"This is of the utmost urgency. I must see the President."

One of the agents tried to block his entry by stepping in front of the big door.

"You don't want to go there," warned the general, deftly sidestepping the agent and opening the door. His soldiers stayed outside, glaring at the Secret Service guards.

President Douglas Triton was sitting at the Resolute Desk with his back turned when the general burst in. His personal hairstylist was carefully pasting his wispy blondish locks back in place after his daily hair-loss treatment. A makeup artist waited patiently, holding a jar of concealer Triton used to smooth over his pock-marked and pasty complexion.

"Can't you see I'm busy," said President Triton, clearly pissed someone dared enter his domain unannounced.

"Mr. President, my apologies. I just wanted to update you on the operation, as you requested at our earlier meeting, sir."

President Triton threw his arms in the air and ordered the two stylists out. "Leave us."

As he turned to face the general, he picked up a mirror that was sitting on his desk.

"Report," he bellowed, checking his hair from side to side and front to back with the long-handled mirror.

"Mr. President, Crisco should have the job done before end of day. With apologies, we had to double the slimy sumbitch's usual fee, so as to expedite the assignment."

"The money is irrelevant, Pope," Triton said, smiling into the mirror then making his lips pout like a fashion model's while examining his bleached-white teeth.

"The ends justify the means. This woman is a threat to our operation. She needs to disappear. Besides, how many times do I have to remind you, general. We have vaults filled with cash. Do whatever the hell we want with it."

"Yes sir."

President Triton's eyes withdrew into a snake-eyed slant. "Does Crisco know *why* we want her taken out?"

"No sir, not part of his need to know, as you so ordered."

Triton clasped his hands together and smiled approvingly.

"You know what, that redhead's so hot, I'll bet that low-life Crisco will try to screw her before he shoots her. Maybe even after he shoots her. Yeah, I can see the horny little weasel doin' her—hump, hump, hump—Christ, she's melt-in-your-mouth goodness all around. I'd do her."

"Yes, sir," said General Pope, clearly uneasy with the conversation. Yet another president who couldn't keep his willy behind its zipper.

"Power is the greatest aphrodisiac, general. And I'm *The* President. She'd let me do her, alright … come back the next day on her knees, begging for more of The Triton."

"Of course, Mr. President."

General Pope glanced down at the rising ripple in Triton's slacks, then shot his gaze up to the ceiling. "Good Lord," he said to himself. Triton was dipping into the jar where he kept his blue pills again, like they were candy for the taking. Triton listed the pills on his expenses as a "heart medication." No one in accounting ever challenged him, or any other expense he saw fit to lay on taxpayers.

President Triton put the mirror down and quickly straightened himself up in his chair, like he read the general's body language, and realized it was time to bite his flapping tongue. Isadore Pope was an influential Evangelical Christian, the same flock that helped power Triton's surprising election run, granting him victory by the narrowest of margins.

"What's most critical to the operation at this point, General Pope, is the testing," said Triton, nimbly changing the subject.

"When did the geniuses we pay millions of dollars say that's going to happen?" he demanded, using both hands like a puppet master to illustrate his words.

"They seem to have some very grave concerns, sir. The technology is completely alien to them. They say they need more time before testing the weapon."

"Fools! These are the *best* scientists we have? Tell them I said testing has to begin within a week or I will have their little balls tied in a knot. They won't be needing vasectomies," said Triton, forgetting himself again.

"Mr. President, sir, they are the experts, we should heed their concerns …"

"Listen to me, Pope. I know more than the scientists, count on it.

"You tell them they will meet my deadline, or I will have their pampered little asses whipped until they're pink as a pussy."

The President opened a bottom drawer of his desk, pushed aside a vintage Colt .45, then pulled out a medieval-looking whip with copper strands wrapped tightly around its leathery tips.

"Here, take this whip the monks used to whack their genitals with, as punishment for craving young boys," said Triton, heaving it at the general.

"Hold it up to the faces of the weenie scientists as you deliver my orders. Give 'em a reason to call you 'Pope,' other than the obvious."

"Yes, sir," said General Pope, clearly disturbed by Triton's maniacal ranting. It must be the blue pills, he reasoned. His own doctor warned him of the side effects.

Triton hit the intercom button and one of his aides answered.

"Send my stylists back in now and call my wife. Tell her I will be arriving early tonight," said Triton with a fat smile.

"Now, get moving, general. I have an interview with the media in less than an hour, got to continue pushing the message that China needs its cheeky little butt kicked."

***

Alexandra Pope was having another sleepless night. She went downstairs to the kitchen, poured some coconut brandy into a snifter, reached for another sleeping pill, and swallowed everything at once.

On her way back to her bedroom, she heard loud snoring from inside her husband's study. She opened the door to look in on him.

General Isadore Pope was lying face-down on the oak floor, naked. There were whip marks on his back, encrusted with dry blood. To his left was an empty bottle of cognac. Up against his bloated belly was a strange-looking whip, its tips splashed in red.

She started to gag as the muscles in her throat went into contractions. She slammed the door behind her and ran to the bathroom with a hand clasped over her mouth.

CHAPTER 5

Shots in the dark

In the casino's space-age monitoring room, Jimi James headed to a set of screens where the staff had gathered. His boss, Cross-eyed Mary, wanted the techs to review video of the redhead at the roulette table. Jimi looked at his boss and was reminded of why she had such an odd nickname: Both of her beady little eyes were turned inward toward her nose.

The techs were zooming in and freeze-framing the redhead's hands, every time a roulette ball fell on the number she had called.

"Did everyone see that?" Mary asked, pointing to a slow-motion closeup of the redhead's hands.

There were a few nods in obedient agreement.

"Give me a split screen, one with the ball landing on Black 29 and one in tight on the redhead's hands—in the same time frame," Mary ordered.

The tech did as she asked without blinking an eye, then hit play.

"Now, did everyone see that?" Mary asked again.

"See how she rolled her right index finger downward, just as the ball held steady on Black 29?"

The responses varied from, "Ummm … yeah," to "well, sort of …"

"Looks like she is just pointing her finger at the spot for luck's sake," said Jimi. "A lot of the high-ballers do that."

"Blind bats, all of you," cried Mary. "Girl works her hands like an illusionist. Goddamn it, she's a flippin' freak."

Mary turned to face Jimi. "Get that redheaded bitch. Now. Jimi, bring her to me."

***

The doting pack watching the redhead win spins on the roulette wheel had since gathered at the crap tables, where her improbable good fortune continued.

The jackpot was beyond huge when it was the redhead's turn to roll. She kissed the dice handed to her, called for a "seven," and tossed.

The onlookers froze, eyes glued to the dice as they tumbled down the table. One turned up five dots and it looked like she was going to miss, but the other die teetered before dropping flat and becoming a two.

The redhead smiled, like she knew it all along.

"Drinks are on me!" she yelled, flinging a stack of chips high in the air directly above the cheering onlookers.

***

Back in the monitoring room, Cross-eyed Mary was reading replies to emails she sent to security chiefs at other casino houses in Vegas. Three told her a woman fitting the redhead's description was in their establishment recently, winning huge jackpots, then disappearing without a trace.

"Mary, you need to see this," one of her tech staff said.

He pointed at his screen, showing a slow-motion close up of the redhead's hands.

"I know she is doing something," said Mary. "Look at the way her fingers curl, like she is manipulating the dice. Crap. The boss will have my ass for breakfast. She is stealing millions from us—we need to shut her down."

***

Jimi and three security agents in identical black suits arrived on the scene, pushing through the harried onlookers who were scrambling like hungry squirrels for the chips scattered all over the floor.

"I don't see her anywhere," one of the agents reported, his head snapping back and forth on his neck.

"Lemme call the cage, see if she's cashed out," said another agent, snatching his phone from his pocket.

Jimi James was already on his phone, urging casino security to fan out, put eyeballs on every exit. Minutes passed. No reports of a sighting. He wondered how the redhead could have eluded the casino's crack security team.

OK, time to put himself in her shoes … If she was going to make a swift getaway, she would head for the underground parking garage, where the only physical security was at the point of entry. The parking-level elevators were 50 feet from the cashiers' cages, Jimi remembered.

As he hurried to the parking garage, he was thinking: Cross-eyed Mary will be smiling the big one when he nabs the runaway redhead. Might be a little "extra" in it for him.

***

In a van in the underground parking lot, Christo Sanchez watched his laptop screen. A grin stretched across his whiskered face as the redhead won another jackpot. When she threw a stack of chips in the air to celebrate, he lost sight of her in the free-for-all.

He'd already hacked into the casino's security system and switched from camera to camera trying to locate her. He thought he saw a blurred image of her racing into an elevator. Impossible, he thought. No one can move that fast. He rubbed his eyes, convinced the hours of screen watching were messing with his vision.

Sanchez looked out the front window, attempting to refocus, give his bleary eyes a break. The redhead appeared in the bottom-left corner of the windshield.

He popped another coca leaf into his mouth and picked up his Glock. He preferred the Glock in this situation. He had modified it so the lighter grain bullets travel faster than the heavier grain bullets of his Magnum. He packed both for every assignment.

He rolled down the driver's side window and switched the laptop's view to display only the cameras in the underground parking lot. There was no one else around. His orders were to get the job done, pronto. Now was as good a time as any.

He saw the redhead coming closer. Despite wearing four-inch-heels, her feet seemed to glide across the concrete floor like it was an ice rink. Oddly, her shoes did not make a sound as she ran. Not a single "click" or "clack."

The redhead turned on a dime and headed for a group of cars in the dead-end corridor close to where Sanchez was parked. Earlier, he'd knocked out most of the lights in the area. She wouldn't even see him coming. Easy pickings.

He quietly left the van, making like a shadow against the walls in the dim corridor. Dressed in black, Sanchez all but disappeared.

***

Jimi James got off the elevator and caught a glimpse of the redhead in the underground parking lot, just as she turned a corner. He started running to catch up to her. When he saw her again, she was walking so quickly her feet were a ghostly blur.

The redhead reached the middle of the corridor, looked around at the parked cars, then went over to a white SUV. It looked like she was fidgeting with the lock before the door swung open.

She must have heard him coming. She closed the door shut again, then turned to face him.

Jimi slowed to a walk as he approached the redhead. He could not help but gawk at the woman staring right back at him. Her eyes, my god, they sparkled like blue diamonds.

Sanchez stared down the barrel of his Glock past the silencer, like he had already sentenced to death the chump making like a statue in front of the redhead.

A silent bullet ripped into Jimi's back at heart level. He slumped forward immediately. The redhead reached out to break his fall.

As he passed out in her arms, rivulets of blood seeped through his white shirt. He saw blinding bright lights and felt himself rising quickly. His life flashed before him like a hell-bound train …

Jimi's eyelids dropped shut. His life went black.

Sanchez fired two more shots.

CHAPTER 6

Shadowy figures

A slow-moving Deon "Jellybean" Carter picked up the pace considerably in the casino's underground parking lot, after hearing what he knew to be the echo of bullets ricocheting off concrete walls.

He rounded the corner approaching the dead-end area in the garage, came to an abrupt stop and pulled out his Smith & Wesson.

Not 30 feet in front of him he saw a man dressed in black with a Glock in his hand, kneeling on the concrete floor.

"*Madre de Dios*," Carter heard him say, making the sign of the cross with the same hand that held the Glock as he lifted his eyes to the ceiling. Carter knew a little Spanish and was bewildered by the man's words, "Mother of God."

It was dim in that part of the underground, but Carter could see there was no one else around. He quickly ducked down behind a sedan parked to his right and watched as the Glock man poked a finger into what appeared to be a small pool of dark liquid near the middle of the corridor. The Glock man expelled what appeared to be a wad of gum from his mouth, then again said: "*Madre de Dios*."

Carter took a photo of the man with his phone, after checking to be sure the flash was off. His dark eyes widened as he observed him get into a black econoline van with a logo on its side that read "Happy Cleaning Services." Carter snapped shots of the logo and the license plate, just as the van disappeared beyond the bend in the underground.

Carter moved toward the dead-end corridor, his experienced eyes scanning the area for clues. He made note of the lone security camera in that part of the parking lot. As he approached the small pool of liquid the man had dipped his finger into, Carter realized it was blood. What he perceived to be a wad of gum spat from the Glock man's mouth was actually a chewed-up piece of some kind of leaf.

His eyes drifted up to the ceiling, just as he had seen the Glock man do. All he saw was a narrow air shaft, stretching about 20 feet straight up, a common element in underground parking lots. Using the flashlight feature on his phone, he aimed the beam up the shaft. There had to be a reason why the Glock man looked up there, Carter figured. But the passageway was clear, with a heavy-looking metal sewer grid at the top of the shaft.

Carter had already memorized the phone number included in the instructions he received from the elegant Rolls Royce woman. After the first few calls, he was given direct access to his employer. He checked his watch. Another report was already more than 30 minutes late.

When Carter was searching for the redhead after she hurled a pile of chips in the air inside the casino, he spotted a small security office on the main floor. He made his way back there, hoping he could review footage of what happened in the corridor, without drawing too much attention to himself.

It was a satellite security office, one of many in the casino's vast complex. Within minutes of showing the Secret Service credentials he still carried with him to one of the two guards on duty, Carter was watching footage from Camera #129.

"You see that, sir, all the lights in that part of the underground parking lot apparently went off a number of hours ago," said the guard. "We can barely make anything out."

"Surely you can lighten up the video and increase the resolution," said Carter.

The other guard said they didn't have time, explaining their boss comes around to all the casino's security stations—even theirs—about this time every night to ask if they have anything to report.

"She's old-school that way," said the guard.

Carter pulled a generous wad of Benjamin Franklins from his inside breast pocket and dropped it in front of the two surprised guards. He knew that kind of money was two months in wages for low-ranking casino guards like them.

"Now do you have enough time?"

The guard's fingers went into overdrive, shutting off the auto function and adjusting the colors and resolution with manual precision. The enhanced footage Carter paid for was still more muddy than clear. The faces were dark but the video was bright enough to make out body movements in the shadows. He asked the guard to sharpen the images even more.

Carter's breathing got heavier as he watched the shadowy figures in the scene slowly come to life. It was definitely the redhead. A man had approached her in the underground as she was about to get into a white SUV.

"Looks like Jimi James," one of the guards said.

The man's body suddenly lurched forward, as if something struck him in the back. As the footage became clearer, blood could be seen dripping down his white shirt onto the floor.

The redhead had stepped into him to break his fall. Her eyes ignited like a flashlight being flipped on. She glared straight ahead at the shooter who was standing about 40 feet away and aiming a big gun with a silencer straight at her. It was the Glock man for sure, Carter thought.

What Carter saw next made his salt-and-pepper eyebrows spasm like a snapped rubber band.

There was a blinding flash of light where the redhead stood holding the man in her arms. When it dissipated seconds later, the redhead and the man were gone.

A bewildered Carter asked the security guard to rewind that particular footage. It took the guard a few seconds to comply, busy as he was staring at his partner, as if to ask, "Did you see what I saw?"

"What's going on here?" a woman's voice barked from behind Carter and the two guards.

"I was just leaving," said Carter, making a dash for the door.

Standing in his way was Cross-eyed Mary, blocking the narrow hallway to the exit door. Carter said, "Excuse me," as he squeezed his way between her and the wall.

"Security!" Cross-eyed Mary yelled as Carter rubbed his massive self against her in order to get to the door.

The last thing Deon Carter needed was for the casino's security people to check the authenticity of the Secret Service credentials he had shown the guards, or have the guards confess they had taken a bribe from him.

He went straight to his car and pulled out the phone he'd been given to contact his client with.

"Yes," said a husky female voice after five rings.

"It's Carter, we have a problem."

"Your report is an hour late ... I'm listening."

"I have lost the subject."

"Details, Mr. Carter."

"She's disappeared, and I think she may have been shot."

"You were explicitly told no harm can come to her. Tell me exactly what happened."

"I was not the one that shot her. It was a situation I happened upon, not a situation that I could control," said Carter, in the kind of tone that said: "Back off, I am not riding the rap for this."

"I paid the casino's security guys to get a look at surveillance video … hard to say exactly what happened."

"Just tell me everything you know, Carter. I have my top people listening in on our conversation now. Together, we will determine the most logical course of action due to this development. Proceed."

Carter told her what the surveillance footage showed. Since he could barely believe what he'd seen with his own eyes, he hoped his observations sounded coherent.

"The camera lens in that section of the underground parking lot only reached until just past the entrance to the dead-end corridor where the incident occurred," he explained. "There was a short, stocky man carrying a gun, his back was to the camera.

"He fired three shots into that area of the underground that was partly in the camera's range. When the shooter half-stepped quickly to his right, for a second, you can see the subject holding a man in her arms.

"I was told that man was named Jimi James, a casino worker, but could not get a firm answer as to what it was he did. I believe him to be dead, or very badly injured."

"We are checking hospital reports for all of Las Vegas, as we speak," said the throaty-voiced woman.

Carter continued.

"Two of the shooter's rounds were fired into what looked like a cloud of silvery haze that suddenly appeared around the man and the subject. When the haze lifted seconds later, the man and the subject were gone from the camera's view. I think the subject released some kind of smoke bomb to veil their escape."

Carter could hear derisive chuckles in the background after he said that.

"We must find out who the shooter is," said the woman. "He's most definitely a pro, won't have left any trace. But we will have him in our sights, very soon. The photos you sent us will help. My people are looking at them right now."

"I checked the area after the shooter left," said Carter. "There was a small pool of blood on the concrete floor, likely that of Jimi James."

"And you are certain, Mr. Carter, the subject did not escape in a car, she simply vanished?" said a male voice.

"Look, there are no exit doors, no way out of that dead-end corridor. There was no car leaving the area at that same time."

Carter could hear the woman conferring with her associates, but the words were too muffled to make out. After a minute, she asked Carter if there was an "exit" somewhere in the ceiling, above the pool of blood, like an air shaft or ventilation vent.

"I do remember looking up and around, checking for blood spatter. Yes, there was a narrow ventilation vent, went straight up about 20 feet, but it was covered at the top with a heavy iron grid."

There was another pause, then Carter heard chattering again.

"Carter, we firmly believe the subject is alive and well. Find her. Fast."

"Where do you suggest I start?"

There was another pause, more background babbling.

Carter waited, his patience tested.

"Go to the airport," the woman finally said. "We have just received information which suggests the redhead will be looking to fly out, likely Europe, as soon as possible."

"How did you come by this information?"

"You have your role in this assignment, Mr. Carter. Rest assured I can afford to have others in different roles as part of the effort. Finding this girl is of the utmost importance. I am leaving nothing to chance."

Carter was about to say, "On my way," then realized now would be a perfect time to ask the question that gnawed at him since the minute he first heard this woman's husky voice.

"Madam, you are paying me a great deal of money. I want to do right by you. If I am to succeed, it's vital I know more about what is going on, who this girl is … and who you are."

"Agreed, at least on the part about knowing who I am, Mr. Carter. I am Samantha Isenberg. I believe you know the name."

Carter's heavy jaw dropped like a ship's anchor. Oh yeah, he knew who she was. Who didn't know the name of the richest woman in America? Hell, he should have asked for triple the fee originally offered him by the Rolls Royce woman.

"One more thing, Mr. Carter. You are quite certain nothing was left behind at the scene?"

"Other than someone's blood, no"

Right then, a thought came to him.

"There was a chewed-up leaf the shooter spat onto the concrete near the blood. Does that mean anything to you?"

"Was it a coca leaf, Mr. Carter?" said a male voice in the background.

"Now that you mention it, yes, it could have been a coca leaf. Do you want me to go back there and confirm?"

Carter was pissed at himself for missing what was now an obvious clue. During down times while he was in the Secret Service, boning up on everything that was going on, from military to FBI investigations, was required reading.

He remembered specific murder investigations of high-profile victims where the assassin left behind a chewed-up piece of coca leaf. None of those murders were ever solved.

"No need to go back there, Mr. Carter. We know who the shooter is, gathering intel on him already."

"That was quick. Do you want me to take him out?"

"No. Find the girl, Mr. Carter. That is your only mission. We will deal with the shooter. He's a dastardly assassin who's only failing is his undying love for money.

"We know how to speak his language."

CHAPTER 7

Land down under

General Isadore Pope marched his way to the Oval Office like his feet were on fire.

"Sir, the President is in another meeting," said one of the Secret Service guards outside the door.

"Out of my way—this is of the utmost urgency!" said the general as he barged through the doors.

"Mr. President, we need to speak."

In the Oval Office with President Douglas Triton was his only child, Olivia. She was sitting opposite Triton, long skinny legs crossed, her pale, never-seen-daylight-without-sunscreen face wearing a frown.

Washington insiders were always quick to stoke the rumor mill when it came to their curious father-daughter bond, especially when Triton publicly referred to her as his "moon and stars," after he spent the night watching reruns of *Game of Thrones*.

Triton and Olivia ignored General Pope, at first, and continued with their heated conversation.

"Dad, I'm telling you for the last time. Now is not the time to go after China, all hell will break loose. You need to back off," Olivia said, glancing over at the anxious-looking Pope.

"This seems important, dad, and I have to go anyway. We'll talk over dinner?"

"China is a vampire, they are sucking us dry, Olivia. Can't do dinner, I have a spa appointment. Call me around 9:00."

"Have a seat, General Pope."

It was a sunny day and the light streamed through the large windows in the Oval Office behind the President, illuminating his backside like a lighthouse beacon.

"Dad, it's time to have your ears waxed again," said Olivia as she kissed Triton on the cheek before leaving. "I can see all the regrowth on your ears because of the sun shining on the back of your head. Kinda gross."

"Like I said, I *have* a spa appointment."

The general waited until Olivia exited the room before speaking up.

"Mr. President, there has been an unfortunate turn of events."

Triton focused his steely eyes on the general's and motioned for him to continue.

"Crisco has disappeared. At first, he did not reply to calls or texts, but now we think he has destroyed his cell phone since we cannot track him. We have reason to believe he's gone rogue. The target has eluded us again, although I think she may be wounded."

The President furrowed his brows and slapped the table with the open palm of his right hand. "Goddammit! Find that slimy little Chico and end him. I am going to freeze his bank account and—goddammit, just take *all* the money back."

"Should we do that, sir? Do we really want to piss off a conniving killer with a temper like he has?"

"It's as good as done. Count on it."

General Pope started thinking that having Sanchez gunning for Triton might not be such a bad idea, after all.

He then explained the CIA operative who was tailing Sanchez was also missing, but he did manage to file a report before vanishing.

"He's most certainly dead, the shadow operative," said Pope. "Crisco likes to shoot before asking, 'Who the hell are you?'"

"Plenty more where he came from," said Triton. "What did he report?"

General Pope proceeded to give the President a recap of all that had transpired since their last meeting, based on the most recent intelligence. The operative shadowing Sanchez said the assassin fired two shots at the redhead, after his first bullet took down a man she was with. He could not see beyond the corner of the corridor from his hiding spot in the underground parking lot at the casino where this all took place, and therefore cannot explain how the redhead and the man were able to disappear.

"Another man was seen checking out the spot where the incident occurred, after Crisco drove off in a black van. Our operative identified him as former Secret Service agent, Deon Carter."

"*Deon Carter*? That son-of-a-bitch, take him out, too."

"What purpose would that serve, sir?"

"I mean it, Pope. I remember Carter, guy's got dirt on every decent man in Washington who ever had problems with his wife, daughter or mistress. Be a blessing for me, and many of my friends, to send flowers for his funeral."

"Of course, sir. Consider it done."

Pope's reply to the President was as far from what he was thinking as Paris is from Pittsburgh. He had no intention of having Carter killed, in fact, he had other plans, put into play just before he came to see the President. General Isadore Pope was done playing court jester to the real fool in the White House.

Pope also remembered "Jellybean" Carter, but did not mention it to the President. Fact is, he was the one that gave Carter the Jellybean nickname, when he was head coach of the football team at the United States Military Academy in West Point.

Carter was his star offensive linebacker. All he had to do was hunker down at the line of scrimmage and nobody was going to knock him over to get to the quarterback. Coach Pope gave Carter his nickname because the muscle-bound giant always kept a five-pound bag of jellybeans to crunch on while he was on the bench. Told the coach they were the source of his energy.

"My people had a look at the scene," Pope continued. "It was a dead-end in the underground lot, there were no exit doors, and they checked all the cars in the vicinity to see if the redhead had hidden under or inside one of the nearby vehicles."

"Hold on, general, let's be quite clear. The two of them, one a dead body, vanished into thin air?"

"Sir, the casino's surveillance footage my men saw shows a flash of brilliant light, then the two bodies vanished. Intelligence says some kind of smoke bomb was used to enable their escape."

"So, they are alive?"

"We believe the redhead is still alive. Rest assured, we will hunt her down, sir."

The general said he'd already put his best operatives in pursuit of the redhead.

"There's something else, Mr. President. Apparently, since this Deon Carter left the Service, he has been operating a security agency in Los Angeles. It appears as if he is also on the redhead's trail."

"All the more reason to snuff that doughnut head. Who hired him, and for what reason?" Triton asked, showing a keener interest in the details.

"Intelligence tells me Carter was hired by Samantha Isenberg."

"THE Sam Isenberg?"

"It's been confirmed sir, yes."

"That bitch, she gave hundreds of millions to the opposition during my election campaign, trying like hell to railroad me, now this? How could she possibly make the connection between the redhead and our operation?"

"Mr. President, as you instructed, only a handful of my most trusted military and intelligence people are aware of our operation. Intelligence suggests, and I would agree, that Isenberg wants the redhead for reasons unknown, at this point."

"But, if she *does* know about our operation, there may be others who know. Find out who she deals with regularly here in Washington. I smell a mole, general."

"Agreed, sir.

"Here's what we have on Isenberg, fresh off the Intelligence desk," said Pope, handing a heavy file marked "Top Secret" to the President.

"You know I don't read those, you read it to me, just the good parts," said the President, handing the file back to Pope.

The general proceeded to brief Triton on Samantha Isenberg, and what her massive corporation was currently engaged in.

Isenberg was holed up at her 500-acre stronghold, in the hills northwest of Denver near Lookout Mountain. Her complex is heavily guarded and remote, with state-of-the art surveillance that can spot anything coming their way more than 60 miles out.

"Bomb the place." The President looked dead serious.

"Sir, that is not an option."

"We can always make it look like another radical Islamic terrorist attack."

"I do think we have pushed that tactic to the limit, sir. Hard to sell this as Islamic radicals taking out the richest woman in America. The bloody press would be all over it, like rats on cheese."

"Find a way, Pope. I don't give a goddamn as to the how. Won't have to worry about the blasted media for too much longer. My buddies and I are slowly buying our way in, we hope to have a controlling interest in every big media syndicate in the country, soon, very soon. Count on it.

"Then we'll see if any of them dare to print bad things about me."

"If I may continue, sir. At the end, I will give you my recommendation for how we should be dealing with Samantha Isenberg."

Triton was listening to more of the intelligence report when his carefully coiffed eyebrows jumped high on his forehead.

"Wait, stop right there, general: She's building a *bunker*?"

"Yes, sir, 200 feet below ground, under the hills in her compound. Massive undertaking. All hush-hush."

Triton gave Pope the "tell me more" look.

"Some 10 years ago, one of Isenberg's companies tested and patented a new laser drill that makes conventional tunneling methods obsolete. Reports say it cuts through solid rock like a blow torch through butter, Mr. President.

"We have reason to believe Isenberg is building a titanic underground bunker—in that very spot where testing was done years ago and a large underground cavern was already carved out. They are just making it a hell of a lot bigger.

"Most recently, we have learned that many of the world's top minds, from scientists to surgeons, from agricultural specialists to environmental experts, are now living inside Isenberg's compound. They even brought their families; elaborate tents are everywhere, scattered all over the property.

"One of the things Intelligence finds most peculiar about the collection of specialists Isenberg is assembling at her compound, Mr. President, is the number of filmmakers, writers, musicians and artists that have arrived in the last week or so."

"Creative types—you know what I think of that useless bunch! Gotta find a way to obliterate Isenberg's compound, Pope. Two birds, one bomb?"

"This isn't your standard family campout," Pope continued, ignoring Triton's last remark. "Intelligence speculates this is some kind of 'Doomsday' bunker Isenberg is building. The families in tents are waiting for the construction to be finished before moving in."

"Don't want speculation, general, spell it out for me."

"Sir, our satellite scans of Isenberg's compound are being largely bounced back into the atmosphere by some kind of deflection beam. The FBI techs *can* make out the shadowy image of a huge underground cavern under construction, but given the signal interference, they cannot confirm exactly what is going on down there.

"However, by piecing together information from various intelligence sources—which only came about this morning—the FBI estimates the underground cavern to be the size of 10 football fields."

Pope also revealed that Isenberg had brought in her own construction crews, all sworn to secrecy, and not allowed to make contact with the outside world until the project was complete.

"Apparently, sir, the crews abandoned a number of ongoing construction projects Isenberg had on the go, at her implicit direction. This implies there is some urgency for the bunker project."

"So. If we can't drop a bomb on Isenberg's compound, how do we take her out?" said Triton.

"She has a daughter and two grandchildren living in Seattle. FBI snoops have been monitoring every call in and out of the daughter's house. Sir, it seems the daughter and the kids are also headed for the compound, in just a few days.

"As you know, we have those specially trained agents who look, talk and operate like Islamic terrorists. Let's have them capture Isenberg's daughter and her kids, on the pretense of asking for ransom money.

"They have returned from the last mission you ordered and are ready to go, at your behest, Mr. President."

"Yeah, I call them 'The Towelheads,' love that name. That was one helluva of job they did in France, the goddamn frog-eater had no idea it was really us," Triton chuckled. "Serves him right for making a pass at my wife when he was here visiting the White House."

"Sir, by all accounts, it was in jest, a response to your comments about how hot *his* wife was."

"Nonsense, Pope. ... So, tell me, how does kidnapping the daughter and her kids rid us of Isenberg?"

"Sir, the plan is to draw Isenberg out from her heavily guarded compound. Make it clear she has to personally hand-deliver the ransom money, or the family will be executed, the video posted online. Word is she would do anything to protect her family."

"Once she is out in the open, we take her down?"

"Exactly, Mr. President."

Triton leaned back in his chair and clasped his hands together. A Cheshire Cat smile took over his floppy face.

"Sweet payback for what she tried to do to me during the election.

"Bitch won't know what hit her."

CHAPTER 8
Leaving Las Vegas

Jimi James came to slowly. His head was pounding like a heartbeat, his vision was hazy, but he recognized his bedroom. He gradually raised his head and realized that he was lying in his bed, naked. There was no sign of blood.

"I remember being shot, I remember all the blood, I remember leaving this Earth … could this be heaven?"

Jimi sat up and searched with his hands for the wound that he remembered being in his upper back. He felt a large gauze bandage, but there was no pain, other than that steady throbbing in his head.

The time showing on the router unit under his television showed just past five in the morning.

He heard the shuffling of clothes hangers. Someone was inside his closet.

A few seconds later, the redhead emerged from the closet, stark naked and holding up a pair of Jimi's jeans. She placed them against her tiny waist, like she was wondering how they would fit.

"Good, you are awake. Do you have anything smaller?"

"What …no … wait," Jimi said, shaking his head.

"What the hell happened yesterday? I was shot, I should be dead."

"Silly boy, the bullet just grazed your back, you fainted like a schoolgirl."

"Seriously, that's what happened? But why would anyone shoot at me in the first place?"

"Perhaps a jealous husband?" the redhead smirked, hands on her shapely hips like she was taunting him, after dropping the jeans to the floor.

Jimi knew that was a plausible motive, as his thoughts rambled through some of the women who told him that, if their husbands ever found out, they would not attend his funeral.

"Maybe what happens in Vegas doesn't always stay in Vegas," said Jimi.

But how would the redhead know details like that about him, he wondered.

"Anyway, not to worry, the police are on it. The man who shot at you did get away, but security has a good description of him."

"I see. How did I get back up to my room?"

"A security guard helped me bring you here. I put a bandage on your back from his first-aid kit."

Jimi wasn't buying her 'explanation,' even though she appeared to be speaking with candor, not a hint of invention. First of all, security was hunting for *her*. How did she evade them? Something was off here, really off.

"My clothes, what did you do with them?"

"I, um, sent them down to Housekeeping for cleaning. Hope you don't mind. My dress as well."

Jimi looked at the redhead. She was lying again. Why? He knew for a fact there would be an immediate investigation if clothing was sent to the laundry room with blood on it. And, there *was* blood on his white shirt, of that he was certain.

"You undressed me?"

"Of course," she smiled, stepping closer to him on the edge of the bed. "You have such a pretty body."

Jimi got a rise out of that remark. Standing before him was one of the sexiest women he had ever seen. And he'd seen a lot of them.

She looked Jimi in the eyes, he gazed right back. The spark between them was palpable.

"Another time," the redhead said, still smiling.

Jimi felt a sudden surge of uncommon modesty. It was time to get up—and get dressed. He walked over to the closet. The redhead stepped aside as he poked around to find something to wear.

"I see you read science fiction," she said, as her eyes scanned book titles on the large wooden shelves Jimi had set up next to the closet door when he first moved into the suite.

"Not so much, lately."

"You have a collection that any sci-fi fan would envy—Philip K. Dick, Ray Bradbury, Jules Verne, Lester Del Ray, Arthur C. Clarke—so many of the old classics."

"Started collecting when I was nine years old, used to spend hours daydreaming about the stars, space travel, life on other planets, all that kinda stuff. Always thought I would be a sci-fi writer, when I grew up."

She smiled sweetly, like she approved of his yearning.

"So, what happened to that dream?"

"Well," said Jimi, "I discovered how much fun girls can be. Got sidetracked."

"We all do. But you should never let go of your childhood dreams. You have them for a reason."

"Someday, I *will* go back to that dream. Right now, that drum just keeps banging me to a different beat.

"By the way, I'm Jimi. We never officially met."

"I know who you are, Jimi James. Call me Delia."

"Last name?"

"Just Delia."

"Uh-huh."

Jimi stopped rummaging for something to wear and went to the bathroom, but the urge to pee suddenly left him. He turned his backside to the massive mirror hanging over the sink and saw a big square bandage. He peeled it back, still feeling no pain. He removed it completely and looked at it. There was no blood, it was clean.

He looked at his backside in the mirror again and saw a small, round scar, still showing pink. He knew it was not there yesterday. Delia told him the bullet "grazed" him, but this scar was already healed, and pinpoint round.

How is any of this possible? Delia was lying to him.

He came back to his bedroom, a big bath towel wrapped around his waist.

Delia, still naked, was digging through the drawers of his dresser.

"Why do you have a drawer full of women's underwear and bras?"

"I um ... sort of collect them," Jimi said, ever so sheepishly. "Some of my guests left them behind ... had to leave in a hurry sometimes."

"If I find one my size, may I wear it?"

"Sure, and you'll find some clothing that should fit you in the bottom left drawer."

Delia opened the drawer. Blouses, skimpy summer dresses, skirts, a few pairs of pants. All neatly folded.

"Some of your 'guests' did indeed leave in a hurry, Mr. James."

Jimi pulled on a comfy pair of jeans as he watched Delia trying on clothes she pulled from the drawer. He was very particular about his choice of pants. He only bought ones that fit just so, with enough give so that the outline of his manhood was hinted at, but not overly obvious.

Delia found a pair of dark blue slacks that fit her and wiggled into a matching half-sleeve pullover, struggling mightily to jerk it over top of her now bra-held breasts.

When her arms were in the air to pull the tight sweater through, Jimi could not help but notice the track marks on her arms. They were healed over, but clearly visible. Jimi knew from drug addicts. They were everywhere in Vegas.

Jimi decided it wasn't the right time to get the truth out of Delia. She was certainly clever, had a response for everything. He would wait until she had a few cocktails, then resume his interrogation. Always a better result with a few drinks in them.

After checking her new outfit in the mirror with a "will do for now" look, Delia drifted towards the wall in Jimi's living room that displayed his multiple-component stereo system and vast record collection.

"Wow, you *are* a 'collector.' I love that wall of vinyl, Jimi. Thousands of records … do you have any David Bowie?"

"*Do I have any Bowie?*" said Jimi, with all the incredulity his voice could muster.

"I may have been a kid when he was nearing the end of his career, but it did not take me long to discover his work. I am a huge Bowie fan, have a look at my collection. I have *all* his 25 studio albums, 10 live albums, 22 of his 51 compilation records, and about 60 of his 128 singles—some releases you just can't find anywhere anymore, mainly cuz no one is willing to part with them, especially after his death."

"Of course, you do. … You rarely see vinyl collections of this magnitude. Seems the whole world has embraced digital as the standard."

"Maybe so, but you can't beat the pureness of vinyl, the music sounds as the artist intended it to sound. Digital music has been converted to numbers and it just isn't the same, it loses the human element, that organic quality that only true audiophiles can appreciate.

"What's worse, is that so many people listen to tunes with ear buds these days. I tell you, music is only real when you can feel it passing through your body, not just ringing in your ears."

"You are certainly passionate about music."

Jimi's face turned red.

Delia began fingering her way through Jimi's vast repertoire of vinyl.

"Your collection does not have much that is current, don't you like the new music?"

"Well, not enough artists release vinyl versions of their work these days, although I admit more of them are doing that now then say, 10 years ago. I love new music, you will find it stored on my hard drive, digital versions," Jimi said, pointing to the MacBook Pro that was part of the array of electronic modules stacked against the wall.

"Glad to see your taste in music is eclectic, Jimi. Some people tune out, only listen to one style of music, and ignore everything else."

"They're not *true* music lovers, obviously," Jimi said with pious conviction. "Real music lovers have a respect and appreciation for its incredible variety, they celebrate country music as much as they do rap music. My humble opinion: Music should just be music. I hate all these limiting categories and genres."

"I don't see how hardcore country fans could even begin to get rap music," Delia countered, "even though they sing about many of the same things: pain, heartbreak and drugs. But, I see your point about musical genres being limiting, to the fans and the artists."

Jimi was impressed. The girl knew her stuff.

"I'll bet you show this off to all the girls … so many control functions," Delia said, pointing to a vintage 24-track mixing board that topped the stack of intricate stereo components at the center of Jimi's record collection.

"Actually, you are the first girl I've had in my suite that's given that wall more than a passing glance. Really, not kidding," Jimi stammered.

"Well, with your looks, one can only assume they had more *pressing* issues on their minds," Delia smiled.

Jimi knew his cheeks must be glowing with embarrassment, a reaction he usually reserved for the chamber maid, when she came to tidy up the morning after one of his lively liaisons with a perfect stranger.

"It's early morning but there's a restaurant just off the lobby that never closes, Delia. I need a good, stiff drink and maybe something to eat. You hungry?" said Jimi, eager to get things going his way.

"Delia?"

The redhead was just standing there, motionless, arms at her sides, staring up at the middle of the ceiling. Her eyes were as open as they could be. They were so shiny, Jimi thought he could see actual light being emitted from them. He shook his head, realizing he must be seeing things.

Jimi put a hand on each of her shoulders and looked right at her.

"Delia?"

"We have to go," she said, snapping out of her trance-like state. "Now."

"What? So, you do want to go down to the lobby, get something to eat?"

"No. I must get to Europe, next plane out. I need you to come with me, Jimi. I can pay you, I have money, lots of it. I will pay for everything."

"This is crazy, I can't just up and fly to Europe."

She grabbed his right hand with both of hers and squeezed. She was much stronger than she looked. Her eyes appeared a more normal deep indigo.

"You *must* come with me, I need you," she said.

Jimi lost control. What he was feeling suddenly swept all logic from his mind. The urge to go with her was overwhelming. Damn the consequences. No, he did not trust her, but it felt like destiny was cashing in its chips.

"OK, let's talk money. How much will you pay me?" He could not believe those were the words that spilled from his mouth.

"I have millions in winnings, all from the last week in Vegas. I will share some with you."

"Really? Where are these millions?" said Jimi, every word doused in doubt.

"Most in an offshore account that I can access from anywhere. A million or so in cash in a locker at the airport."

"You will show me the money in the locker, before we get on the plane?"

Jimi thinking it best to keep spinning the "I only care about the money" line. Actually, aside from his now routine escapades at the casino, he had never experienced *real* adventure. He felt a gnawing hunger for change. His buddy Hugo was right, he *was* wasting his life away at the casino.

"Yes, I will show you the money, another reason why we must leave, immediately."

"OK, lemme just pack a few things."

"NO, all you need is your passport, Jimi. I will buy you everything else you may need along the way."

Just like a good sugar mamma should, Jimi smiled to himself.

He pulled her in close and kissed her softly on the lips. She kissed him back. He kissed her again. He felt sharp flashes of pure pleasure. Delia made him feel so alive. Right then he decided that nothing would change his mind about going with her. Money, or no money.

Jimi grabbed his carry-on from the closet and quickly stuffed some socks and T-shirts inside as Delia urged him to hurry it up. He grabbed his wallet, found his passport, checked to see when it expired, then said, "We are good. Let's go."

Jimi thought about leaving a note for his boss Cross-eyed Mary, or at least telling someone at the casino he would not be around for a while, but decided against it.

Too much to explain, they wouldn't understand—hell, he didn't even understand. Jimi took Delia by the hand and said, "Let's take the elevator down to the lower level, leave through the service exit. Always a cab there waiting for staffers that need a ride home."

What Jimi was really thinking was more along the lines of, "No way I am going to risk bumping into the crazy husband that's got a gun aimed at my ass for doing his wife by venturing out front of the casino to hail a cab."

He took one last look around his suite before closing the door behind him. A strange sigh escaped his mouth.

The feeling that he would never see his home again creeped him out.

CHAPTER 9
Needles and pins

At the Vegas airport, Delia took Jimi to the locker where her cash was stashed, then fished out the key from her handbag.

Jimi made sure no one had eyes on them before opening up. When he unzipped the gym bag inside, his eyes did a happy dance. No time to count up the stacks, but he figured the total was easily in the hundreds of thousands.

Jimi grabbed a couple of fat wads from the bag and stuffed them into his pant pockets, telling Delia they needed some cash to exchange for Euros. Had to have some "walking around money."

Delia said that was a good idea and went to book their flight. Jimi was to go to the currency exchange, then meet Delia at the bar they saw near the locker area. He hoped they served good bourbon there, snap back a few while he waited for her.

The cashier at the exchange carefully checked each of the hundred-dollar bills Jimi handed her under some kind of counterfeit-detecting device. Within minutes, he walked off with an envelope crammed with Euros, and the satisfaction that his tactic worked. The cash in the locker was not counterfeit. Jimi also kept the locker key for "safe keeping." When he returned to Vegas, the locker would be his first stop.

They were, in fact, headed for Lisbon, as Delia informed him on their way to the airport, after she experienced another trance-like episode.

After tossing back a couple of shots, Jimi checked the time. Where was Delia? He found her at the American Airlines wicket, where she told him there were no direct flights to Lisbon from Vegas until later in the day.

She booked two seats on the next plane to London instead, as it was departing in under an hour. From Gatwick in London, there were flights to Lisbon almost hourly, the airline clerk told them.

As they headed for customs, Delia explained that in Lisbon they were to meet a man who had a package for her. She wouldn't say what was in the package.

"Jimi, I know we just met and you have questions I can't answer. But you need to trust me. I will let no harm come to you. I promise to tell you everything, absolutely everything, once we have the package."

Jimi was careful to give her a nod with a look that implied he bought in, but he was still uneasy with every logic-defying incident since he first saw her at the casino.

Despite his misgivings, he did sense a growing comfort in her presence. He would let her have her way with him, for now.

Once the flight was underway, Jimi wanted to know more about Delia, but she deflected every question, telling him they should get some sleep, as there would be little time for rest once they reached Lisbon.

He *was* feeling drained and it wasn't long before his eyes shut down and a slight nasal snore could be heard beneath the noise of the plane's engines.

Jimi woke up when he felt Delia's body bumping up against him. She was shivering. Her face was flushed and sweaty. Her arms made random motions, suddenly swinging in the air when her body twitched. He did not need to remember seeing the track marks on her arms to recognize the symptoms.

Before he moved into his suite in the casino and starting working full-time, Jimi spent a month shacked up with an exotic dancer who loved the needle more than life. Jimi went to hell and back with her while she tried to kick the horse.

Her co-workers found her lifeless body in her dressing room at the strip club one night. She spent the next day in a hospital, Jimi holding her hand until her skin felt like ice …

A steward came by, asking if there was anything he could do to help Delia, as passengers all around them looked on with concern.

"She's an epileptic," Jimi said. "It's just a minor seizure, she will be OK in a few minutes."

The steward seemed relieved, nodded his head and went back to his station.

Jimi wondered if this was why Delia wanted him to accompany her. The real reason why she "needed" him? She may have lured him on board with the promise of big cash, but a different reason for his crazy decision to go with her snuck up on him. It made him feel light-headed, like he could fly to the Moon if he wanted to. But it was also frightening, like he was roaring down a freeway at 200 MPH, a hairpin turn away from certain death.

Delia's tremors began to ease. Jimi pushed her bangs away from her face and gently wiped the sweat from her skin, drying his hands on his pant legs. She opened her eyes to look at him, then took his hand.

"This body is frail, it needs to heal," she said softly.

"'This body?'"

"Soon, you will understand, Jimi … soon."

Delia's eyes closed again. When her body started shaking, Jimi drew her closer, their bodies touching from head to toe.

***

Jimi and Delia booked a flight to Lisbon from Gatwick within 45 minutes of arriving. As they touched down at the Portela Airport, Jimi said they had to hit the airport shops before finding a hotel. He wanted bourbon; she went on the hunt for burner phones.

When they met again, Delia had purchased six prepaid burners made by different manufacturers. She told Jimi to junk his phone, insisting it was critical no one could track their movements.

He refused, saying he could disable it by turning it off.

"Who the hell would be tracking *our* location? That's just nuts. I'm keeping my phone."

She snatched it from him. He gave her his 'what the hell' look as Delia put his phone inside a plastic bag the burners were sold in, then filled it with water from the bottle she had on hand. She twisted the end of the plastic bag into a small knot, then heaved it into a garbage container.

"This is bullshit. Do you know how much that phone costs?"

"Don't be a fool, Jimi. Here, take one of these burners. We'll toss it and use a new one, every time we change locations."

Jimi shook his head as he grumbled mightily about the years of contact information he just lost.

"Trust me, Jimi, all those contacts you had on your phone, you won't be needing them, ever again."

There was something about the tone in Delia's voice when she said those words that made Jimi's spine tingle.

Delia wanted a hotel close to the airport, saying they may have to leave again, at a moment's notice. She ignored Jimi when he gave her the "we just got here" line.

At the Tourist Information kiosk, Delia asked the clerk for advice on decent hotels near the airport. The young man was all eyes. He opened his mouth to speak, but nothing was heard. She had to repeat the question before he finally suggested the Proximo Rio Hotel.

Delia checked the hotel's location on a map and said it was "perfect, just minutes away." Jimi called to book a room with the burner Delia forced on him.

As their cab headed east towards the Tagus River, Jimi marveled at the beauty of the city

"First time in Lisbon?" the well-groomed cab driver said in near-perfect English.

"Yes, and it's gorgeous, a magnificent mix of the old and the new," said Jimi.

Delia stayed silent.

"You know, Lisbon is one of the world's oldest cities," said the driver. "Older than Rome."

"Wow, look at that bridge," said Jimi.

"This beautiful bridge you see," the driver explained, "crosses the mighty Tagus River. It is the Vasco da Gama Bridge, the longest in Europe, was named after our famous Portuguese explorer."

Jimi said one thing he knew about Portugal was that drug use had been decriminalized, including heroin. He looked over at Delia for a reaction, but she was unmoved.

"That is true, but our drug issues are much better now than before decriminalization, and traffickers still get arrested here."

Jimi really wanted to ask Delia if that was why they were in Lisbon, to pick up drugs, but thought better of it. She had assured him she would tell him everything. He wondered how long his patience would hold out.

At the hotel, Jimi asked for a suite with a view of the water and got a polite chuckle from the attendant at the front desk.

"Sir, as you can see from our brochure," he said, handing one to Jimi, "all of our suites have 'jaw-dropping' views of the river.

When they entered their suite on the 32nd floor, Jimi let got a huge "Wow."

The breathtaking views of the river and the gleaming Vasco da Gama Bridge spanning it were spread right across the floor-to-ceiling windows which wrapped around the suite.

There were two cocoon-style swing chairs hanging from the ceiling to relax in, and a luxurious whirlpool tub to soak in, all while taking in the spectacular scenery.

"Look, there's even an espresso machine," said Jimi.

"We'll need that in the morning. Right now, I need to rest. Tomorrow, we will meet with the man who has my package."

Jimi went to kiss her, knowing what he wanted to happen next. She gently pushed him away.

"Sorry, Jimi, but I seriously need to get some sleep."

Jimi gave her a disappointed eye. She undressed and got under the covers. Jimi pulled the bottle of bourbon from his carry-on and filled a glass he took from the counter up to the brim. He chugged it back and refilled it.

He saw that Delia was out like a light and turned his gaze to the stunning view beyond the windows. The sun was setting, dipping below the horizon across the shimmering waters like it was slowly drowning.

Jimi sucked back a couple of glassfuls as he marveled at the sight, all the weighty thoughts slowly leaving him as the drink overpowered his senses. He had another glass before feeling the dizzies. He took off his clothes and lay down on the king-size bed next to Delia.

She woke up for a minute and looked at him. There was calm in her eyes, Jimi could sense the quiet. He fell asleep minutes later, curled up against Delia like a kitten to its mother.

CHAPTER 10
Girl gone wild

On the flight to Lisbon, Deon Carter did his due diligence. He had to know more about the elusive redhead. Samantha Isenberg and her lot were hiding something from him. That was as obvious as a kick in the nuts was painful.

Thanks to a former colleague that owed him some favors, Carter had the latest password to the Secret Service's database. The Wi-fi on his flight was slow as molasses, but Carter had nothing but time to kill before landing.

He already knew Isenberg was the richest woman in America, but was surprised to discover the reclusive tycoon had interests in firms all around the globe. The Service's financial experts believed she vastly understated her true wealth, pointing to a number of so-called shell companies that could be traced back to one of her corporate holdings.

Over the last few years, Isenberg had been liquidating her biggest assets. No one seemed to know why.

Isenberg was also very active politically but never publicly showed her hand, refusing interview offers from the media, preferring to let anonymous donations from one of her companies do the talking.

Most of the groups Isenberg was known to fund were affiliated with the so-called Green movement, even more so after President Douglas Triton declared that global warming was "a nefarious hoax perpetuated by a mainstream media that is dominated by lying liberals, and greedy scientists who had invested heavily in developing alternative energy sources."

The screen on Carter's cellphone suddenly flashed a warning: "You are not authorized to be on this site. Cease and desist immediately. Criminal charges may be pending."

Took them nine minutes to shut me down, Carter was thinking. They are getting faster. He knew they would trace the IP address and discover it was him. What they would do about it was another issue. Carter didn't really give a damn.

When he was at the Vegas airport, Carter texted a contact from his time in the Secret Service. Like other big-money organizations, the Service had numerous "information providers" on its clandestine payroll, and over the years Carter developed a great rapport with the cream of the crop.

"This girl can get you in the back door of anything," is how agents depicted the skills of a Dark Web hacker known as Bonnie Best.

"Like the tomato variety, but nowhere near as sweet," Carter used to joke with his fellow agents.

Bonnie Best replied to Carter's request with the same code they used for secret communiques when he was with the Service. She demanded payment upfront, since Carter was no longer an agent with the authority to engage her services. Bonnie Best told him she was making herself available out of appreciation for how Carter helped her out when she was a fledgling hacker seeking high-stakes, big payday action. Long gone were the days when she would work for a hot meal and a cold drink.

Carter knew there would be serious repercussions for her if the Service discovered she was helping him. But he wasn't about to remind her of that.

By now, the wire transfer Carter sent to Bonnie Best's offshore account should have dropped. It wouldn't take her long to get him answers. Carter needed to know why Isenberg wanted the redhead brought to her, without a hair out of place.

A message finally arrived from Bonnie Best, asking him to dial into a radio station livestreaming from Bern, Switzerland. After entering the password she sent, he was to look for a file called "Bern Playlist." This was a new tech trick for Carter. Essentially, the information she sent "piggybacked" on the radio station's bandwidth. It couldn't be detected, unless one used the specific login she provided.

In seconds, the file appeared. Carter got reading.

The redhead was Delia Cassavetes, born in San Francisco 28 years ago. She was originally a brunette. Tall and athletic, she excelled at sports in school. She was also on the Berkeley swim team. During a competition in Los Angeles, she was approached by the father of a competing Cal State swimmer. Said he was a photographer for big-ticket clients. She declined his offer to do some test shoots at Dockweiler Beach the next day. On Facebook, she told friends the guy gave her the creeps.

There were other offers during her freshman year, most from characters claiming to be agents looking for new talent. "Get lost, creep" was a term Delia used often.

Her parents were from Athens, immigrated to America a year after their wedding day. Delia was born shortly after the couple settled in San Francisco. She was an only child. Her mother was unable to bear children following treatment for uterine cancer. Delia's father wanted her to be the second lawyer in the Cassavetes clan, and had already preordained she would take over his small tax law firm.

But the modelling offers didn't stop, becoming increasingly enticing after one of her guy friends posted pictures of Delia in a string bikini all over social media. Against her parents' wishes, Delia dropped out of Berkeley after signing a lucrative contract from an A-list modelling agency when she was 19.

At first, the diamond-in the-rough Delia was loved by all and hailed as the next Big Beauty. Interviews with film directors and producers were easily arranged and she was told small parts in upcoming films were being written specifically for her.

Delia was excited about her future and even managed to get her father's blessing, after showing him the check she received for a modelling assignment in Palm Springs.

Popular rising star Delia was being invited to parties all over Southern California, her handlers insisting it was in her best interests to attend.

"And don't be a wallflower," they told her. "You have the best body in the business. Flaunt it."

There were social events almost every night and Delia had difficulty coping with the expectations and demands from her agency. She was out past the witching hour almost daily, and up with the sun to prepare for shoots, go-sees and auditions. She kept telling everyone the pace was too stressful, and she was always tired. They told her to take an assortment of vitamins and consume more lean protein.

Then it happened. Delia started friending it up with the permanently un-sober, life-is-an-endless-carnival crowd in Los Angeles. There were pills for when she was fatigued and pills for when it was time to sleep. She began to favor parties where the drugs were as overflowing as the Grey Goose and Dom Perignon.

Delia became extremely difficult to manage. She was late for assignments and messed up promotions during the agency's premier showcases.

She was eventually dumped by her management team, who went out of their way to let other agencies know that drug-head Delia was as reliable as an expired condom.

The final curtain came down after the wife of an influential media magnate walked in on Delia and her husband. She snapped a photo of a topless Delia, passed out in the hot tub, with her naked husband all over her. The wife threatened to divorce him and post the grubby photograph all over the Internet, unless he made sure Delia never worked again, unless 7-Eleven or Wal-Mart were hiring.

Delia followed that up by falling off the catwalk during a fashion show organized by one of her few remaining friends, specifically to mark her comeback. She picked herself up, then berated the organizers, claiming they gave her the wrong size shoes to wear. A number of high-brow fashionistas were in the audience, bearing witness to her drug-fueled tirade.

The take-no-prisoner's paparazzi hounded Delia like never before after that self-inflicted debacle. Unflattering photographs of the doped-out former beauty queen were posted on those hussy online sites that celebrities fear more than they dread trashy scripts. The offers dried up for good. She did not.

Delia was desperate and broke. She dyed her hair red, hoping the paparazzi wouldn't recognize her. A few months later, she was knocking on her parents' front door in San Francisco. She had lost everything.

Carter was at a loss to explain how Bonnie Best managed to get hold of such personal details, but remembered that, when it came to data mining, she was the best driller in the business.

The last few snippets of information on Delia Cassavetes were puzzling to Carter. Her last known address was an apartment above a restaurant on 16th Street in the Mission District, where she lived when she was arrested for shoplifting from children's apparel shops in the neighborhood.

"Shoplifting from kids' clothing stores? Why in hell would she do that?" Carter wondered.

During her trial, Delia managed to stay cool and tight-lipped. Her father had connections and hooked her up with a clever criminal attorney. Delia got off with probation and community service.

The final item in the report was even more bewildering to Carter. Medical records from San Francisco General Hospital revealed Delia was dropped off by persons unknown near the emergency entrance a few months ago, apparently suffering from a heroin overdose.

An ER doctor recorded that she was on the verge of death. Another report indicated that, three hours after being admitted, Delia suddenly got up from her gurney, yanked the IV tubes and monitors from her body, declared that she was feeling fine, and literally vanished before hospital security could track her down.

Bonnie's report ended there, leaving Carter with questions still unanswered. Why would a sharp businesswoman like Samantha Isenberg pay millions to get her hands on a washed-up former model with debilitating drug issues? And why was someone hired to kill a down-trending loser like Delia Cassavetes?

Carter was so preoccupied with the report that 20 minutes passed before he noticed a message had dropped. It was from General Isadore Pope.

"Call me, ASAP."

Carter knew the general well, and not just from his time playing college football when Pope was his head coach. These days, the general was not someone you wanted to mess with.

There were many hushed whispers about the 'Dark Pope' in Washington watering holes, where media gadflies kept distilleries in the black. Tales were told of those who voiced opposition to the general suffering untimely accidents. Some were fatal.

Most recently, Carter read about the accidental death of the Secretary of Defense. General Pope was named as a temporary replacement. Maybe the rumors were true, maybe they were smears. The only thing Carter knew for certain was that, in Washington, D.C., the line dividing truth from lies was purely imaginary.

What the hell did Pope want with him after all these years? As he walked through the Arrivals terminal at the Portello Airport, Carter's giant knees began to feel small.

CHAPTER 11

Downward spiral

When Jimi woke up the next morning, Delia was in the bathroom. He could hear the shower running. He got dressed, made some espresso, and went out to the balcony to embrace the sunshine. Down below, people holding cellphones like they were cameras dotted the grounds of the hotel.

"Tourists, they're the same everywhere they go," he said out loud, recalling the tourist-littered streets of Vegas.

His gaze drifted south. Lisbon was one hilly place, some looked as steep as cliffs. He saw an historic-looking building on one of the hills, figured it was the Sao Jorge Castle he'd read about in the hotel brochure.

He finished his espresso and put his hands on the railing as he looked around the city. He thought the railing height was lower than the ones in the States but figured, from what he'd seen, the Portuguese were definitely a tad shorter than the average American.

He started hoping he and Delia would have some time to play tourists, explore this enchanting city on foot, although trekking up and down those hillsides would take a slice off the soles of his shoes.

When he saw people lined up to get breakfast at a sidewalk café, his stomach talked to him. He went back into the suite and looked over the room service menu. The *frittata* sounded good, but he'd never tried something called "baked eggs."

"We have to leave, as soon as possible," said Delia as she emerged from the bathroom, a fluffy white towel wrapped snugly around her torso, still combing her wet hair out with her fingers.

"Can we at least eat first?" Jimi flashed the menu in her face.

"We'll eat on the way."

"Where are we going?"

"South, to Albufeira, in the Algarve region. We'll rent a car and get there in just a few hours. Be quicker than going to the airport and hoping there's a flight to Faro right away, then we'd still have to drive 40 minutes to get to Albufeira."

"Why are we going *there*? You said the package was here in Lisbon."

"The man who has my package left Lisbon last night. Creep didn't bother waiting for me. Plans have changed, I got a message. Unfortunately, this man is a snake, I have no control over the meeting place."

"But that means we won't have time to explore Lisbon. This is my first time in Europe, you know."

"There are more important matters at hand, Jimi. Look, the drive to Albufeira will have to do for your 'sightseeing tour.' The rolling countryside and quaint villages will be very pleasant for you to look at during the drive."

Jimi reached for the half-empty bottle of bourbon, took a quick hit and packed it in his carry-on. Delia laid out the plan as they readied to leave.

After checking them out, Jimi was to head straight for the car rental shop they saw on the way to the hotel.

"Get a fast car, Jimi—a BMW or an Audi. The highways here are like race tracks."

"So, you have been in Portugal before?"

Delia just kept giving Jimi instructions.

"I have some contacts to make, then I will get dressed and meet you out front of the hotel in 20 minutes. Don't just stand there, go, 20 minutes. Don't be late. Fast car."

After checking them out, Jimi made quick strides across the hotel lobby, swinging his carry-on as he hurried to the front doors. The carry-on smacked into a young girl in his path who was eating a pastry. The vanilla custard filling was splattered on her cheeks.

"I am so sorry," said Jimi, not even knowing if she understood English.

"You broke it," said the girl, who looked around seven years old.

Jimi bent over and tried to wipe the custard from her face with his free hand.

"What are you doing to my daughter!" screamed a woman running toward them.

"Help—security!"

"It was an accident, ma'am, please, happy to get your daughter another pastry. Where did you buy it?"

The little girl told her mom what happened. The mother calmed down, gave Jimi the quick once over, then smiled. She told him the pastry was called *pasteis de nata* and came from the hotel's breakfast buffet.

"Wait here, I will be right back with another pastry for you," said Jimi, thinking he would grab a couple more for himself and Delia. Hunger was starting to cramp his thoughts. Plus, it would be good to find out if the brochure was right about the "mouth-watering" little pastries.

***

Delia was out on the balcony, still wrapped in a bath towel. She was in a trance-like state, like the one Jimi witnessed back in Vegas. She didn't notice the man who stepped through the sliding doors onto the balcony.

"Delia, my name is Deon Carter. I was sent by Samantha Isenberg. I need you to come with me."

Delia appeared to be looking right through him as she stood with her back to the balcony railing. Her eyes were a bright, beaming blue and she was motionless.

"Miss? … Delia?"

Carter put his right hand on her left shoulder and in a much louder voice he said, "Miss?"

Delia broke from her trance and instinctively pushed Carter away from her with both arms. His massive frame stood firm, whiplashing her body backwards. She rolled over the railing and plunged head-first to the waters below.

CHAPTER 12
Little red Peugeot

After giving the little girl a fresh pastry, Jimi ate one of the others he'd purchased as he exited the hotel. He came upon a large group of people, speaking excitedly and pointing at the river. Jimi did not recognize the tongues being spoken, but his ears picked out a familiar few.

"Oh me godt, I can no believe what me eyes 'ave seen."

"It's a miracle," came another voice.

"I got it all on video as I was shooting the hotel to show how it sits right on the water," said another.

"I wanna see it," a woman said.

Much of the crowd gathered around a young man who was cueing up a video on his phone.

"*Inacreditavel!*"

"*Incrivel, meu Dios!*"

Jimi had to know what all the fuss was about and started across the road toward the growing crowd.

A little red Peugeot almost smacked right into him as it came to a screeching halt, inches from his knees.

"Get in!"

It was Delia, still wrapped in a bath towel, her flaming red hair a flying mess over her face.

"Delia? What the hell …"

"Get in, we have to get out of here," she said, reaching over to open the passenger door.

"I just want to see what all the commotion is about over there," Jimi said, pointing to the circle of people by the hotel.

"Be right back."

A silver Mercedes stuck in traffic behind the Peugeot started honking its horn, the driver rolling down her window and yelling, "*Mova-o estupido turista!*"

Delia jumped out of the car, shoved Jimi into the passenger seat, then punched the gas pedal with her shoeless foot.

"What the hell is wrong with you?" said Jimi, sounding pissed.

The other *pasteis de nata* Jimi bought was crushed to his left hand, vanilla custard ready to drip on his pants.

"This one was for you," Jimi sighed.

Delia pulled into the lane that would take them across the Vasco de Gama bridge and cursed.

"Goddamn stupid little car has no guts."

"I would have got us a fast car, if you weren't in such a goddamn hurry," said Jimi.

"I, umm, sort of *borrowed* this one. It was handy."

"What? Why? What the hell is going on? Why didn't you get dressed before leaving the hotel—or is that a new style you are plugging, bath towel chic?"

"Do you really think I'd parade around town in a towel, Jimi?" Delia sounding peeved.

"I had unexpected company. I had to improvise. I will explain later. Right now, use the GPS to find out how to get us to Albufeira as quick as possible."

Jimi was tired of hearing Delia say she would "explain later." This girl was a mess. What the hell had he gotten himself into?

Delia looked at the clock on the dashboard and shook her head.

"Crap. In this gutless little car, we won't make it on time."

Jimi swiped most of the crushed pastry on the side of his car seat, wiping the rest away on his pant legs.

He saw no navigation features on the Peugeot's dashboard so he used his burner phone.

"There's an exit after the bridge that will take us to highway A2. From there it becomes a toll road, but it looks like the quickest route to Albufeira."

Delia cursed the car again, as if she could shame it into picking up more speed.

Jimi, noting that Delia was wearing just a towel and driving a "borrowed" car, said: "I don't think we should be speeding."

"We will have to stop and rent a faster car, once we are well out of the city," said Delia. "I will also need to dye my hair."

"A cool platinum shade would be a perfect match for your eyes," said Jimi. "But don't you think some clothing would be top of your list right now?"

"We'll find a clothing shop along the way. You can buy me something to wear."

"I thought the whole trip was on your dime?"

"Listen, Jimi. I left everything—including my purse—back at the hotel."

Jimi said they were lucky Delia gave him her passport to keep with his, then pressed her to explain why she left the hotel without her stuff.

"Not now," she snapped.

Little was said as they travelled, save for the odd "crap" from Delia, when another vehicle went blasting by them.

They stopped at a small town called Alcacer do Sol, about 25 minutes south of Lisbon. Delia told Jimi to fill up with gas while she waited in the car.

"And ask the guy over there where the nearest clothing shop is," she said, pointing to a man filling up next to them.

"The guy spoke English, said there are shops and restaurants just a few streets over, near the river."

Delia browsed the shops as they drove by, parking in front of one that had female mannequins wearing blue-jean-style jeggings in the front window. She made sure the bath towel was wrapped snugly and went inside the shop.

The two girls in the otherwise empty shop appeared stunned by the nonchalant manner in which the barefoot and towel-wrapped Delia fingered through a rack of colorful summer dresses, but said nothing. Both were young, one short, one taller.

When Jimi turned to watch Delia, the shorter clerk whispered to the other, "*Uau, ele tem um corpo sexy.*"

The taller clerk whispered back: "*Gostaria de ter relações sexuais com ele.*"

They both giggled.

Jimi had no idea what they were saying, but it made his cheeks turn red.

"Do you ladies speak English?"

The taller clerk responded with, "Yes, a liddle beet." The shorter clerk nodded no.

Delia quickly settled on a pale blue sundress and a white cotton sweater, suitable for the cool late-April evenings in southern Portugal.

"*Você não deseja experimentar em primeira, senhora?*" the shorter clerk asked Delia.

Delia pressed the sundress against her body for a second, then replied, *Onde está a sua mudar de quarto?*"

"*Na parte de trás da loja, à sua direita.*"

Jimi's surprised eyes gave Delia the "you speak Portuguese?" look. She waved him off with the flick of an eyelash and headed for the back of the shop.

Jimi asked the taller one for a translation.

"Your gurl, she is sizing dress in changing room."

When Delia returned a few minutes later, the shorter clerk said: "*É perfeito para você. Você surpreendentes. Temos uma excelente selecção de brás e roupas íntimas bem, Senhora.*"

"*Obrigado perca, nenhum que não será necessário,*" Delia said.

The clerk's eyebrows raised high at Delia's response. She then pointed at Delia's bare feet and said: "*O que sobre um bom par de sapatos?*"

"*Há uma loja com tênis de corrida para venda do outro lado da rua,*" Delia replied, pointing through the shop's window to a shoe store across the street.

Jimi figured they were talking about shoes, but his eyes never looked at her feet.

Jimi paid for the sundress and sweater, the girls smiling as they counted the euros. Delia was already out the shop door when he heard the shorter clerk say to the other with a tone of condemnation: "*Que mulher vestidos como uma vagabunda.*"

"I think they were saying something nasty about you," Jimi said as they crossed the street.

"I heard. They said I dress like a slut, but they liked you ..."

"Oh?"

"They said they wanted to have sex with you ... wanna go back inside?"

"Yeah, the line starts here," Jimi smiled, pointing to Delia.

"Easy, pretty boy. But nice of you to put me at the front of the line."

"You never told me you could speak Portuguese."

"Actually, I have not told you *anything* about myself, Jimi. Now, let's go buy some running shoes."

"Why running shoes, I love my shoes, super comfortable."

"We may have to do some, ah, 'running,' Jimi. Better to be prepared."

Jimi wondered if she was referring to 'running' from the cops when they located the car she stole.

They were in the shoe store for all of 10 minutes before walking out wearing shiny new Pumas. Jimi spotted a little restaurant called Casa de Churrasco across the street and remembered how hungry he was.

"Come on," he said, grabbing her by the hand. "If we don't eat something right now, I am going to faint on you."

Inside the restaurant, Delia said the food must be good since the place was full of local-types, chowing down on heaping plates of piri-piri chicken, salted *bacalhau* with chopped onions and parsley, and sizzling chorizo sausages.

"I've had the piri-piri chicken in Vegas, I should try some while I am here, see if it's as good as what we get back home," said Jimi.

Delia explained that, although piri-piri was available around the world, it was actually Portuguese cuisine, suggesting he try something he could *not* get back in the U.S. On the menu, she pointed to a dish called *espada maltratado*.

"I'm always willing to try new eats, Delia, but you have to tell me what that is. Sounds like something you put on leather shoes, not in your mouth."

"It's absolutely delicious, you won't regret it."

Delia ordered two *espada maltratado*, with rice, boiled broccoli and roasted baby potatoes, standard Portuguese side dishes.

"First you try some *espada* ... then I'll tell you what it is."

While they waited for their food, Jimi and Delia played footsies under the table and smiled bashfully at each other, like they were love-struck teenagers on a first date.

Jimi was loving this side of Delia, playful and full of tease. She could go from dead serious to schoolgirl silly in the blink of an eye. It was like she was two different people.

When the food was served, Jimi cut a piece of the crisply-battered *espada* and forked it onto his tongue. At the first chew, he told Delia it was "the best fish I ever had."

"*Espada preta* is actually a black eel with a menacing face, like a barracuda, called black scabbard in English."

"That's crazy—I am eating *eel*? I feel sick."

"No different than eating slimy snails or other unpleasant-looking creatures like octopus, is it?"

"I do like octopus ... and squid. OK, going to finish this *espada*, it really is lip-smacking good. Once you get that black eel with a barracuda head thing out of the way," Jimi laughed.

As they enjoyed the rest of their meal, Delia told him more about the bizarre black eel.

"*Espada* lives deep in the ocean. It rarely rises above 2,000 feet below the surface, until the sun goes down. This is why it is usually fished at night."

Jimi was feeling good, enjoying the meal and Delia's company. He never thought about ordering a drink, until he saw a man at the next table, pouring the last drop from a bottle of *vinho tinto* into his glass. It was as if Delia could read his mind ...

"No time for drinking, Jimi, we really have to go."

While they were paying the bill, the waiter told Delia there was no rental car agency in town, so back onto the highway in the sputtering Peugeot they went, Jimi at the wheel this time.

Delia told him to floor it, Jimi replying his foot was flat with the floor.

"Crap. We will never get there on time. We took too long to eat. Jimi, pull over, we have to lower the car's weight."

"Say what?"

"Less weight will give us more speed, it's basic science."

Jimi pulled over and Delia quickly got to work. He watched, shaking his head. Delia the lunatic was showing her face now.

First, she took out the spare tire and jack. She removed all of the floor mats, tore off the sun visors, emptied the little glove compartment, and threw out any loose items from within the vehicle, save for Jimi's carry on. Then off came all of the car's metallic branding.

She also ripped off the bumper guards on both sides and snapped off the windshield wipers. Using a ballpoint pen she found in the glove compartment, Delia poked two holes into the soft plastic of the windshield wiper canister and let the fluid drain.

After kicking out the headlights, glass and plastic falling under the front tires, she said, "Get in, Jimi, I'll drive."

Jimi said the speedometer didn't go any higher, but Delia insisted the car was travelling faster and would definitely have more juice going up hills. All Jimi could see was other vehicles still leaving the Peugeot in their dust.

Jimi put the seat back to help his full belly digest. Delia was focused on keeping as straight a line as possible, hugging every curve to the inch, telling Jimi a straight line was the shortest point between two distances.

Jimi trained his bleary eyes out the window. The landscape was changing from green, rolling hills to small farms and orchards as they drove farther south. He spotted what he thought to be cork trees, some with their trunks ripped open. He saw olive trees, walnut trees and small vineyards. He saw Delia grit her teeth as she saw another car zoom past them.

The silence started to get to Jimi after a while. He wanted to talk to Delia, get some real answers, but held back. She was on edge about something, he could sense it.

They were still miles away from Albufeira when Delia broke the silence.

"Back in your suite, you told me when you were young, you would spend hours daydreaming about space travel, life on other planets …"

"I did, had a lot of time on my hands back then."

"What would you do if you actually met a being from another planet?"

"I would have a lot of questions, that's for sure."

"You would not be frightened?"

"Hell no."

"Seems to me, most humans would be afraid, to the point of panic. What kinds of questions would you ask a Cosmic visitor from another galaxy?"

"Well, before I answer that, you should understand I don't think like most people. I'm self-taught, quit school in Grade 10. Never did graduate from one of the 'education sweatshops' that churn out cheese heads from the same recipe. That's why I drink, you know. It's my escape from a world which wallows in ignorance. It's depressing to hear about all the wars and killing, because our leaders are fools. It makes me so angry."

"I know you are an intelligent man, Jimi, I sensed this from the beginning. There is more to you than what your alcohol-fueled, playboy lifestyle implies.

"You say you are a free thinker? I am curious as to how that makes your views different."

Jimi glanced over. Delia looked like she meant what she said. He felt encouraged to continue.

"OK ... The way I see it, our scientific principles and our system of beliefs are flawed by our failure to grasp what is so obvious."

"What is 'so obvious?'"

"Simple. We're at a primitive point on our evolutionary path. Using the Cosmos timeline, hell, we stepped from our caves like, a second ago. We don't understand the Universe and our place in it. We don't understand the things we see. Sadly, we *think* we do.

"Our science is based on how things work on Earth, but we know the rest of the Universe is infinitely more complex. We are like children, singing nursery rhymes we think are real, because we don't know any better.

"In reality, what we call 'truth,' is more like fiction, something we make up as we go along."

"But it is your truth for *now*, a basis upon which you can plan for the future."

"If there weren't so many prevailing 'truths' out there—thank you Internet—I would agree with you, Delia. But there is no singular truth on Earth, no singular vision. That's why we go to war, to force the vanquished to believe what the victors tell them to believe. Beneath our clever, sophisticated veneer, we are ignorant and cruel creatures at heart."

"Are you suggesting humanity will *never* evolve beyond that?"

"Not with the so-called *truths* humans currently hold dear. Things like nationalism and religion are barriers to our spiritual growth, keeping us controlled and infantile. We will never realize our potential as a race so long as our leaders go out of their way to keep these blinkers on us.

"We have smoke detectors in our homes and safety features on our cars to protect us from bodily harm, but there is nothing to protect our minds from the lies of industrialists, politicians and men of the cloth. This is why meeting aliens from another planet, another reality, would be such a benefit to us. Don't you agree?"

There was no answer from Delia. Jimi let the discussion fade to black. He'd learned from past experience that his self-righteous lectures fell on deaf ears. People are more inclined to accept principles that support what they already believe in, instead of exploring opinions that disrupt their reality. Henry David Thoreau nailed it when he said, "The mass of men lead lives of quiet desperation and die with their song still inside them." It's been some 200 years since *Walden Pond*, not much has changed.

"Jimi, I think we are being followed."

"How can you tell?"

"Well, I've seen a black beamer behind us a number of times for the last hour or so. It never passes us, slows down going up hills like we do … seems to fall way back, but when we approach any kind of exit off the highway, it comes within visual range again."

"That's all I've seen on this highway, dark-colored BMWs flying by us, for hours."

"Like I said, Jimi. This one, does not pass us."

"If it was the cops, they would have arrested us by now for stealing then trashing the crap out of this car. Who the hell would be following us in this part of the world?"

"Not to worry. I know who it is," said Delia.

A loud popping sound startled both of them. Delia lost control of the Peugeot and veered off into the ditch.

CHAPTER 13
Gravity Girl

Deon Carter's size-20 loafers inched their way to the edge of the balcony. His arms and legs got the shakes as he leaned over the railing and looked 32-stories down to the river.

There was no sign of a body, or a towel, bobbing in the rushing waves below.

He had killed the woman he was hired to protect. What would he tell Samantha Isenberg?

There goes the million-dollar bounty. He had planned to retire, somewhere warm, with palm trees swaying and blue waters kissing the shoreline … Barbados, where his family was from.

He knew he had to call Isenberg, but needed to come up with something better than Delia Cassavetes plunged to her death because he messed up.

"Oh my god, this is crazy. Oh my god … she bounced right off me."

Everything was going so well. Earlier, he asked a young man at the airport's Tourist Information kiosk if he'd seen a pretty woman with long red hair passing through recently, saying he was a co-worker here for a convention.

"Really beautiful lady, with eyes you can't forget? She's at the Proximo Rio Hotel, on the river."

Even the hotel clerk was helpful, giving up Delia's room number after Carter slipped him a 20.

Back in the suite, he sat on the couch facing the river, still playing out scenarios that might have Isenberg take pity. He noticed a handbag on the coffee table. He opened it up. Inside was Delia's ID, and a few hundred euros. Carter pocketed the euros, sighing, "She won't be needing these."

A search of the suite turned up little else. There was a pair of dress pants and a sweater on the bathroom floor. Delia's, he assumed. He fingered through the pockets. Empty.

There was no sign that Jimi James had left anything behind. Carter wondered where he'd gone. Was he coming back to meet Delia?

He checked the time. His next report to Isenberg was more than two hours late. He had delayed the call, figuring he would soon have the redhead in hand, better to call then. He might as well just phone Isenberg now. Get it over with.

She answered at the first ring.

"Mr. Carter. You are late, I have been waiting for your report."

"With apologies, Ms. Isenberg. I am in Lisbon, tried to call you earlier but I must have been in a dead zone, did not have a signal."

"Uh-huh ... were you under water or something, Mr. Carter?"

That was a dumb thing to say, he realized. Of course, she didn't believe him. Now what ... keep it together, man, don't panic. Carter took some deep breaths. His mind was racing.

"Is something wrong, Carter—what are you not telling me? Where is the girl?"

"I have not found Delia Cassavetes, yet."

"Really? She and Jimi James checked into the Proximo Rio Hotel near the airport—yesterday, my people tell me. You should have reported to me on time, I would have told you this. We could have her by now."

Isenberg sounded more disappointed than angry, but definitely both.

"Very well, I will go there immediately."

"Do it, Carter. Report back the minute you find her."

Carter hoped it would be days before Delia's body was discovered, if at all, given the Tagus River's strong push to the Atlantic Ocean. He should have enough time to set something up. If and when the body was found, he would then tell Isenberg that, based on his investigation, it looked as if Jimi James had killed her. Damn, no good, the police would investigate, the clerk at the Proximo Rio would definitely remember a giant black man asking for Delia Cassavetes's hotel room number.

Carter had another look around, then tore Delia's clothing into small pieces with his bare hands, and flushed them down the toilet bit by bit. He scooped up her purse on his way out the door and left the hotel using the service exit.

He had a plan. Get the hell out of Lisbon. Deal with the consequences later.

Within a few hours, Carter was in a restaurant at Gatwick in London, waiting on the cajun chicken with a side of Moroccan meatballs he'd ordered. He had an hour or so to kill before his flight to Los Angeles.

Should he return General Isadore Pope's call from London, or wait until he was back home? Hell, maybe Pope had an assignment for him, wouldn't be that far-fetched. Then he could tell Isenberg he left Lisbon on orders from the highest-ranking military official in America. This just might work, he reasoned, tucking into his first meatball. But, better to call the general when he was back in the U.S., then he wouldn't have to answer any questions about why he was in Europe.

Back home in L.A., Carter was about to hit the ignition button in his late-model sports car when his cellphone went off. Carter fumbled to dig the ringing phone from his jacket pocket. It was Bonnie Best.

"Jellybean, have you seen the video?"

Carter was more surprised at the excitement in her voice than he was by the fact she actually phoned him, breaking a longstanding protocol.

"What video?"

She told him a video had gone ballistic online, featuring a woman in a bath towel that had plummeted down the side of the Proximo Rio Hotel in Lisbon.

"I have confirmed it was Delia."

Jesus, it's over, they found the body. I am royally screwed, Carter thought.

He wanted to tell her Delia's death was a freak accident, but bit his fat tongue, hard. Trust no one. There was no way of knowing to whom Bonnie Best ultimately reported. She was always evasive whenever he dared ask. Not only that, talking to her about this on an unsecured connection was an arrest waiting to happen.

"Should we be talking on an unsecured line?"

"It's all good, Jellybean. I scanned your phone and disabled the apps with covert listening. You're clean, for now, but word of advice … be wary of installing updates to apps on your cellphone. In fact, don't use *any* apps, unless it's absolutely critical."

"You scanned my phone—remotely? How is that possible?"

"Have you forgotten who I am? You were in the Service; you know what cellphones are *really* used for."

That reminder made Carter even more nervous. Could he really trust Bonnie Best? Better to proceed with caution, watch every word that came out of his mouth. Or maybe he should switch to the phone Isenberg's people provided. Isenberg guaranteed him it was untraceable. No, better not, Isenberg's phone may be secure, but surely not out of *her* reach.

"How did this video get online, who shot it?" Carter stammered, hoping his edginess went unnoticed.

"Tourists who were also staying at the hotel. You should look it up, see for yourself."

"I will. Any idea who was responsible for her death?"

"Death? … *No*, no, Jellybean. Delia survived. She was somehow able to use the towel like a parachute, stopping her fall, inches from hitting the water. It's all on the video."

"*What*? That's impossible. Are you fffing pulling my chain?"

"You know I would never do that. Look, this girl has skills I haven't seen written about anywhere on government dispatches—Top Secret or otherwise. I'm pretty sure she's one of the Super Soldiers the military has been secretly developing. No wonder everyone is after her. She must be worth millions."

Carter heard rumors about the Super Soldier program when he was in the Service. Genetically engineered humans with advanced biogenic implants, by way of Japanese scientists the military kept on its pay-in-cash-only payroll. He never heard they succeeded in creating a working model, but that was years ago. The science behind the venture was evolving faster than any other part of human endeavor.

"Wait, you said 'everybody is after her?'"

"There has been chatter about this woman all over privileged CIA dispatches that I regularly monitor, Jellybean. General Isadore Pope's name is mentioned on some of these dispatches, you know him, right?"

Carter's face froze over.

"Jellybean … you still there?"

"Yes, I'm listening …"

"While we were talking, I tuned back in to my news feed. Worldwide media is all over this story, it's everywhere. They are calling Delia 'Gravity Girl.'"

Carter dropped the phone and slumped forward against the steering wheel.

"*Lord Jesus*. Who the hell is this woman?"

CHAPTER 14

Black magic woman

Delia spotted the problem right away. The left front tire had popped off the rim.

"See that?" said Jimi. "Looks like a shard from the headlights you kicked off the car."

"The tires are old and worn out, but you could be right."

"Damn, if you had not chucked the spare tire …"

"Get your bag, we can walk the rest of the way."

"How long of a walk?"

"About 20 minutes. I can see the Albufeira sign off in the distance."

Jimi couldn't see the sign, but took her word for it, saying, "OK, bright eyes.

"But why walk? Put your thumb up. With your looks, some guy is bound to pick us up."

"Hitchhiking is not an option, Jimi. There is a description of me all over the news by now. Someone driving by while I stand there with my thumb up will use their cellphone to alert authorities."

"Yeah, your flaming red hair is like a neon sign, that's for sure."

"How about this," she said, "so no one can see my hair as we walk to Albufeira."

Delia placed the white sweater she purchased in Alcacer do Sol over her head like a bonnet, tying the ends around her neck, then tucking her hair up and under it.

"Now people will just think you are an idiot," Jimi scoffed. "Look, do you really think someone saw you steal the car? And why the hell would the police issue an alert for you? I'm pretty sure cars in a big city like Lisbon are stolen by the minute."

"Perhaps. Jimi, start walking."

"You *are* crazy. 'Be on the lookout for a good-looking insane woman walking with a white turban on her head.' That's what a police report would say."

"Shut up, walk faster."

"The only good thing about this situation is that we have comfortable shoes—and don't say 'I told you so,' psychic turban girl."

Delia ignored Jimi's silliness and started walking at a brisk pace. As they approached the outskirts of Albufeira, Delia stopped an old man carrying bags of groceries.

"Excuse me, sir. How far is the Nomar Beach Hotel?" she asked in Portuguese.

"*Nomar? Não muito longe*," said the man, pointing down the road.

"What did he say"

"It's not far, let's go."

When they arrived at the hotel, Delia asked Jimi to book their room.

"You have money, I don't. Ask for the highest floor—a room with a balcony."

"Where are you going?"

"To find the man with my package. We are really late in arriving, but maybe this time he waited a little longer," said Delia, moving away quickly.

She went out to the narrow road with cars parked on the left side and looked it up and down. She walked a big circle around the hotel, ending up at the front entrance again.

"Bastard."

***

Jimi told the hotel clerk he was coming in from Lisbon and had walked the last half hour because their car broke down.

"From Lisbon?" said the clerk. "Then you must have heard about the naked woman who jumped from the top of the Proximo Rio Hotel and survived."

"I was at that hotel this morning—is that what all the commotion was about?"

"Must be, that's when it happened, this morning. There are videos on the Internet and the story is making international headlines. Pretty amazing. You should definitely watch the video, especially in slo-mo," said the clerk with a wink.

After getting his pass key, Jimi looked around the lobby for Delia. He noticed a bunch of people crowding into the far corner, watching something.

"*Senhora de Gravidade*," one of the men said softly, like he was praying in church.

"*Senhora de Gravidade*," another voice echoed with the same reverence.

Jimi wondered what all the fuss was about, but couldn't see what they were watching from behind all the bodies. He turned away and headed for his room. He was tired, and the thought of a comfortable bed sounded like heaven. But what he needed most, was a drink.

When he got in the room, running shoes and socks were first to go. There were two drinking glasses on a small wooden table beside the television, so he flipped it on, surfed for English channels, then poured some bourbon.

He settled on the NOA news network, figuring it will have a report on that naked hotel jumper the clerk told him about.

"We have an update on the incredible story out of Lisbon, Portugal," NOA's Larry Wolf was saying. Jimi was all ears.

"NOA correspondent Lindsay Buckingham recently arrived at the hotel and is live with this latest report. Lindsay …"

"Well Larry, I have to say, it is absolute mayhem here at the hotel. Looks like media from all over the world have descended like vultures. We had to walk a mile just to get near the hotel, as Lisbon Police have cordoned off the area and are preventing anyone from driving anywhere near the scene of this miraculous event."

"Lindsay, any reports of anyone having seen the so-called Gravity Girl?"

"None that can be substantiated, but you can bet every woman in the area with long red hair is getting the once over by police, and the media, for that matter."

Jimi gulped down the bourbon and refilled his glass, spilling some on the tiled floor, as his eyes never left the TV screen.

"Amazing," he said, between big sips.

"Can you explain to viewers around the world, who may be seeing this report for the first time, why everyone is calling the jumper 'Gravity Girl.'"

"Of course, Larry, we have a better handle on that now. From what we have uncovered so far, the video that's online was posted by a Portuguese man, who tagged the video "Senhora de Gravidade," comparing it to the miracle of Our Lady of Fatima, 'Nossa Senhora de Fatima,' as they refer to her in Portuguese. As you know, Larry, the video went viral to the *extreme* with billions of views already. Someone who shared the video even added a soundtrack to the footage, from an old Santana song called *Black Magic Woman*.

"When the first English media started reporting on the story, *Senhora de Gravidade* was translated as Gravity Girl. The name stuck, and media everywhere are now referring to the redheaded woman by that name."

"Lindsay, are there any leads as to who this Gravity Girl is, do we have a name?"

"She has not been identified as of yet, Larry, but police tell me they have some leads they're chasing down. In fact, one of the French reporters here just filed a story claiming he spoke to an eyewitness who saw the Gravity Girl getting into a little red car with an unknown accomplice, a man."

Jimi was going through the bourbon like he had a thirst that wouldn't stop.

"Oh. My. God."

"Let's show the video, one more time, Larry."

"Before we roll the video again, a reminder to viewers around the world of NOA's policy against showing gratuitous nudity. However, given the nature of this story, the brevity of actual nudity, and the fact that billions have already viewed it uncut, NOA producers made the decision to air the video as is."

The footage was just a few seconds long. It showed a woman with red hair falling backwards through the air down the river side of the hotel. The rushing wind unravels the bath towel wrapped around her body. She grabs it before it flies off, straightens her body upright, then spreads her arms outward like a bird does its wings. She stops falling, just before her feet touch the surface of the water.

Hovering over the river, the waves lapping at her toes, the woman ties the bath towel back around herself, then darts quickly across the water like she was stepping on solid ground.

Jimi did not hear Delia enter the hotel room. She stopped about six feet away, off his right shoulder. When he noticed her, his breathing got heavy.

"Who, the hell, are, you?"

"You don't recognize me as a blond, Jimi? I dyed my hair in the hotel's little spa. No one was using it, the door was unlocked, so ..."

"NO! *Who the hell are you!*"

Delia came as close to Jimi as she could without touching him. Her eyes grew brighter.

"You look tired, Jimi. You should go to bed."

"I won't be able to sleep until you tell me who you really are."

"You know that already, don't you, Jimi?"

"I don't know what I know."

"You must rest, Jimi. You will sleep now."

Delia's eyes emitted a beam of blue, right into Jimi's eyes. His head started to feel warm.

The glass slipped from his hand. His eyes rolled back in his head. He dropped to his knees and rolled over.

CHAPTER 15
My blue angel

The richest woman in America stands just over five feet and makes a shoelace look thick. As a teenager, her peers joked about her elfin stature, saying things like: "Sam's still here. She's just turned sideways and disappeared."

Young Samantha Isenberg hated shopping for clothes, nothing looked good on her bony frame. It was an exercise in embarrassment for her, having to buy boys' shirts and pants. In high school, she watched with envy as other girls wore sexy outfits, flaunting their budding breasts and curving hips. Every time she saw her child-like body in the mirror, she cried.

To this day, she still has no need for a bra, and feels uncomfortable in the company of women with breasts larger than a Florida grapefruit.

Her parents, both plump and puffy, kept saying when she got older, being thin would be a blessing. She hated when they said that.

Medical experts cited issues with little Samantha's hormonal balance, as a result of disorders with her endocrine and thyroid glands. They suggested various treatments, but her parents said they couldn't afford the costs.

Isenberg may have been unhappy with her feminine features, but she felt superior to her classmates in other ways. She was smart, really smart, achieving the highest marks throughout her public schooling, without really trying. She was the envy of every nerd in her school. She found out later in life her intelligence quotient tested higher than Einstein's.

Her academic brilliance won her a scholarship at the Massachusetts Institute of Technology when she was 16. In her sophomore year at MIT, she began to have "visions" while she slept. She believed they were too *real* to be dreams, and the notion that she was losing her mind prompted her to seek professional help.

She described the visions to her first psychiatrist as visits from a "blue supernatural being." When she claimed the visits didn't frighten her, the shrink didn't believe her.

"Anybody would be frightened by a blue monster, surely you were, too," he insisted. Isenberg found a different psychiatrist. The visits continued.

After a while, the blue visitor revealed that it was a female. For the first time in her life, Isenberg felt like she had a BFF. They engaged in long conversations about her future while Isenberg slept.

When the third psychiatrist in a row prescribed drugs used to treat schizophrenia and dementia, Isenberg stopped seeing them altogether.

The visits continued.

One morning, she woke up to find a piece of paper on her night table. There was a complex set of mathematical equations written on it. It was her handwriting. Memories of her conversation with the blue visitor that night told her what to do next. By late afternoon, she was able to decipher the figures. She soon realized the resulting formula could be used to create a revolutionary new plastic-like material that would have 10 times the tensile strength of steel, yet one-third its weight.

The next night, the visitor told her the product could be made using common chemicals drawn from compounds in the air produced by the burning of fossil fuels. In effect, the extraction process to create the product also helped rid the atmosphere of pollutants. Isenberg was flabbergasted. She was also told the new material was invulnerable to the damage sunlight usually wreaks on plastics and had an R value of 40.

Isenberg and the blue visitor talked until morning light. She said her name was "Mother" and urged Isenberg to patent the formula. She was also given the details for accessing a Swiss bank account established in her name. There was $10 million in it.

On the next visit, Mother provided the engineering specs to build the "extractor," the device that removed compounds from the air to create the material Isenberg dubbed "10-Steel."

Isenberg dropped out in her third year at MIT and began building her empire. With the seed money, she hired a team of experts in a variety of fields and founded Isenberg Industries.

10-Steel was snubbed in the West. Architects were confounded by the material's applications and skeptical of its strength. Then there were building code regulations to deal with. Government officials in the West refused to certify 10-Steel for construction purposes, despite the specs that demonstrated its viability as a replacement for steel, wood and concrete. It didn't take long for Isenberg to discover the real reason 10-Steel was disregarded.

Because 10-Steel could be mass-produced onsite and snapped together like giant building blocks—saving natural resources, hauling fees and man-hours—projects could be completed in a quarter of the time and a tenth of the usual costs. Since most construction trades based their fees on a percentage of the project's total price, their profit margins would be severely impacted.

So, Isenberg was left with little choice. She started her own construction company, designing and building small bridges and apartment complexes in Asia and Africa, using 10-Steel. Before long, interest in the material was unprecedented.

More unique inventions followed, thanks to Mother. Isenberg licensed her patented inventions for lucrative sums to new and growing fields, including robotics, space craft construction, medicine and the manufacturing of hand-held devices.

The old expression, "Like printing money," was never more apropos.

One of the more innovative products that sprung from Mother's mind was self-charging vehicles. The concept was simple: As the tires turned on a vehicle rolling down the road, the kinetic energy generated by the spinning motion was fed back to the vehicle's battery, continually charging it. One could conceivably drive for months without stopping.

Predictably, the blow back from petroleum conglomerates and automakers was enough to hurricane the idea into oblivion. Undeterred, Isenberg went ahead and built her own prototype, selling it to a Chinese electronics tycoon for half his net worth.

The first $10 million became $100 million in six months. By the time she turned 25, Samantha Isenberg joined the Billionaires Club, and never looked back.

As her wealth grew, Isenberg became suspicious of men who asked her out. She even turned down three marriage offers. But the desire for an heir haunted her.

She tried invitro services, but doctors warned her petite size made giving birth a precarious situation, for her and the child.

While in Somalia on a business venture, she visited an orphanage that was funded by her personal donations. She fell head over heels for a beautiful little girl with big black eyes, abandoned that same day by a woman who left her husband for another man.

It was a sign, Isenberg thought. She adopted the 10-year-old and renamed her Keltie. Today, Keltie has twin boys and lives in Seattle.

For her birthday three years ago, Isenberg's long-time chief executive officer took her out for lunch. He joked that she had enough money to fill Lake Superior.

"Good, because it's time to start spending it," she replied. "Get the lawyers together. Begin liquidating my assets. Start with everything worth more than half a billion, work your way up. The small stuff, it's irrelevant.

"Don't look at me that way. Just do it."

Her CEO was shocked and continued to ask why. He knew Isenberg well enough to understand this was not a passing fancy.

"Yours is not to question why. You will be well compensated for your loyalty over the years. Anything worth under a half-billion is yours to keep.

"Let me know when the paperwork is ready."

***

Samantha Isenberg was having lunch in her kitchen. Two fast-fried free-range eggs laid by her own hens, a side of steamed spinach from one of the greenhouses on her vast estate, and a thick slice of heavily buttered quinoa bread, homemade by her personal chef, and fresh from the oven.

She cut through the eggs with a fork, digging into the spinach before each mouthful, to add flavor to the unsalted eggs. A red lighter sat on a pack of cigarettes beside a steaming cup of black coffee, waiting to be her desert.

"How do you like the quinoa loaf, Ms. Isenberg?" her chef asked.

"Delicious, Ida … is this from the same harvest that we have in storage for New Eden?"

"Yes, Ms. Isenberg. I thought you might want to sample it before the agriculturalists seal the containers."

"Very good of you. Have some served with dinner tonight. There will be six of us now. Chief engineer Holt will be joining us, he has an update on the construction timeline."

"Actually, Ms. Isenberg, Mr. Holt was here just before you came for lunch. I asked him to return when you were finished."

"Oh … did he say why, Ida?"

"He can tell you himself. I just saw him through the window, headed for the front door."

Isenberg took the first sip of her coffee. Jack Holt was at her side by the time she lit up a cigarette.

"Thought you were giving up smoking, Sam," said Holt.

"I will when we move underground. Until then, I'll do as a chimney does."

"You're not a very good liar, Sam," Jack smiled. "I saw one of your people lugging cases of smokes through the underground entrance late last night. I'm told he stashed them in the closet of your private quarters."

"No, Jack. You did *not* see cases of cigarettes. Neither did any of your crew. Do we understand each other?"

"As always, Sam. You're the boss."

Isenberg nodded in approval, as she exhaled smoke in his direction.

"You wanted to discuss something with me before the dinner meeting, Jack?"

"Yes. We have a problem with the numbers. This morning, I went over the final figures with my crew. We only have living quarters for 1,500. I need to know who we are going to cut from the list."

"You jest with me? My plan was for 1,800 people, you told me no problem, just last month. There will be no cuts."

"To be fair, Sam, that was before you added that little concert hall to the mix, saying the artists and musicians must have space to hone their craft, remember?"

"I never forget a thing, Jack. Do you have a solution in mind?"

"Yes. If you won't cut numbers, we'll have to scale back on the recreation facilities, fill in the nearly completed swimming pool, and the size of the playground at the children's school will have to shrink by half."

Isenberg stood up to face Jack. He was a stout man with a beer-lover's belly but she stepped right into him, her face angled up toward his chin.

"Listen to me, Jack. Those recreational facilities will remain as planned. Cuts are out of the question.

"I have already paid these people millions of dollars to take part in the experiment. They are out there, camped all over the place, waiting for you to finish building New Eden. More are coming in every day.

"I will not send any of them away. They are excited about taking part in this research and have committed the next six months of their lives to be a part of this ground-breaking work. There is no turning back. No one will be sent home."

"But we *have* no more space, so what do you suggest?"

Isenberg visualized the blueprints for the complex, with total recall.

"Extend the south wall of the cavern. There will still be 200 feet of headway if you take the floor down 20 feet; just install stairs down to that level."

"But I can't meet your deadline if we expand. Can't be done, Sam."

"Bring in more personnel, double the current shifts *and* double the salary of every worker on the ground. That's an order."

"So, my salary gets doubled as well?"

"I'll *triple* your original fee, throw in a million-dollar bonus. The money means nothing to me. Do we understand each other?"

"Consider it done, Sam. Hell, I am going to retire after this project. See you at the meeting tonight."

Jukka Sarensen, one of Isenberg's inner circle of four, entered the kitchen while she was giving Holt his orders.

"You still haven't told Jack this whole thing is not an 'experiment,' have you, Sam?" said Sarensen after Holt exited the house.

"I have no intention of doing so, until the day is upon us. Jukka, you know it has to be like this."

"If you say so. You're the boss."

"Listen to me, Jukka … I attracted some of the world's brightest people to New Eden by luring them with more money upfront than they could expect to make in their entire lifetimes. They have brilliant minds. Best on the planet.

"If an 'eccentric billionaire' like me told them we were actually preparing for the end of the world as we know it, how many of them would stay? How many of them would take me seriously?"

CHAPTER 16
The Coral Castle

In their room at the Nomar hotel, Delia lifted Jimi up and laid him out on the bed. She walked out to the small balcony facing the Atlantic Ocean and looked straight down at the rushing whitecaps striking the rocky shoreline.

The hotel was built on the cliffs that protect the region from the angry waters. The whole of Portugal's Algarve is perfectly angled to pick up pounding Atlantic swells from all directions.

She felt herself drawn to the sea. The rhythm of the waves was intoxicating. Nature's never-ending symphony. Her eyes hitched a ride on each incoming wave like a thrill-seeking surfer.

A noise from the bedroom brought her back inside. Jimi had rolled onto on his side and knocked over a glass of water she placed at the edge of the night table. She sat beside him and gently stroked his forehead, pushing back the long bangs fluttering over his sleeping face.

"You have feelings for me, don't you, Jimi James. I sensed it when we linked."

Delia learned much about Jimi while restoring him after the fatal gunshot back at the casino, absorbing his life like snapshots as she combed through his thoughts. He was born James Archer Fitzpatrick, to a woman who was abused by her disturbed husband. The couple married late in life, both close to 40 by the time they celebrated their first anniversary.

James was their only child. His mother reluctantly agreed to have a baby, believing a child would soothe the beast in her husband, and end his demands for an heir. At the very least, a child would give her husband a choice of battering rams. "Besides," as she told friends, "I did not want to miss my window."

Love and kindness were rarely shown in the Fitzpatrick home. Dinner was always a tension-filled ordeal, James wondering if his father would take his anger out on his mother, or him. His father regularly whipped little James with his leather belt, until the welts on his backside ran red. Some nights, the neighbors took to pounding the walls from both sides of the Fitzpatrick's tiny row house in the Bronx, hoping to stop the violence without confronting Mr. Fitzpatrick face-to-face.

When his parents argued, James would hide under his bed, reading books about space travel and alien worlds by flashlight, his great escape from the madness. On nights when his parents' arguments became raging battles—his mother used to hurl plates and fire cutlery at his father to defend herself—James would put his hands over his ears, until all he could hear was his mother softly crying.

The fainting spells started early in life for James. At first, they seemed triggered by his fear of being beaten by his father. The family doctor, who never saw James while he was still black and blue from an assault, was at a loss to explain the blackouts, determining they were likely sparked by a lack of blood and oxygen to the brain. He wanted to run some tests on the boy, but his father refused, insisting his son was a "wimp," and that was why he fainted so often.

James never knew what it felt like to be loved, but he grew well-acquainted with pain and sorrow. When he was 11, his mother didn't come home after work one day. James never learned what happened to her. She left a letter behind, addressed to him, but his father tore it up in disgust after reading it. James never learned what was in the letter.

His father beat him to near death that night, blaming him for his mother's desertion. James knew the neighbors must have heard his blood-curdling screams through the thin walls, but no-one banged on the walls like they had in the past. No-one knocked on the door. No-one called the police.

When he was 14, James packed a duffle bag while his father was at work, got on a Greyhound bus headed south from New York City, and never looked back. He got a job working for room and board in a family-owned car wash in Miami's Little Havana, vacuuming the floor mats and helping put a shine on the vehicles after they were waxed.

He told the family he was 16 and had quit school. They didn't doubt him; the hood was heavy with high-school dropouts. He knew his Latino-loathing father would never look for him there. The family he lived with encouraged James to learn Spanish, and he was a quick study, at least when it came to cursing.

James slept in a tiny room at the rear of the house, enough space for a single bed, a small dresser and a rusty metal shelving unit he retrieved from the trash. He started collecting books to fill the shelves, most from second-hand book shops. He read everything from science fiction to psychology and sociology manuals that were part of university-level courses.

When he wasn't working, James spent hours at the local library, feeding his curious mind. He loved reading about how different societies evolved and how religion adapted over time. After a few years of exploratory reading, James began to postulate his own theories about life, as he tried to understand why the world was rife with hatred and violence.

The crux of the problem, he reasoned, was the way in which we identified ourselves based on nationality, religion and race—a sure-fire recipe for conflict, as history demonstrated time and again. He envisioned a day when people referred to themselves as human beings *first*, placing greater importance on that association than they did on their country of origin, religious affiliation or their skin color.

In his late teens, James hung out with a gang called The Minks, so named with boundless homage to Willy Deville, front man for Mink Deville, the '70s band that recorded the classic *Spanish Stroll*—a song every gang member had to memorize, from guitar licks to lyrics. It was their brand, a tradition passed down through The Minks since the early '80s.

On Saturday nights, the pugnacious Minks would pull off pranks in the hood, everything from slashing the car tires of thugs who were banging one of their sisters, to stomping on the flower gardens of uptight spinsters who gave them disrespectful looks as they cruised the streets. When they were really bored, they smashed streetlights or left burning bags of dog shit on the front porches of those they felt deserved special treatment.

The gang had a ritual they performed after every prank, taking to the streets of Calle Ocho strumming air guitars and proudly singing the lyrics to their signature song: "*He's a razor in the wind ... he got a pistol in his pocket.*"

When he was 20, he legally changed his name to Jimi James, telling friends it was "cuz I like the ring to it." The real reason was that he despised his last name, Fitzpatrick. It reminded him of his father, the sorrow of his childhood, and the mother who abandoned him.

After he turned 22, Jimi James left for California with the $5,000 he'd saved up, tending bar in a little joint where married men went in with $100 dollars in their wallets, and the ladies got free drinks. The El Marachi Taberna was also where Jimi learned everything about women.

Delia lay down next to Jimi. She kissed him softly on the cheek then whispered, "You are all that is beautiful."

He slowly opened his eyes.

"Delia? ... Where am I?"

Jimi shook his head violently, as if the rattling would bring him to his senses. He stood up and stepped back quickly from the bed, making a face like he was remembering something.

"You were in my head ... how did you do that?"

Delia hesitated, wondering where to begin. Then she remembered Jimi's science fiction collection.

"I told you I would explain ... it's time."

"Tell me, tell me everything."

"You're a big reader of science fiction novels. You told me you always wondered what it would be like to actually meet someone from another world, right?"

"Well ... yes, that's true."

"Let's make believe that you are indeed meeting someone from another planet ..."

"This is not pretend—you *are* an alien. Oh my god ... oh my god, a real alien."

Jimi started pacing back and forth in front of Delia, a bundle of nerves ready to snap.

"You are right. I am from another world."

"I knew it—nobody on Earth can do what you do."

Jimi's face was flushed and his knees looked ready to buckle as he shuffled barefoot about the room. Delia asked him to lay back down on the bed, she would tell him everything he wanted to know.

"You won't hurt me?"

"Never. I need you."

"You 'need me?'" Jimi said, as he let Delia help him lay down across the bed.

"So ... Are you one of the evil aliens? Are you here to take over our planet?"

"Please listen to my story, Jimi. Stop me every time you have a question. Don't judge until you hear me out. Promise?"

"I'll try."

Delia smiled, took Jimi's hand in hers, then said, "I am not here to 'take over' your planet. I don't even own a 'ray gun.'"

It seemed to calm him down.

"Jimi, I am not an 'evil' alien. Evil aliens, as humans define them, don't exist in the Universe. That perception is an invention of the creative human mind. On Earth, you hear so many crazy stories about evil aliens, perpetuated by your writers and filmmakers for so-called 'entertainment value,' and used as a fear-mongering tactic by those who are eager to develop space weapons.

"In reality, it's a view that reflects human anxiety over how little they understand about the forces at play in the Cosmos. The Universe is populated by benevolent, peaceful species. We do not conquer or assimilate other forms of sentient life."

"But you could, if you wanted to, right? Take over whole planets, enslave the inhabitants …"

"That kind of thinking is foreign to us. It's that fear of the unknown that has led your people to assume evil lurks in deep space—scaly, reptilian-skinned monsters with malicious eyes, armed with vastly superior weaponry, out to conquer the human race. I have read the books, seen the movies, found them quite amusing.

"Believe me when I tell you this evil alien concept is simply historic human behavior that's been unjustly transposed. It is *your* race that has made the assumption aliens are evil. That fear is really a mirror of human conduct, not seen outside of your planet."

"So, you are saying *real* aliens are more like the ones in the movie *Close Encounters of the Third Kind*? Friendly creatures, that mean us no harm?"

"Yes. Like them, we are a supremely benevolent race. Words like war and hate only have meaning on Earth."

Jimi buried his head with his hands. Delia could sense his bewilderment. Before that feeling became fear, closing his mind like a steel door, she knew she had to keep the conversation alive.

"Jimi, stay with me … what more would you like to know? What does your curiosity say? You told me on the way to Albufeira that you would *not* be frightened about meeting someone from another planet, remember?"

Jimi slowly lifted himself, sat on the edge of the bed, but kept his gaze to the floor.

"I … I need a drink."

Delia brought him what was left of the bourbon. Now was not the time for a lecture on alcohol abuse. Jimi sucked most of it back with one gulp. He drained the bottle with his next swallow.

"Feel better?"

"No, need more."

"You talk to me for a bit longer and I will get you another bottle, OK?"

"I don't care what you say, you *are* scary, you know that? I'll have my bottle, and I want it now."

"Ask me a question first, deal?"

"What is the name of your race … Where is your home world?"

"We are called the Deus. My home world? Let's just say it's somewhere central in the Cosmos, compared to Earth's location. It's hundreds of millions of light years away, out of range from the telescopes and space probes Earth currently has. It's unlike any other planet, eleven times larger than your Jupiter. We call it Caelum."

"What does Caelum mean in English?"

"Heaven."

"You said you are Deus. I know a little Latin, my father tried to get me to be an altar boy when I was a kid. They rejected me because I missed too many classes … due to, um, illness. Deus means god in English, doesn't it? Are you a god?"

"No, not in the way humans define what god is."

"Then what kind of *god* are you?"

"I will explain, Jimi, but keep in mind there are so many events in human history that contributed to this misunderstanding.

"Latin is the mother tongue of the Deus. It became a universal language billions of years ago, as my race used it to facilitate communication with all sentient species in the Cosmos. We also taught it to some early human civilizations who spoke a variety of parochial tongues, so the tribes could communicate with one another, as well as with us.

"So you see, Jimi, the human notion of god derives from an inadvertent translation. When we explained at the time that we were the Deus from the planet Caelum, early humans took that literally. We became known as the 'gods from heaven.'

Jimi shook his head in utter disbelief and said, "No. *No.* Not buying it. Not possible.

"You are God, sent from heaven? You know what, this is as nuts as it gets—I'm going to get some more bourbon—now. Before my head explodes."

"In the strictest literal sense, what you say is accurate. However, Deus, or God, is simply what my people are called.

"I understand that it's difficult for you to grasp how this concept came into being and developed into a system of worship here on Earth. Of all the other worlds in the Universe, Earth is the only place where this desire to worship, to serve some kind of imaginary entity, has come to pass, Jimi."

"I know about the origins of religion. I'm not an ignoramus."

"Then you know that human thoughts and actions are impacted by so many variables. Be they emotional or mystical in nature, the human mind is not a logic-defined platform when it comes to establishing Truth. The Deus 'brain'—for lack of a better human description—*is* a logic-based platform."

"Logic-based? You mean like the Vulcans, like Spock from *Star Trek?*"

"Why, yes, something like that," Delia smiled.

"Well, I am still confused ..."

"Jimi, I am going to tell you a story. Lay back, close your eyes, pretend you are listening to an audio book. A new science fiction novel you just purchased."

"There is a big fly on the ceiling, directly above us," Jimi said as he stretched out on the bed.

"Don't worry, flies don't bite," Delia smiled, without looking up.

"Flies buzz around and always go toward the light. This one has not moved since I first noticed it, some time ago."

"Shush."

Delia waved a hand over Jimi's eyes. In seconds, he appeared relaxed and ready to listen.

"On this visit to Earth, Jimi, my ship was hit by a barrage of missile fire from your flying battleships. I was not aware that humans had developed technology which could detect my arrival, let alone missiles that could impair my craft.

"The missiles did not penetrate my craft's exterior, but the vibrations from the collisions were powerful enough to misalign the gyroscope on the hyper drive. It will be a challenge for my ship to break free of Earth's gravitational field upon my departure.

"However, there is an anti-gravity device here on Earth that I can employ to help my ship break through the atmosphere. It was once in the possession of a man I knew, a long time ago. He was angry with me and stole it, brought it with him to America.

"He used it to move giant pieces of coral rock to build a castle in Florida. Now the anti-gravity device is owned by a nefarious individual who wants millions of dollars before he will give it to me. This is why I was in Las Vegas, to win enough to pay him. This is also why we came to Europe, to meet this man."

Jimi's eyes opened wide when he heard the part about the anti-gravity device, used to move giant rocks.

"I used to live in Florida, so I've heard of the Coral Castle, but I don't know much about it. Sounds fascinating. Tell me more."

"Jimi, I have a message coming in. This time, I must respond. Why don't you search for Coral Castle online? I am sure you will get the information you seek."

Jimi reached for his burner phone and looked up Coral Castle. He got thousands of results. After clicking on a few, he found a story with a subhead that really intrigued him: "The Church of Mad Love, is such a holy place to be."

He began reading.

He was five-foot tall and weighed 100 pounds, yet single-handedly lifted 30-ton rocks while building Coral Castle, an engineering feat which boggles the imagination.

His name was Edward Leedskalnin, a Latvian-born immigrant with a fourth-grade education who moved to Florida in 1919. As the oft-told story goes, he began building the cryptic Coral Castle shortly after, and continued working on it until his death in 1951, taking the secret of its construction with him.

Today, you can visit Coral Castle in Homestead, Fla., where it remains a top tourist attraction.

Townsfolk of that era say that Leedskalnin worked alone and always at night, so as to mask his construction methods from curious onlookers. His only visible equipment was a primitive tripod with a hand-pulled chain hoist. Actual photos of the tripod show a "mysterious" black box at the top of the hoist.

Many pundits have speculated the black box contained an anti-gravity mechanism Leedskalnin invented, that gave him the power to move the giant rocks perfectly into place without the assistance of modern machinery. Others claim the black box was a secret alien device the little big man used to move the rocks with.

There are numerous published accounts that seek to unravel the techniques Leedskalnin used to build the massive monument. Leedskalnin also published documents with vague scientific details about his construction methods, but the shroud of mystery has yet to be lifted.

In response to questions about how he was able to move the giant rocks, Leedskalnin made the bold claim that: "I have discovered the secrets of the pyramids, and have found out how the Egyptians and the ancient builders in Peru, Yucatan and Asia, with only primitive tools, raised and set in place blocks of stone weighing many tons."

Some of the structures in Coral Castle are apparently calibrated to celestial alignments, and it has been reported that Leedskalnin said he believed the Universe was made up of magnets. He argued that by harnessing the flow of these magnets he could defy gravitational forces, allowing him to move large objects without exerting any significant physical energy.

Leedskalnin also claimed that he could actually see "beads of light" on physical objects. These beads, he said, were the physical manifestation of nature's magnetic forces.

The legend goes that Leedskalnin was inspired to build Coral Castle after being abandoned at the altar back home in Latvia by his 16-year-old sweetheart, Agnes Scuffs. Little is known about the mysterious Scuffs and what happened to her, although some say she was part of the

Latvian resistance during World War One. Leedskalnin set out to win her back by proving that he could do something incredible.

The seeds for Coral Castle were sown.

Ripley's Believe It or Not has dubbed Leedskalnin's 5,000-pound, heart-shaped rock at Coral Castle the world's largest valentine. He also built a 24-ton replica of the planet Saturn and a 23-ton Moon crescent.

Sadly, Leedskalnin died knowing that, despite his historic achievements, the love of his life never came back to him.

"Mystery solved," said Jimi. "So, this is how Leedskalnin *really* built Coral Castle, using your anti-gravity device?"

When there was no reply, Jimi looked directly at Delia. Her eyes were glowing and she appeared frozen. He touched her hand and shook her arm.

"Delia? Is something wrong?"

A few seconds later, she spoke.

"Jimi, we have to leave, immediately. Grab your things, we need to get to the airport at Faro as soon as possible. Call the front desk and ask them to get us a taxi. Time is critical."

"But we just got here, and I'm really tired," Jimi whined, laying back down on the bed.

"Now, Jimi. Get moving."

"Where the hell are we going this time? I need to eat something and you know I hate airplane food."

"To the Madeira Islands. It's a short flight. We'll eat at the airport."

"Did you see that, Delia?"

"See what?"

"The big fly on the ceiling above us that I mentioned before. Its eyes suddenly glowed."

Jimi stood up on the bed and jumped up at the fly, swatting it hard with his hand.

The fly dropped to the bed. Delia picked it up and examined it, then turned to look at Jimi.

"This is not a fly."

CHAPTER 17

22 years ago ...

US Air Force pilot Alpha 1 was on a reconnaissance mission over the North Pole, a flight that had become so routine, she could do it with her eyes closed. Something peculiar appeared on her radar screen. She radioed her cohort in the SR-71 Blackbird on her port side for confirmation.

"Alpha 2, do you see what I see?"

"I see it, Alpha 1. It's not a craft I'm familiar with. We better call it in."

"You call it in. In the meantime, protocol is to follow it."

"Jesus—there it is Alpha 1. We have visual. Alpha 2 to ground control, over."

"Ground control to Alpha 2. What is your status? Over."

"We have eyes on an unexplained aerial phenomenon. Do you have it on radar?"

"Roger that. None of our own is in that area. Tracking it now, just appeared a minute ago."

"What are our orders? Over."

"Get closer. Shoot video. Await further instructions."

"Roger that."

Two minutes later, the Blackbirds were within visual range of the unidentified craft and let ground control know.

"Ground control to Alpha 2, describe the vessel, over."

"It's an ovoid shape. About 500 feet long, seems to camouflage itself by reflecting the sky and clouds around it. It's truly astounding."

"Alpha 2, continue—without the theatrics. Over."

"Understood ... The elongated egg shape is more tapered at the nose. No visible windows or portals. No visible engines, no contrails, no visible emissions whatsoever. Over."

"Roger that, Alpha 2. It's cruising at Mach 5. How much longer can you match that speed before your fuel gets to the point of no return? Over."

"At Mach 5 we are good for another 42 minutes, over."

"Roger that, maintain velocity. Await further orders. This one is getting kicked upstairs to General Slaight. Over and out."

"Roger that."

"Alpha 1, have you ever seen anything like this before?"

"Hell no. I've been briefed on a lot of UFO intel, but this one is unlike anything in those reports."

"Holy crap, Alpha 2, that thing just hit the hammer. Call it in."

"Alpha 2 to ground control. The aerial phenomenon is quickly picking up speed. We won't be able to keep pace much longer. Our top speed is Mach 7, almost there now. Over."

"Roger that. We have patched in General Slaight direct from the Pentagon. Over to you, general."

"Alpha 2, how long before the object is out of missile range?"

"Less than a minute, general. Over."

"Then shoot it down—now. Those are your orders."

"Roger that, general."

Within seconds, both the Blackbirds fired AGM Mavericks at the speeding craft.

"General, sir, the missiles literally bounced off the object without detonating. Over."

"Fire the whole damn payload—now!"

The two pilots followed the general's order.

"General, sir, the missiles seemed to bump the craft slightly off course, but no detonation. Over."

"Follow it for as long as you can. We are calculating a trajectory and ..."

"Sir, our instruments are no longer reading the craft. It disappeared, just plain disappeared."

***

At the Pentagon, General Slaight was waiting for a report from NASA, which had 17 orbiting satellites tracking the unexplained aerial phenomenon. When the report came in, his eyes bulged from their sockets.

"General Slaight, is everything alright, sir?" his aide asked.

"This can't be possible ..."

"What can't 'be possible,' sir?"

"NASA says they tracked the unexplained aerial phenomenon leaving our atmosphere, accelerating from Mach 7 to well beyond the speed of light in seconds."

"Must be a malfunction, sir. Their instruments need recalibrating."

"No, this is not an error. At least 12 different satellites recorded the exact same data."

The aide watched as the general paced the room, shaking his head and muttering words that made no sense.

"Sir, if there is nothing more, I will log this incident in the standard unexplained aerial phenomenon folder."

"No, wait. This one is different. Open a new file, in an 'Eyes Only' folder. Highest security level. Even the President must never see this."

"As you wish, sir. What should I call this new folder?"

"Let me see ... let's go with Stairway to Heaven."

"Like the song, sir?"

"No. Like the book."

CHAPTER 18
Noah's Ark

Viktor Kozlov watched the news, pounding a fist to a knee every time he cursed. A red-headed woman had miraculously survived a 32-story fall down the side of a hotel in Portugal. The planet was abuzz. The video was viewed by billions.

"Blyad! ... *Blyad!!!*"

Mother put their mission in jeopardy with that stunt. Journalists looking to make a name for themselves will never let the story go.

Kozlov cursed again.

The blabbering media, always eager to post stories before the facts are known—so long as they're first to report it—had dubbed her 'Gravity Girl.' If they only knew who Gravity Girl really was, their tiny brains would explode. There would be chaos everywhere.

The depth of human knowledge is as shallow as the graves they dump their bodies in to putrefy for decades. And always will be. Kozlov had been convinced of that for more than a thousand years.

He had been trying to make contact with Mother since he saw the video. Why was she was blocking him? Something must be very wrong.

Kozlov looked out the window and opened his eyes wide again. They grew shiny, brighter as he beamed his message to her, making the signal as strong as possible. He must get through to Mother.

"There has been another change in the plan to obtain the anti-gravity device. Mr. Lam is up to something. We must talk."

He repeated the message three more times, every 20 minutes. Still no response.

He wondered if Mother was conserving her life force by allowing Delia Cassavetes to take control more often. His own energy level had declined after years of living with his human host. Though he estimated he could remain in Kozlov's body for another two years if he conserved wisely, he yearned to be back on his home world of Caelum long before then.

He once had sympathy for the struggling human species. Millions of years ago, during a meeting with the Imperitus Council, he witnessed Mother urge them to help save the humans, insisting they were not to blame for their inability to evolve beyond the primitive. Mother admitted to the Council the flaw resided in the original double helix she created for her wise ones' experiment. She argued that minor tinkering of the DNA strands would resolve the issue, if they would give her another chance. The humans *did* have potential to be worthy members of the Deus Federation, she pleaded. To no avail.

The Council was unanimous in its conviction that humans, being the only sentient life forms that killed their own kind, should face fate as they veered toward self-annihilation. A destiny deserving of such a brutal and predatory race, they concluded.

And so, it happened. Humans not only destroyed the Martian atmosphere, they obliterated their race in the process. Mother warned them about the irreparable harm they were doing to Mars's fragile ecosystems. But they continued poisoning the air and water, so their factories could manufacture new gizmos and gadgets, in their futile pursuit of bigger and faster means it's better.

The humans in seats of power were beholding to the Lords of Production, who argued their manufacturing methods must continue, saying people needed jobs and the economy topped everything. The worker humans eagerly bought into this economic model, hooked as they were on shiny new trinkets to pacify their unquenchable desires, never realizing they had become enslaved by the process.

The ruling classes expended enormous resources to build towering edifices on vulnerable land, proclaiming their dominance over the natural world on Mars. Meanwhile, half the population struggled to feed their children and lived in conditions considered unfit for the ruling classes' livestock.

The humans also upset the Imperitus Council by creating artificial boundary lines to mark what they called nation states, so as to sustain what they believed to be precious cultural differences. The Council viewed this division of humans based solely on cash, creed and color as horrifying. No other sentient beings in the Universe even had a word to define "racism" or "poverty" in their language.

Mars became a total disaster. Humans in wealthy nation states began producing ever more deadly weapons to fortify their artificial borders, keep out the ones that were not like them. It didn't take long before tensions were so high between opposing nation states that war broke out everywhere. Massive exploding bombs ripped apart the immaculate planet. Injured civilians were left dying in the streets, innocent children starved to death.

Unbeknownst to the Council, Mother hijacked a male and female pair from Mars, just hours before warring nation states unleashed a torrent of lethal chemical bombs at one another. The toxic gases that were a side effect of the relentless bombing slowly ate away at the planet's thinning atmosphere, until every human perished. Oceans and lakes evaporated into space. Flora and fauna became extinct. Mars was dead.

Despite their appetite for destruction, Mother refused to give up on humans. Unlike the Council, she believed the human soul was innately pure and virtuous, and blamed her own scientific errors in the initial genetic design for their self-destructive behavior. She must make amends, no matter what the cost.

She transported the human pair to the nearest planet which could sustain such fragile life forms. Urantia, third planet from the yellow star in that solar system.

She called their new home the Garden of Eden, and christened the two humans Adam and Eve. Mother made sure the young couple had everything they needed to flourish and, after 20 orbits around the star, she left Urantia. It was time for her to regenerate under the blazing blue star back on her home world. After that, she was duty-bound to return to other parts of her life's work; there were 75 other worlds in various stages of development that she was 'mothering.' That was more than one million years ago.

Mother returned to Urantia, in the year humans call 5010 B.C. The Garden of Eden colony had prospered and spread. There were many thriving civilizations on the planet. She visited all of them and, although troubled that conflict and violence still dominated their cultures, Mother was pleased to see that the arts and sciences were flourishing.

The location where she established the Garden of Eden was known as Mother Land by the locals. Nearby, a promising group of humans had settled along the Nile River and called themselves Egyptians. In their language, Mother Land translated to "Africa," and the continent is still known by this name. Oddly, the humans referred to their planet as "Earth." She hoped that wasn't a sign they would treat Urantia like dirt.

Confident her second chance with the human experiment was in a manageable state of evolution, Mother returned to her home planet Caelum for regeneration.

Upon her arrival, the Imperitus Council chief summoned her for a private meeting.

"I know what you did, Mother. Why do you continue to defy the will of the Imperitus Council?" said Artemis Prime, the Council chief.

"I am are grief-stricken. If word gets out among the Deus populace that humans still exist, I will have no choice but to remove you from your duties."

"Why am I not able to address the *full* Council? I would prefer to state my case before all of the officials."

"It was decided I alone should meet with you. Too many of the Council are despondent over this. No one can recall ever having to condemn a sentient species to extinction—a second time! It is not our way."

"I was counting on that," said Mother.

"You attempted to deceive us. We had asked you to terminate your human experiment, yet, thanks to the latest report from our friends the Angelus, we have discovered that it continues on Urantia ..."

"The humans call it Earth, Consul Prime."

"We are the Watchers of the Universe—everything, all in one, the entirety—we will refer to that tiny blue planet in the 944th Solar System of the Milky Way galaxy by its proper name."

"Of course, Consul, Urantia."

"On second thought, I will make a note of this. We will use 'Earth' as a secondary identifier."

"Thank you, Consul, the humans would be pleased."

"It is not my intent to 'please' them. This savage species has already destroyed one planet and is clearly out of sync with the essence of benevolent harmony that prevails throughout the living Cosmos."

"The humans *can* be assimilated, become one with our harmonious principles, Consul. I truly believe this."

The Consul shivered blue with disagreement.

"The Imperitus Council asked for opinions regarding the humans from all Federation worlds, Mother. The reply was unanimous. There is no space in our Universe for such a vile and unsophisticated species. They must be eliminated before they destroy another beautiful world. That is our ruling."

"Can we instead move them to a small moon that has a similar atmosphere to Urantia, perhaps Yum Kaax, which orbits Yumil Kaxob in the Alpha Centauri system? I will move them there myself, Consul Prime. Watch over them, guide them ..."

"It was also decided that we cannot have you defying our Prime Directives, especially when it concerns the humans. However, I will ask, purely out of respect for the great work you have done on thousands of other worlds. But don't get your hopes up.

"A species must be self-aware, enough to understand life is too precious to delete with impunity, as humans do, murdering and maiming their own kind—even innocent children! The Council has viewed those damning reports, courtesy of the Angelus. Many of us became violently ill."

Mother's blue shine faded. It was how the Deus showed embarrassment.

"The humans *had* their opportunity to be members of the Deus Federation, Mother, now Mars is dead. The Council has delegated Mars to the Kukulcans. They will repair it, but millions of solar cycles are required before its atmosphere is even partially restored. It will be red and dead for eons to come."

The Consul stopped, his form becoming brighter as a message came in.

"I have a reply from the Imperitus Council to your request about moving the humans. It pains us to render such a verdict, but there can be no second chances and no requiem for the humans.

"Instead, there will be a cleansing of Urantia, in the form of a great flood, to disinfect the planet of humans."

"A 'great flood?' Consul, how is that possible? I know the Imperitus Council would *never* approve of such intervention."

"It's not our doing, it's the force of the Universe. Our astrophysicist unit has confirmed that, in five Urantian solar cycles, a large meteor shower will pass the planet's orbital plane. It will create a mass extinction event. Their projections indicate the biggest of the meteors will strike near the center of Urantia's largest ocean, creating a tidal wave that will flood more than half the planet, specifically the low-lying areas that humans currently inhabit."

Mother asked to see the projections for herself, but the Consul was adamant the astrophysicist unit was never wrong about such matters.

"You will let go of the human experiment. The Council's decision is not open to discussion."

Mother assured him she would abide by the Imperitus Council's wishes but asked if she could make one last voyage to Urantia.

"The Council appreciates the love you have for the humans. They are your children. We will not stand in your way, but I would urge you to forgo a final visit. It will be excruciatingly painful to watch. The experience of seeing them drown will be horrific, it will impact you, in ways we have no data to foresee."

"Your concern is noted, but I *must* see them, one last time, Consul."

Kozlov remembered when Mother came to him after that meeting. He had never seen her so distraught. She told him about all that was said, her thoughts filled with dread when she spoke of the coming flood that was sure to wipeout the humans.

Mother was not like the others in their race. She created life. The Deus are immortal, they did not mate, there was no need for offspring.

They could never understand the bond between mother and child. He knew Mother felt such a connection with the humans. It changed her.

"So, I *do* have to remind you ..."

"Remind me of what, Xeno?"

"When the humans destroyed Mars and you smuggled Adam and Eve to Urantia, you said this to me: 'Xeno, you are my partner. Whatever happens, never let me forget that failure is not an option.'"

Mother's body glowed brighter, followed by a brilliant surge that made Xeno move away from her.

"I have an idea," she said. "No one else can know."

***

Mother's vessel left Caelum and hurtled through the Thales worm hole, a channel through cosmic time that bypassed three-dimensional space travel. The ship re-entered the intergalactic plane at a point near Saturn. From there, the shimmering blue planet was just hours away.

After landing on Urantia in a region known as Mesopotamia, Mother cloaked her ship and moved among the human population undetected. She had engineered the human eye to see but a narrow band of the electromagnetic spectrum; visible light for humans fell between 390 and 700 nanometers, the Deus became visible at 1,000 nanometers, rendering them invisible to humans. Likewise, the human ear can only detect a small fraction of the audible scale, mother reasoning that if they could hear every possible sound echoing throughout their environment, their brains would be overwhelmed with data.

Mother and Xeno observed the humans toiling in the wheat fields, the sweltering Sun baking their skin ever darker. In the evenings, they watched humans caring for their families.

"Why couldn't they be this caring all the time?" she said to Xeno. "Why do they become like raging beasts when conflicts arise? It's my fault. I did this to them."

Xeno knew there were nothing he could say that could ease the torment Mother was feeling.

As the humans slept, Mother finalized her plan to save them, at least the ones who seemed most pure and loving. They would go forth and breed, passing on the genes she hoped would kindle behavior which fostered peace and harmony. It was a theory she was willing to risk everything for. Reason enough for her to defy the ruling of the Imperitus Council. Again.

Mother appeared in the dreams of a local leader who was noble of spirit. She tested his DNA for purity. It was free of defective genes. She told him to build a giant water ship, for a great flood was coming that would swallow the lands. He had been chosen to save his people, she told him.

Night after night she appeared to him, detailing plans of how the great ship would be built. She told him it had to be large enough to house many different species of fauna. She would gather the animals in male and female pairs and bring them to the great ship once it was completed.

Noah, as the man was known, began gathering materials to build the big boat, explaining to other humans that it was "god" who appeared before him and ordered the ark be built.

It was what Mother had come to expect. Primitive intellects could never grasp her true being. She *was* a 'god' to their simple minds.

Noah, his family and most of the animals survived the flood, roiling across raging waters for 150 days. When the waters subsided back to the oceans, Mother and Xeno scouted a sheltered valley that would be suitable for a new settlement. She came to Noah in his dreams again and told him what to do.

When she returned to her home world, Mother kept news of the surviving humans from the Imperitus Council. She provided video evidence of deep waters washing over the planet, choking out all life. She told the Angelus scouts to take a pass on Urantia for now, urging them to visit some of the other worlds she had seeded instead.

When she returned in 100 B.C., her hopes for the humans were high. There were thriving civilizations everywhere. She was pleased, until she began visiting them. Only a few were peaceful and lived in harmony with the natural world. Most were overtly hostile and aggressive with their neighbors. She was despondent as she watched villages plundered and innocent humans slaughtered by conquering hordes.

On their way back to Caelum, Mother began formulating a new plan for the humans. Xeno was alarmed by the details. What she proposed went against everything the Deus stood for.

He was also concerned that Mother was becoming increasingly distant from him. He knew what he had to do. When they arrived home, he secretly reached out to members of the Imperitus Council.

It would be hundreds of years before Mother and Xeno returned to the third planet from the Sun.

CHAPTER 19
Murder in Madeira

The unveiling of Madeira as the jet descended below the mushrooming clouds was a wake-up call for Jimi's weary eyes. The island rose above the Atlantic like a sparkling jewel, lapped on all shores by the pounding surf, as if the sea was determined to take back the land.

At the airport in Faro, Jimi had picked up a tourist brochure. During the flight, he gave Delia a recap of the highlights, never noticing her 'been there, done that' expression.

The Madeira Islands are an archipelago of volcanic origin, 540 miles southwest of Lisbon and 360 miles west of Morocco on the African coast. Only two of the four islands are inhabited, Madeira and Porto Santo. Originally known to the Romans as the Purple Islands, they were rediscovered by Portuguese explorers in the early 15th century, who dubbed it the "Island of wood," Madeira in Portuguese.

During the Napoleonic Wars in the early 19th century, Madeira was briefly occupied by the British. Today, U.K. tourists flock to the island renowned for its perfect year-round weather.

As the jet approached the airport in Funchal, Madeira's capital, Delia had eyes on Jimi as he looked out the window. She could see his hands grip the seat handles as the jet made a sudden turn out over the sea and, for a second, looked like it was going to plunge into the Atlantic. But the plane's nose veered suddenly downward and the runway appeared, seemingly from out of nowhere.

Jimi breathed a sigh of relief when the wheels hit the tarmac.

"It's a short runway here, Jimi," Delia explained, after seeing the terror in his eyes when the jet dropped from the skies to make its landing.

The tiny airport was renamed in 2017 to honor soccer legend Cristiano Rinaldo, who was born in Madeira, Delia told him.

They had just stepped out the exit doors when a long limousine with black windows pulled up. It was their ride. Delia wondered how the driver knew who they were. Jimi's eyes were on the limo, a vintage Mercedes-Benz S-600 Pullman.

"Saw a few of those in Vegas. Hear they go for about a million bucks. Got some serious armor plating, bullet-proof windows … mafia types love them," he said to Delia.

The driver's side window rolled down about five inches. A female voice said, "Get in, please," just as the back door swung open. Jimi hesitated. By the time he turned to look for Delia, she was already seated, gesturing for him to come in.

Jimi sat in the rear-facing seat next to Delia. Sitting across from them were two, identically dressed young women, plain white short-sleeve blouses tucked neatly into the thin waists of knee-length black skirts. They had big smiles, perfect white teeth and long, dark hair parted in the center.

"Hello, my name is Kimmy and this is Tammy," said the woman on the right.

"Welcome to the beautiful island of Madeira," said Tammy. "How was your flight?"

"Short, but scary … are you twins?" Jimi asked.

"Not even sisters," Kimmy said.

"I think you will find Mr. Lam's emissaries look much the same," Tammy said.

"Mr. Lam only hires women of a certain look to be his personal attaches," Kimmy added.

"He has good taste," Jimi smiled, winking at them.

Both the women took to giggling, eyeing Jimi like he was something they wanted to sample. And they looked hungry, too, Delia thought.

Tammy offered them drinks from the built-in bar between her and Kimmy. Jimi eyed the selection and asked for the Glenlivet, neat. Delia declined the offer.

Jimi tipped his glass back like it was already empty, Tammy poured him another.

"Won't you ladies join me?" said Jimi.

More giggles from the near-twins, Tammy stretching her long legs out, one deftly placed between Jimi's.

It was then Delia noticed a mini-revolver strapped to the inside of her left thigh. These smiling bimbos were more than "personal attaches."

"Where are we going?" Delia said, thinking it was a good time to break up the party, before the girls started ripping Jimi's clothes off to see what they could find.

"Mr. Lam has a property here in Madeira, way up in the hills overlooking Funchal," said Tammy. "We will arrive there in about 20 minutes. It is just a few miles from the airport, but the roads up the hills are slow and winding."

"Where is the item?" Delia said.

"We are hospitality staff, here to welcome and comfort you," smiled Kimmy. "We do not talk business. Only Mr. Lam talks business."

"Time is of the essence, tell the driver to kick it up," Delia ordered. The less time spent with these Jimi-hungry bitches, the better.

Kimmy tapped two times on the dark glass separating the driver from the passengers. The limo sped up, everyone leaning left as it whipped around the next curve.

Delia heard Mother tell her to put a check on her jealousy. Delia replied she could tell by the look on Tammy's face that if she wasn't there, Tammy would be yanking at Jimi's zipper.

Delia reached over to Jimi and snatched the glass from his hand, just as Tammy was going to pour him another.

"Jimi, you've had enough to drink—we are here to do business."

For the rest of the drive, Tammy and Kimmy sat with hands folded in their laps, four dark eyes wandering all over Jimi. Delia wanted to smack both of them silly, then spank their tight little butts until they were purple.

The limo climbed the steep hills with ease, its powerful engine barely revving. It pulled up to a large gated residence, oriented on the cascading hillside to face the colorful city below. There were stunning views of the crescent-shaped bay, dotted with sailboats and yachts bobbing along the shoreline.

The actual size of the sprawling manor was largely obscured by Canary date palms, native laurel trees and towering Norfolk pines. A rugged, eight-foot natural stone wall encircled the residence and its grounds.

"Please follow me," said Tammy, leading the hike up to the massive front entrance along a tiled pathway lined with stately dragon blood trees and flowering orchids. Two women dressed in the same 'uniform' as Kimmy and Tammy stood guard on both sides of the giant double doors. No visible weapons, they just stood at attention, smiling.

Once inside, Delia could hear loud voices and bellicose laughter echoing through the expansive entry hall from a room at the rear. As they walked down the marble-floored hall, Kimmy explained that Mr. Lam had a fondness for Madeira and learned to speak Portuguese as a child in Macau, which was owned by Portugal until 1999. "Knowing the language allowed Mr. Lam to negotiate the purchase of a number of prominent properties like this one on the island," said Kimmy.

With an eye to reselling them to his well-heeled friends, Delia figured. For a handsome profit. She knew something of this. The wealthy had been buying up prime properties all over the world for decades, real estate being a good place to park money, before governments could take a cut.

Mother told Delia Mr. Lam operated out of gambling mecca Macau, the Vegas of the East, exporting cheaply made pharmaceuticals and dangerous narcotics from the mainland to Australia, Europe and the U.S. That's how he made his first million, on the backs of drug mules and addicts.

A woman dressed in the same uniform as the other Lam associates approached them, smiling from cheek to cheek.

"Welcome, my name is Casey. Mr. Lam will greet you in the entertainment room. Please follow me."

As they continued through the gallery-like hallway, the voices grew louder. Jimi looked at Delia and said, "I recognize that voice—it's John Travolta!"

"You are correct, Jimi," said Casey. "It's John Travolta playing Chili Palmer. Mr. Lam is a huge fan of Elmore Leonard, and *Get Shorty*, the movie he is watching now, is his favorite of all the films based on Leonard's novels. He has seen it at least 100 times, knows every scene by heart."

"It was a terrific movie," Jimi agreed, "cutting edge in its sneering take of Hollywood insiders."

"Mr. Lam likes it because he thinks it is incredibly funny," Casey said. "He laughs all the way through it."

When the visitors entered the great room, Jimi said, "Look at all that food."

"Mr. Lam's personal chefs have been in the kitchen for hours preparing this feast, in anticipation of your arrival," Casey smiled.

On a 12-foot-long coffee table that would look more at home in a royal palace, there was Russian caviar, Japanese sushi, frog legs a la Provençale, Buffalo-style chicken wings, Italian meatballs and Singapore spring rolls. Steamy aromas wafted to the top of the 20-foot ceiling like mini-clouds of gastronomical joy.

A short, chubby man with a big face, dressed in loose-fitting blue track pants and a white T-shirt sprinkled with food stains, sat on a 10-seater couch, rubbernecking at the theatre-size screen on the facing wall. He had sparkling diamond rings on most fingers and a thick, rapper-style gold chain dangling from his blubber-bound neck.

In between hearty chuckles, he took a big bite from a chicken wing, chucked the rest back into the same bowl, then grabbed a spring roll and forced the whole thing past his fleshy lips.

To his right and left sat two more 'uniformed' women, passing him food with chopsticks from all corners of the coffee table, and smiling. Always smiling, like the rest of the Lam crew, as if they'd had their lips permanently stretched. Like the Joker in the Batman comics.

"Oh, my favorite part of the movie," the jolly round man hooted, oblivious to the three that had entered his realm.

He was watching the scene where the character played by John Travolta was trying to get the character played by Danny DeVito to look at him like he was a shylock. Travolta mocked DeVito's attempt.

The round man burst out laughing. Chewed-up pieces of meatball flipped from his rolling tongue, spraying much of the food on the table.

"I am so sorry to interrupt, Mr. Lam. Your guests have arrived," said Casey.

Immediately, the two uniforms on each side of Mr. Lam stood up, facing Delia and Jimi with scrutiny in their eyes, atop bloody big smiles.

"Ah, you finally arrive," said Mr. Lam, suddenly looking serious as he turned to his guests, then motioned for one of his crew to turn the volume down on the TV.

"We should have met in Lisbon, then Albufeira ..."

"That was due to circumstances beyond my control, not to mention your habit of jetting off to another city without notice."

"Look at me, Delia," said Mr. Lam, doing a paltry imitation of *Get Shorty* shylock Chili Palmer.

"No—you look at me, Mr. *Lamb Chop*," Delia shot back, doing an admirable impression of Travolta playing the shylock.

Mr. Lam immediately aimed a finger toward Delia and Jimi.

Tammy, Kimmy and the two other uniforms reached under their skirts on cue, like they had practiced the move a million times, and snatched up their little revolvers. Three of them aimed heart-high on Delia, the other pointed at Jimi's stunned face. They held onto their smiles the whole time.

Jimi's arms shot up in the air, like he was being held up by thieves. Delia glanced over at him, spotted his eyes starting to roll and his knees beginning to buckle. She reached in and snapped his arms back down, telling him, "Now is not the time to faint on me, Jimi."

Mr. Lam's associates inched toward them, smiles looking creepy now, no longer showing their white choppers.

"Tell your smiley-faced clones to back off, Lam, I'm not here for fireworks. Tammy—if that is your name, I can't tell you freaks apart— aim your little baby gun at me, sister, not Jimi."

Delia pushed Jimi behind her.

Tammy looked to Mr. Lam for direction.

"OK, everybody take a step back," he said. "Take it easy. Let's work this out."

He ordered the ladies to put their guns back in their holsters. They obeyed like trained soldiers.

"My apologies," said Mr. Lam. "The girls get a little excited, sometimes."

"Don't you want your money, Mr. Lam? I can transfer funds to your account, in seconds."

"Yes, let's conclude our transaction, Delia. Kimmy, time to do business—fetch my laptop, over there on the end table."

"First, show me the item, Mr. Lam."

"Actually, before we continue, you must satisfy my curiosity, Delia. Why is this little black box so important, that you would pay me … \$10 million for it?"

Jittery Jimi's mouth snapped open as he gave Delia the "are you f-ing kidding me?" glance.

"The deal was for \$5 million, Mr. Lam. And why I want the black box is none of your concern."

"I charge *fat* interest rate; you are two days late. … No explanation, no black box," said Lam, gesturing with his hands to his girls. On cue, they pulled Black Widows from between their legs again.

"You know, I had my people find top scientists to examine that box, it was a great expense for me, another reason you need to pay me more."

"You're a shylock, just like in that movie," Delia said.

Mr. Lam continued, ignoring her comment.

"The scientists were metallurgical experts, yet they could not force the box to open, they could not even scratch or dent its surface with the most powerful laser cutters or diamond-tip saws. The biggest bullets bounced off the surface without leaving a mark. None of their high-tech scanning methods were able to penetrate the metal to see what was inside. Tell me, how is that possible?"

"As I said, it's none of your business," Delia said, like she meant it, her blue eyes becoming brighter.

"The box is also virtually weightless and has no visible seams," Mr. Lam went on. "Even under an electron microscope the scientists could not determine its chemical structure or how the box was constructed. It was clearly not welded in any manner known to them. And how is it possible that a metal so impossibly durable has no mass or weight?"

Delia seemed intent on stonewalling.

"What we should be discussing, Lamb Face, is why you led me on a wild goose chase to acquire the black box."

"It's some kind of revolutionary new material, isn't it?" Mr. Lam continued. "This is why you are willing to pay millions for it. ... Perhaps we can be partners? The patent alone would be worth a fortune."

"No deal Lam, I wouldn't trust you with my lunch order. In fact, I'll bet the reason you had me chase you all over the map to pick up the box is because your people were still running tests on it, right? You needed more time, didn't you?"

"Perhaps ... My scientists hit a dead end, told me they could not replicate or decipher the material the box is composed of. So, if we can't be partners, I *will* sell it to you. But we can negotiate a better price for me, yes? How does $12 million sound?"

"You found the box in Florida, didn't you, Lam?"

"How did you know that? ... Yes. I had bought some property near Homestead, two acres with a crumbling house. We tore it down to build an enclave of luxury homes. In an old suitcase with a faded tag labelled "Property of Edward Leedskalnin," my workers found the box and numerous note pads with odd mathematical equations scribbled on every page.

"My contractor brought the box to my attention when one of the workers threw it into a garbage bin and it put a dent in the metal."

Mr. Lam passed his laptop to Delia.

"Last chance to consider a partnership ..."

"Forget about it, Lam."

"As you wish. But you will be sorry for not partnering with me.

"Whenever you are ready, Delia. I have entered my banking credentials and password."

Delia keyed in the information to complete the transaction, but before she passed the laptop back to him, she said, "If you are messing with me, Lam, you *will* regret it. Now, hand over the box."

"Do not be worried, I am an honest man. You will get your black box. It has just been placed in a locker at the airport in Lisbon."

"In an airport locker?" said Delia. "You fool ..."

"My people will have eyes on the locker, day and night. No need to be so concerned."

Mr. Lam fished a key out of his pocket with the numbers 308 on it and showed it to Delia. When she stepped forward to reach for the key, he slipped it back into his pocket.

"Not so fast, I need to be sure it was $10 million you deposited."

"The deal was $5 million. You said you were an honest man," Delia snapped back.

After checking Delia's deposit, Mr. Lam put the laptop down on the couch.

"Ladies, we have $5 million, that's not enough. Tie them up until they agree to pay the rest."

A muffled shriek, followed by a heavy thud, echoed from the front of the residence. Mr. Lam's four women moved like ninjas toward the noise.

"Stop, only two of you go," Mr. Lam ordered. "I will not be left alone with these scoundrels."

Two of them bolted for the front door, Tammy and Kimmy hung back.

"I do not think we have rope strong enough to tie them up with, Mr. Lam," said Tammy.

"The chefs in the kitchen have rope, but you are probably right, it won't be strong enough. What the hell, shoot them in the legs so they can't run off."

Jimi looked down at his legs. Delia held steady, her eyes glowing.

There were two more shrieks followed by the sound of bodies hitting the floor originating from the front hall.

A panic-stricken Mr. Lam pointed at Delia and screamed, "Shoot her first—now!"

Delia evaded the bullets by jumping straight in the air, nearly hitting the top of the 20-foot ceiling. A dumbfounded Mr. Lam watched her gently land back down. His two sidekicks were stunned.

"Looks like I am just in time for lunch," rang a voice from behind Mr. Lam.

It was Christo Sanchez, who seemed to appear out of nowhere, his Glock aimed at Mr. Lam's head.

Mr. Lam's girls spun around, weapons raised. What followed was like a scene from an old Jackie Chan movie. In one nimble move, Sanchez flipped forward and drop-kicked the guns from each of their hands. He stood in front of them, a big sneer marking his mouth.

One of Mr. Lam's girls seemed to distract Sanchez with some dazzling hand movements, just as the other girl took out his legs with a swinging side kick to his knees.

"My mother does not like me to hit ladies," said Sanchez as he jumped back up, "but you *biatches* are not ladies ..."

The girls erupted with a flurry of kicks and punches, thrashing on Sanchez multiple times before he countered with blazing fists and powerful leg strikes of his own.

There was a full two minutes of back-and-forth jabbing, spinning and kicking, Sanchez looking like he was toying with the girls, enjoying himself. When one of them landed a strike to his genitals, Sanchez let his might ignite, grabbing each girl by the neck and snapping them like twigs.

Delia was trying to waken a fallen Jimi, slapping him hard on the cheeks, as she watched the rapid-fire display of martial combat.

Mr. Lam stared in horror as both his girls wilted to the hard floor beneath them. "Tammy! Kimmy! Oh my god. … Somebody help me!"

"No one will be coming to your rescue, unless the dead can walk," said Sanchez, dusting off his hands like a baker shakes off flour.

Three men in white aprons carrying big knives and chanting "*Ni hui si*" entered the room like a pack of wolf cubs and surrounded Sanchez, circling him like he was prey.

"Nice toys, boys. I hope they are sharp," Sanchez snickered, looking at the knives. "Which one of you wants to get carved up first?"

Mr. Lam cried out, "Don't hurt my chefs, please, I beg you!"

Three seconds later, one of the chefs was on the ground clutching the carving knife that had been rammed through his gut. Sanchez eyed the other two, in no hurry, smiling like he caught a buzz from the dread in their faces.

"Stop—*no more killing*," Delia said.

Sanchez spun on his toes with the speed of a ballerina and when he stopped, he had both the chefs' knives in his right hand.

"As you command. I am here to serve you."

"What is your name?" Delia wanted to know.

"Those who pay for my services call me Crisco. But you can call me Sanchez. I know who you are. I am your humble servant."

"You are a killer!" screamed Mr. Lam. "My girls, my girls … I will hunt you to the ends of the Earth!"

Sanchez knocked Mr. Lam to the floor with a heavy slap to the back of his big head.

"Shut your face, stoopid, or I will snap your piggy neck in two."

"That's *enough* violence, Sanchez, let him be," said Delia.

"I know who you are now. We met in the underground parking lot at the casino. You tried to kill me."

"I was on a mission. Forgive me," Sanchez said, almost pleading. "Things have changed. Samantha Isenberg sent me. I am here to protect you."

Sanchez made the sign of the cross and got down on one knee facing her.

Delia tilted her head to confirm a sound she just heard, approaching the Lam residence.

"We have to leave, now."

A suddenly alert Jimi said, "Jesus, what is it with you and the 'We have to leave, now' line? Everywhere we go, this shit happens."

"She is right," said Sanchez. "I hear the sirens, too. Let's go … Little piggy can explain what happened here to the police."

A freaked-out Mr. Lam yelled, "No, take me with you—I will return your $5 million!" His begging eyes looked ready to pop from their sockets.

"I can't explain this mess, all these dead bodies—they will never let me go."

Delia forced the key from Mr. Lam's pocket and demanded to know where the locker was.

"At the airport, like I said … in Lisbon."

"Christ—we can't go back to Lisbon. They'll arrest us," Jimi cried.

"I will go there, for you," said Sanchez.

"We can discuss that on the way," said Delia. "Move it, Jimi."

As they hurried off the property, high-stepping over the fallen bodies, Mr. Lam followed close behind, still pleading with them.

Sanchez suggested they take his rental car, parked just around the corner.

"No. Let's take the limo," said Jimi. "It's bullet proof and it has a bar. I really need a drink right now."

"Do you have a key for the limo?" said Sanchez.

Delia touched the driver's side door handle. It opened.

"Get in everyone."

She dropped into the driver's seat, started the engine with a wave of her hand, drove the pedal to the floor and screeched away, just as a police car rounded the curve right in front of them.

"Pass me the scotch, Sanchez. Forget the glass. Gimme the bottle."

Sanchez handed it to him, then rolled down his window and spat out the spent coca leaf from under his tongue. He reached in his pant pocket for more.

"Here, chew on this instead," said Sanchez. "It will help you relax, make you feel better."

"You want me to chew on a freakin' leaf—do I look like a rabbit?"

"Yeah, a scared little rabbit, missing its momma. Go ahead, keep sucking on that bottle like it's a tit. I should turn you over and give you a spanking, sissy boy."

Delia snapped her head around to confront the bickering twosome, even as the limo raced down the snaking hills of Funchal.

"You do not lay a hand on Jimi—ever. Understood, Sanchez?"

"As you command."

When they reached the airport, Delia told them to wait in the limo while she enquired about flights off the island.

"You stoopid fool—don't you know who this woman is?" said Sanchez, as soon as Delia disappeared through the airport doors.

"Sure I do, that's why you should listen to her—touch me and she'll take you out, asshole," said Jimi, still taking slugs from the bottle, his face looking redder with each mouthful.

"You ungrateful little cockroach—I saw her back at the casino, flying up the air shaft with your dead body in her arms. And now you live. That fly on the ceiling in your room at the Nomar, it was one of my drones. I heard everything. I spoke to Samantha Isenberg, I know what is *really* going on here. I have pledged my life to protect Delia.

"Why do you drink so much and act so stoopid at a time like this?"

"You look like Fidel Castro when you get angry—anybody ever tell you that, Sanchez?"

Even if Jimi wasn't half sloshed, he wouldn't have ducked the lightning-quick fist that pounded him in the forehead like a hammer.

Jimi's near-empty bottle dropped to the floor, his head slumped back against the headrest.

Sanchez slapped his cheeks hard with a flattened palm. When there was no response, he placed another coca leaf under his tongue, and made the sign of the cross.

When Delia returned, she opened the door that Jimi was crumpled against, saying, "Everybody out, next flight for Lisbon leaves in 25 minutes."

She looked at Jimi, then over at Sanchez.

"He's out like a light. What happened?"

"He's drunk. Sucked the whole bottle down his throat while you were inside. We should leave him behind. Guy's a useless tool. He'll only slow us down."

CHAPTER 20
The cross I bear

At first, Viktor Kozlov was relieved. Mother finally responded. He sent her his thoughts and they mapped out their next steps. But when he asked what took her so long to get back to him, she broke off communication.

How could she treat him so callously after all the sacrifices he'd made for her? The feeling welling up from his human host made him experience anger like never before.

He couldn't wait until their mission was over, he was done with humans. The human body is a frail vessel, permanently in need of nutrients and sleep, oxygen and H2O. Such were the flaws that plagued carbon-based beings. He felt vulnerable in human form, a feeling other Deus could never understand.

Xeno joined with the human named Viktor Kozlov 18 years ago. Kozlov was 21, and dying of severe anemia from a hookworm infection when Xeno found him in a Moscow hospital. Doctors believed the source of the infection was related to Kozlov's summer job, maintaining portable toilets for a huge government-owned construction firm.

The seconds before the human soul leaves its failing physical body is the optimum time for a Deus of Xeno's abilities to merge with a carbon-based host. If the soul had already departed, the precise linking of minds would miscarry. Xeno timed the union perfectly, just like Mother had done with Delia Cassavetes.

Xeno as Viktor Kozlov became a member of the Russian foreign intelligence agency known as SVR. He rose quickly in the ranks and lay the groundwork for his eventual transfer to the United States, in keeping with the plan concocted with his two co-conspirators on the Imperitus Council, who were members of The Salvatores.

He joined the staff at the Russian Consulate in Washington, D.C., where he had easy access to American military leaders. Until yesterday, the plan was proceeding on schedule. That's when Mother threw a wrench into the works with her 'Gravity Girl' fiasco.

Xeno warned Mother about bringing an outsider like Jimi James with her to Europe. He didn't understand why she healed Jimi after he was shot. She refused to explain her motives, telling Xeno all would be revealed "soon." He reminded Mother that such expenditures of energy would weaken her life force; she would need to regenerate much sooner. She didn't seem concerned, and that worried Xeno. Mother was always cautious about her energy use during past missions.

He wondered how much of Mother's life force was left after the Gravity Girl stunt. Such a strain on the feeble human form would seriously weaken it, snapping tendons and muscles like overstretched rubber bands.

As Viktor Kozlov, Xeno was acutely aware of the human body's physical bounds. Sure, he could make the body leap 100 feet straight in the air or run faster than a cheetah, but Kozlov's frame would be a mangled wreck if he did so. Not to mention the unwelcome attention such exploits would bring from stupefied humans ...

Xeno's current mission took him by surprise. He and Mother were about to leave for a world called Indica when she came to him, her aura beaming blue. She was nervous about something.

"That mission to Indica is delayed—start preparations to leave for Earth, instead. I will explain later."

She had a plan, but gave him few details. Mother had never been this secretive before. He had observed variations in his own thought patterns and behavior since interacting with humans, but the changes he saw in Mother were much more profound. She didn't deny she had incorporated some distinctly human strategies into her planning when Xeno challenged her, but insisted this gave her advantages which were critical to her success.

Before he left for Earth with Mother this time around, Xeno had a secret meeting with two prominent members of the Imperitus Council. They were, in fact, Salvatore 2 and Salvatore 6. Like other Deus, Xeno was unaware a powerful clandestine society like The Salvatores even existed.

It was then he committed to their quest to cleanse the Cosmos of the human scourge. With Xeno's help, The Salvatores would have a direct hand in their annihilation. He was sworn to secrecy. His betrayal of Mother was devised and activated. He was told the fate of the Universe depended on him.

In return for his cooperation with The Salvatores, Xeno had one condition: Mother was never to learn of his betrayal. He was certain she didn't know. She would have confronted him by now.

Despite his growing aversion to being trapped in a human host, Xeno vowed to persevere. The end game was worth his sacrifice.

Mother would be with him again, once the umbilical cord to the human distraction was cut. Partners once more, like they always had been.

During his years with Kozlov, Xeno's loathing for modern-day humans festered like a cancer as he observed their daily lives. They were not logical. Their days were filled with mindless pastimes, like watching sports, playing video games and posting photos of their food on social media. They knew more about sport statistics and the makeup tricks of celebrities than they knew about where their food came from or how their governments worked, opening the door for manipulation on the grandest scale. He did not understand how a life so precious could be so squandered.

Xeno and his co-conspirators knew that if Mother discovered their plan, she would find a way to save the humans again. Just like she did on Mars and with the giant water vessel on Earth.

Failure was not an option.

If left unchecked, humans would eventually make their way to other solar systems, bringing their machines of death and destruction with them. To conquer was all they understood. The humans must be stopped, before they became too powerful to contain. The Deus and their allies would be defenseless against the ruthless warrior race from Earth.

A mass extinction event was the only logical solution.

CHAPTER 21
Human guinea pigs

Samantha Isenberg was on the phone with her White House mole, getting updates on Deon Carter and Delia Cassavetes. It was as secure a connection as possible, the mole assured her. The signal was bounced to 23 far-flung countries employing nine communication satellites, making it an onerous task for anyone to trace the call, let alone eavesdrop.

There was a four-second delay because of all the re-routing, but Isenberg would rather that inconvenience than gamble with New Eden's security. They never spent more than eight minutes on a call, the mole warning that, any longer, and the authorities would have time to trace the signal.

Her mole was a colleague she'd known since her time at MIT, now the senior technician for the internal White House computer network. In order to troubleshoot software and hardware issues, his security clearance inadvertently granted him access to sensitive information shared by those in the House of Power.

Isenberg called him "Sonny," but his real name was Theodore Liston. He'd been on her payroll for two years.

"We lost track of Deon Carter shortly after you spoke to him in Lisbon," Sonny explained. "Word is that General Isadore Pope is on his tail. I think Carter is a lost cause for our mission. A million dollars, up in smoke."

"Oprah and I could care less. Very soon, thousand-dollar bills won't be worth the ink used to print them. She arrived here yesterday, brought her own food, said she couldn't make it through this without her cauliflower dough and vegan pepperoni."

"Save some storage space for me, Sam. I wanna bring some Texas steaks. Most tender, lip-smacking corn-fed beef you've ever wrapped your teeth around."

"Absolutely not. There will be no animal flesh at New Eden. Mother's rules."

"What? That's blasphemous, the Bible references all kinds of meat-eating ..."

"God did not write the Bible, we did," Isenberg countered. "The new humans will respect *all* animal life—from the seas to the skies, to the valleys and the hillsides. No more barbaric hunting, not for sport or for sustenance."

"I can't live exclusively on roots and berries, Sam, I'll wither away to skin and bones."

"Nonsense, Sonny. Why the strongest mammals on Earth are vegetarians—gorillas, apes, elephants, to name a few. The choice is yours. Nobody is twisting your arm to join us at New Eden."

"Well, Sam, you know I'll be having ham and eggs for breakfast, steak sandwiches for lunch and roast beef for dinner, every day, until I get to New Eden."

"Good. So when you arrive, I won't hear you shouting, 'Where's the beef?'... Now, back to more serious matters ... About Mother's quest for the anti-gravity device—oh how I wish I had found her in time to give her the money she needed for the transaction, instead of her venturing off to Vegas. But I could not make contact with her."

"We both understand why she does not use a cellphone to communicate with us, Sam, which would have saved her all that trouble, but potentially put our mission in peril. In retrospect, what she did was the safest way, for all involved."

"By the way, Sam, have you heard from Sanchez?"

"Sanchez just checked in," Isenberg replied. "They have the device, picked it up in Lisbon. He says they are heading back to the States."

"That's good news, Sam. So, Sanchez will be joining us in New Eden?"

"Yes, he is."

"You know, the deal you made with Sanchez, I think you will regret it once he gets to New Eden. We should have him taken care of, before he gets there."

"On the contrary, Sonny. I have given this some thought. The colony will need a 'heavy' like Sanchez, someone who can help maintain order, especially in the beginning. After I reveal New Eden's true purpose to everyone, we may have a small rebellion to deal with. He will prove useful, trust me."

"But is Mother OK with this, Sam? You remember how firm she was about the selection process for the colony. Sanchez's DNA profile is sure to pollute the purity of the gene pool Mother so ardently insisted upon."

"That won't be a problem ..."

"Oh? Why do you say that?"

"It's simple, we'll have him fixed. He won't be able to breed."

"He will be pissed … I have to ask, Sam, how did an outsider like Crisco Sanchez get wind of our operation?"

"That was my fail. The little weasel hoodwinked me. He's a sly one. Claimed he already knew everything about Mother's plan, gave me enough to convince me he did. I should have known better. In the end, I had no choice but to guarantee him a place in New Eden, in exchange for protecting Delia from Triton and Pope."

"Don't blame yourself, Sam, he is renowned for his cunning. Hell of a lot smarter than the military could have imagined when they brought him here from Colombia to work for them. Plus, as you said, he will be a useful asset.

"One more thing, Sam. I am getting really anxious about the President's timeline for testing the wave bomb. It may happen, sooner than we think."

"We are very close to completion, Sonny. If pushed, we could be ready in five or six days. Look, I have a meeting with my senior staff, they have probably started without me. Let's talk again, later tonight."

***

Chief engineer Jack Holt was buttering a slice of warm quinoa loaf when his fingers dropped the knife to his plate. He looked around the table, where Isenberg's senior team was meeting over dinner, with a dumfounded look on his face.

"This better be a joke," said Holt. "I was told, and therefore planned, for a six-month project. The batteries will hold for that long. I stake my reputation on it."

Isenberg couldn't believe what just happened. Did her staff intentionally sabotage her? Or did they simply forget that Holt was not part of New Eden's inner circle?

Everyone stopped eating. Isenberg's tiny eyes glowered at renowned oceanographer Jukka Sarensen, New Eden's director of environmental projects. He was the one that dropped the 'doomsday' bomb, during a discussion on whether the underground colony's network of batteries would have enough juice in them after one year.

"Also, let's keep in mind that our ability to produce solar power will be severely compromised," Sarensen had said.

"My weather models predict at least six months of continuous cloud cover after the Earth is flooded. Much longer if, after the tides smack the continents and tectonic plates rattle in the lithosphere, the planet's axis tilts more than 0.0225 degrees."

Sarensen glared right back at Isenberg, saying, "I told you, we should have been straight with Jack about New Eden's true purpose, Sam."

"I agree with Jukka," said geologist Heidi Merkel. "It was foolish of us to think we could keep this from the rest of the senior staff."

Isenberg stiffened her back and clasped her hands together under her chin as the other five looked her way.

"Jack, you are here to give us an update on the construction schedule," she said firmly. "What you just heard is mere speculation on potential scenarios, the kind we discuss at *all* our meetings. It's an integral part of the research we have undertaken.

"Please give us your report, then I must ask you to depart, Jack. You can take the rest of your dinner with you, if you like."

Holt was quick to respond.

"Look Sam, you hired me, not only because I am the best at what I do, but also because I am totally trustworthy—how many times in the past have I proven that to you?

"Now, it appears to me like I am being left out of a critical part of this project. Unless you bring me up to speed, I will tender my resignation. Effective immediately."

"You're not going anywhere, Jack," said Merkel. "Sam, if you don't tell him, I will."

Nods of agreement circled round the table.

"The time has come, Sam," said Sarensen.

"OK. Where do I begin?" said Isenberg, to no one in particular.

"Try starting at the beginning," said Holt. "I don't think any of us have anywhere else we need to be any time soon."

Isenberg was seething inside. She did not trust Jack Holt, beyond his ability to do the job she hired him for. Perhaps there was a way to test his impending allegiance to New Eden, before the truth came forward. Then the staff would understand why Holt must remain an outsider.

"Alright Jack," Isenberg said, "I know that you are a very religious man … your brother is a priest and your father runs a charitable organization for the Catholic church, yes?"

"That is correct, Sam. 'The Lord is my shepherd; I shall not want.'"

"Yes, of course he is. … What we are about to tell you, Jack, is in the strictest confidence—none of the others in the compound are to hear a single word of our conversation. Agreed?"

"You have my word on that. Everyone here at the table will serve as witnesses."

This is *too* easy, Isenberg thought. She had Holt right where she wanted him and, at the same time, she would stealthily rebuke her staff for undermining her authority. She had to place a quick hand in front of her mouth for a second, so no one could see her spiteful smirk, one that was already anticipating payback. She knew she had to wipe it from her face before continuing.

"So, Jack, you are obviously a Christian, but have you ever really examined *why* you believe what you do?"

"I can say with certainty that my belief in God is beyond scrutiny, there is no faith stronger, or more spiritually rewarding. Why would you even ask such a question, Sam?"

"I am interested in knowing *how* you learned about your faith, Jack. Allow me to illustrate why I ask: If you were born in the remote African rainforest to a family of pygmies, odds are you would never hear about Christianity. Your creator would be a god named Bembe who lived in a parallel universe, and the rainforest would be a realm of ghosts whose wrath you would fear. You wouldn't know any different and these would be your beliefs because you would have been taught them throughout your childhood. The tenets of your faith are learned the same way, through indoctrination."

"That is the silliest thing I've ever heard, Sam. I was not born a pygmy, so of course I believe only in the true God."

Isenberg smiled and looked around the table to note the reactions from her inner circle. So far, so good, she thought.

"Do you believe there is life on other planets, Jack?"

"Of course, that's a given, Sam. As an engineer, I may be a man of science, but I am also a man of faith. I believe those two realms are indivisible, they are One. As such, only a fool would believe otherwise. And, if you are a 'believer,' as I am, you *have* to trust in God's ultimate wisdom. He would *never* create such a vast Universe and put life on just one single planet. What a waste that would be. It's just not logical that almighty God would be that thoughtless.

"We know for a fact there are billions of solar systems out there and even more planets, likely trillions of planets, many of which are inhabited. That I say with certainty."

"NASA's latest findings reveal there are more than two trillion galaxies, each like a little island Universe," said Anaki Washimba, a theoretical physicist on Isenberg's team.

"That means the number of planets in the Universe borders on the infinite."

"Yes, and every time a star explodes its material is spread throughout the Universe," Merkel jumped in.

"We are all made from stardust. We are composed of materials that are billions of years old."

"Like I was saying, before Neil deGrasse Tyson and the *Woodstock* woman interrupted," Holt said with contempt.

"God created a vast Universe and there is no chance whatsoever he only put life on *this* planet. No way Earth is that special, no way our Creator is that short-sighted. It just does not make sense that my God would ignore everything else he has created and only focus on one tiny speck of a planet," Holt concluded.

"Glad to see you have an open mind about this, Jack," said Sarensen, smiling at Isenberg like he knew what she was up to.

To Isenberg, Holt's position that science and faith are 'indivisible' was as absurd as adding hot sauce to jalapeno peppers. Science and faith are wholly *incompatible*. Faith is belief in something without empirical evidence, science is logical reasoning based on empirical evidence. There is no objective truth in faith. Science is constantly evolving and its knowledge base expanding. Faith, and its basic tenets, remain relatively static over time.

"What we are about to tell you, Jack," Isenberg said without flinching, "will brutally test the mettle of such convictions."

"Wait," said Merkel, "before we say another word, has anyone checked the electronic dampers that block signals from leaving the compound today?"

"Of course," said Isenberg. "And it's automated, remember? Warning signal goes off if anyone manages to penetrate our shielding."

"What about your household staff?"

"All the servants follow protocol to the letter, Heidi. You know all this, don't be so anxious. When we have our meetings, they are required to remain in the guest house. That's why we always clear our own table after our dinner meetings."

Merkel apologized for her paranoia, explaining she was horribly concerned, "That crazy President Douglas Triton would send bombers" if he had any inkling of what their project was about. Isenberg assured Merkel that a trusted confidante says all is going according to plan.

Isenberg continued. She told Holt that, during the last 18 years or so, she and her cohorts were visited in their dreams by what they thought was a ghost, at first.

"For me, it was frightening. I had horrible nightmares," said Sarensen. "I thought I was losing my mind, mostly because, in my early teen years, I was a heavy drug user, including many serotonergic psychedelics like psilocybin, peyote and LSD. But then one night she revealed her true self, this glorious, serene being, bathed in brilliant blue light."

"That kind of hallucination happens when you're tripping out on psychedelic drugs, Jukka," Holt nagged.

Holt's contempt for what he heard so far was written all over his face. He continued.

"Hell, I once believed I actually saw God rising from behind Rick Wakeman's keyboards at a Yes concert in New York, courtesy of 'window pane' acid ..."

"I was in my first year at the University of Helsinki at the time," Sarensen was quick to counter. "I had quit doing psychedelic drugs long before then."

"And I *never* did drugs stronger than a decongestant," said Merkel. "Mother also visited me in my dreams, for years. I also thought she was a ghost, at first."

"It was the same for the rest of us," said Isenberg. "Through the early years, Mother gave us guidance and direction, especially regarding our career choices. She told us we were chosen for a reason, that the fate of humanity was in our hands."

"But she did not reveal her true plan for us until a few years ago," added Sarensen. "I remember telling a few close friends about Mother— they thought I was crazy, wanted me to see a psycho-analyst. So, I kept it to myself, as Mother had asked from the beginning."

"Of course, they would think you were a nut bar, who wouldn't?" said Holt. "I get it now, you are all part of some kind of doomsday cult, right?"

"Enough, Jack," said Isenberg. "You asked for the truth, zip it and listen up."

Holt glanced around the table. Everyone looked as serious as Yogis at a metaphysical conference.

"OK, please continue, Sam."

"We all rose to become leaders in our fields, as a result of Mother's guidance," Isenberg said. "I am the financier of project New Eden, which is why I was directed into the business world, and eventually became a multi-billionaire."

Merkel said she was fascinated by how the Earth works as a teenager, and when Mother started visiting her in her dreams, she was encouraged to study geology and all its related fields.

"Today, Heidi Merkel is considered the world's preeminent academic in plate tectonics," Isenberg said.

"Jukka Sarensen, aside from being an oceanographer of world acclaim, is also an expert in climatology. Nancy Pelligrino, my chief botanist and food scientist extraordinaire, is also a geneticist with a compelling knowledge of agricultural practices. Next to me is Anaki Washimba, who has had more breakthroughs in the world of theoretical math and physics than Albert Einstein and Stephen Hawking. I dare say, in terms of IQ, Anaki makes the rest of us look like simpletons."

"That's high praise, coming from you, Sam," said Washimba. "Please allow me to join the conversation.

"Mr. Holt, your skepticism is rational, and not unexpected. Just one reason why Sam and I arrived at the obstinate decision to keep the true mission of New Eden under a shroud of secrecy, until the underground colony was established and the looming cataclysm had befallen us."

"'Looming cataclysm?' What's that mean in plain English," Holt wanted to know.

"We are getting ahead of ourselves," said Isenberg. "Let me dial it back for you, Jack.

"Two years ago, the four individuals you see here, appeared at my front door, within hours of one another. We had never met before and were completely unaware that we were part of Mother's chosen few. In our dreams that night, she explained why we were selected for this mission: To save humanity, and begin the next stage of our evolution."

Holt was fixated on every word Isenberg said, his eyes rarely blinked.

"She told us she belonged to a race called the Deus, from the planet Caelum. She asked us to gather the finest minds in the world and bring them here. When the rest of humanity perishes after the Big Flood, we will be left to forge a new society here on Earth. A more advanced human race, a people of peace ..."

"Wait a minute—all of you—stop!" said Holt, his breathing becoming heavy.

"You have the floor, Jack," said Isenberg.

Holt shook his head like he was seriously annoyed, saying, "You should hear yourself, Sam. I know some Latin; Deus means God and Caelum means heaven. So, this alien of yours is *God from Heaven*?"

"Mother explained to us how that misconception came about."

"That's total nonsense—you are all out of your goddamn minds!"

Holt's outburst seemed to put the others on edge. Isenberg eyed each member of her inner circle with an "I told you so" frown.

"Jack, if you talked to Mother, as we have, you would understand," said Merkel.

Holt stood up, then paced slowly around the table.

"What I am hearing—with fresh ears, you should all note—is that an alien that calls herself 'Mother' has directed this secret operation for the last 18 years, telling each of you what *her* plan is. Basically, embedding orders in all your thought patterns, like what happens when people are programmed—*brainwashed.*

"Tell me, Sam, who *selected* the people who will become residents of your New Eden? ... It was your so-called alien, right? Of course it was.

"Looks to me like you have been deceived by this alien."

All eyes and ears focused on Holt.

"If her goal is to weed out the weak in humanity that she sees as a hindrance to our evolution, then who's to say she isn't also the one behind the 'looming cataclysm,' this Big Flood you speak of?

"Don't you people see what I see? It's clear as day to me. We're talking about an evil perversion of the human race. You have all been manipulated to do her bidding.

"This isn't about saving humanity. This is social engineering on a grand scale. New Eden is her science lab. Humans are her guinea pigs."

After a brief pause, Holt said, "Screw you and your money, Sam. I am outta here, I don't want anything to do with heretics like you and your fantasies from hell."

He stormed out of the dining room, cursing loudly as he headed for the front door. "Goddamned crazy motherfuckers … freakin' Satan worshippers ..."

Everyone at the table looked like their clothes had just been ripped from their bodies. Except for Isenberg.

Her hand was back in front of her mouth, hiding the biggest smile she ever had.

CHAPTER 22
'Dialogue of idiots'

General Isadore Pope sat on a couch in the Oval Office, hunched forward as he read through a stack of classified documents. Around him, President Douglas Triton and his top-line advisors talked strategy. Pope scribbled notes in the margins as he went through the pages. He would need them when it was his turn to brief the President.

It was early Friday afternoon. Triton had called the meeting before he lifted off in Air Force One with an entourage of 17, not counting domestics and Secret Service agents, for a Saturday of golf, followed by a steak and lobster feast at his sprawling ocean-front estate. Unless a foreign power threatened to nuke the United States, the staff knew better than to disturb Triton while he was engrossed in his two favorite pastimes.

Triton's Chief of Staff Adam Probert was livid over media reports the President's extravagant golf weekends with his billionaire friends were costing the taxpayers millions, money better spent sustaining social programs facing the Triton administration's axe, the media proclaimed.

"The press is disgusting in this country," said Probert. "Sniveling scribes. No respect. I tell you Mr. President, if Russian or Chinese journalists dared to criticize their leader in such a despicable manner, they would lose their fingertips—chop-chop!"

"Should be the same here," said President Triton. "Hold on, once they heal, their stubby little half-fingers would start typing bad words at me again, count on it."

"I would hire a half-blind dentist to pull their teeth out one-by-one, like the scene in *Marathon Man*," said Scott Salter, Triton's press secretary. "See how fast all these Woodward and Bernstein wannabes shut their traps."

"I have a better idea," said Stan Braddick, Triton's chief strategist. "Let's invite the top media dudes over to my place in the Hampton's, very private, right on the water. Tell them we want to have a frank discussion about how the press is treating the Leader of the Free World."

"They wouldn't come," said Triton. "Bad idea. Disaster. And the female reporters would feel left out, accuse me of being a male chauvinist, all over again."

"In truth, they would just be calling a spade, a spade," said Braddick. "Keep listening, Dougie, I'm not done yet."

"I object to your inference about my father," said Triton's daughter, Olivia.

"Oh come on, Olivia, you know what a horny dog your old man is," laughed Braddick.

Olivia was sitting on the couch next to General Pope. "That was a long time ago. My father has changed," she said to Pope in hushed tones.

At the same time, the President whispered to Braddick: "Women can't keep their hands off The Triton. How is that my fault?"

Pope knew all about Triton's affairs. The scandals had been quietly quashed with payoffs, courtesy of Triton cronies with bank accounts bigger than their brains, but Pope knew how to bring them back into the light.

He also had intel on Olivia's troubled youth. Her father was cruel and overbearing; she went through therapists like kids at the circus go through cotton candy.

"The media hacks *would* come, if you lured them with food and booze," said Salter. "Journalists are drawn to free liquor like Johns to street corners."

"Exactly, that's the *hook*," agreed Braddick. "What we do is drink them stupid with doubles, then send them off to private rooms with some super-discreet ladies I know. They've done a lot of good work for me in the past. All my bedrooms are equipped with hi-def, motion-sensing video cams. We can watch the action from monitors in my office there."

"Start them off with a hand party, get them hot enough to wanna get naughty with the ladies—I like it," said Triton. "And it won't cost us a plug nickel. I'll get one of my aides to work all the expenses into the books, somewhere."

"We'll have to spike their drinks with erectile dysfunction drugs," added Salter. "I know the media hacks well enough to tell you, their farts are more dangerous than their dicks."

There was a round of bellicose laughter among the men, with Triton's being the loudest.

"Salter, that's the best one I've heard all week," Triton laughed.

"If life be a bowl of peaches … I be the cream," Salter sailed back.

"Shakespeare?" asked Triton.

The room filled with laughter again, but Pope never parted his lips. He knew the President's question was serious.

"Gentlemen, please, enough locker-room talk," said a frustrated Olivia. "Surely we have more pressing matters to discuss than hookers and hacks."

Olivia understood why her father appointed her the token female in his clique of advisors, more a response to public criticism than it was respect for her opinion. Still, she was determined to make her voice count.

"That's why Pope is with us today," said Triton, pointing at the general. "You ready to brief us?"

The general was waiting patiently for his cue. He knew better than to interrupt the President when the talk turned to sex, scandal and blackmail.

"Let's begin with Crisco, Mr. President. I have an update on his situational status."

"And I can tell *you* that my people went to drain his secret bank account, but the slimy little Chico weaseled the money outta there, minutes before we hacked him," said Triton.

Olivia shook her head in dismay. "Please, general, resume your report."

"Intelligence reports that Crisco is still ignoring us. We tried pinging his phone to track his location, but he's using a next-gen burner. The agents we sent in pursuit have not checked in since they arrived in Lisbon.

"Their whereabouts are currently unknown. Crisco's last confirmed location was on the Madeira Islands. We have no one in Madeira to determine his intentions at this point," the general continued.

"We must decide if we want to risk losing more of our people to hunt Crisco down. Intelligence suggests we leave him be, for now. Wait until he comes back to U.S. soil before taking him out."

"He's a zero to us now, putting him to sleep can wait," said Probert.

"What about the redhead and her accomplice from Vegas?" said Braddick, looking at the file which contained some surveillance pictures of Delia Cassavetes.

"That's a strange one, sir," the general said. "Intelligence reports they were on the same plane to the Madeira Islands as Crisco."

"So, he's still on her trail, it would seem to me," said Braddick.

"That is a distinct possibility," said the general. "And, there may be a legitimate reason why he has gone dark. I am expecting to know more shortly. We have reached out to Portuguese intelligence over this matter. It was not on their radar, of course, but they agreed to report to us ASAP."

"Shame we have to kill her," Braddick sighed, as he ogled photos of Delia.

"This is all new to me," said Salter, who was also looking at the redhead's photos. "And the reason she has to die is ...?"

"No one told you?" asked the general.

Salter responded by shaking his head.

"Those shots were printed from surveillance footage of my home here in Washington," Pope explained. "The redhead somehow eluded security—my men are top-notch pros—figured out the password for the 'impenetrable' entry to my secret office in seconds, and replicated my iris signature to get past the scan that opens the bureau holding plans for a classified mission the President and I have undertaken."

"Right—*that* mission. When are you going to tell the rest of us about it, general?" said Braddick.

"At our next meeting. Those are direct orders, from President Triton."

"I made that decision under advisement," said Triton, looking over at Pope, then back at the others. "Next week, the rest of you will be briefed. It's nothing personal, guys. But it's big, really *big*. Need to know only, for now."

The President's penchant for hyperbole was well-documented. Many of his critics just called him a liar. As such, there was no dissension from his advisors. Only Triton, General Pope and a select few were entrusted with the classified mission. As far as anyone else in Triton's inner circle and the military were concerned, the secret wave bomb testing was strictly routine. Standard protocols were being followed.

Pope thought about what to report on next. He sorted through what to keep to himself, and what he wanted the President to know. Although he was appointed acting Secretary of Defense by Triton, he was not given the respect such a post was traditionally accorded. He despised having become a mere marionette, his strings pulled by these immoral overlords controlling the White House.

Like most of his cohorts in the military, Pope jumped on the Triton bandwagon early, believing he was the straight-shooting President they had been waiting for, a powerful patriot who would advance America's dominance over the rest of the world.

They now realized Americans had been duped. Triton was a maniacal, self-absorbed tyrant, more interested in scratching the backs of his billionaire brethren and the sweep of his hairline, than he was in securing truth, justice and the American way.

With the help of a few trusted allies, Pope had been developing a strategy of his own. In fact, he was the one who leaked the true costs of Triton's golf extravaganzas to the media. Pope was a disciple of military history and studied the downfall of tyrants extensively.

The scheme was to take Triton down after the wave bomb decimated China. All the seeds were furtively planted for Triton and his cronies to take the fall. Pope kept meticulous records and secret recordings of incriminating conversations with the President. He was recording this meeting, as well.

For the time being, he would maintain his cover, playing puppet to the master of showmanship. With the American economy in shambles because of Triton's abysmal economic policies, and an approval rating in a downward spiral, everything was perfectly aligned for the coup.

Pope turned to the matter of a video circulating on the Internet.

"Intelligence confirms the redhead we are after is the same woman the world is now calling 'Gravity Girl.' She survived a 32-story plunge down the side of a Lisbon hotel called The Proximo Rio two days ago. The video shows her miraculously breaking her fall by using a bath towel like a parachute, coming to a dead stop, just before she hit the water."

"How did she do it?" said Braddick.

"Intelligence is working on it," said Pope.

"In other words, they don't have a clue," said Triton.

"No yet, Mr. President."

"I have seen that video," said Salter. "Body of a goddess. Shame we have to eliminate her."

"Moving on then, Mr. President," said the general. "As far as Samantha Isenberg is concerned, we have had a major breakthrough. Intelligence says there is no need for alarm."

"How do we go from wanting to bomb her compound to 'no need for alarm?'" said Braddick.

"Sir, a couple of days ago, Intelligence sent two operatives to Isenberg's compound," Pope explained, "under the guise of being electrical inspection experts. Isenberg's crew had special-ordered 16 state-of-the-art lithium batteries, each the size of a truck.

"We convinced the manufacturer to demand their own people perform the final inspection of the installation. One crossed wire and the whole thing could blow, leaving behind a crater the size of Rhode Island, was the contention used. The server room in the underground bunker Isenberg is building was unguarded. The agents hacked in and downloaded everything on the drives."

"Fantastic work, general," said Probert. "So, tell us, what the hell is Sam Isenberg up to?"

"Most importantly," said Braddick, "why is it we should *not* be alarmed?"

Pope said the stolen documents indicate Isenberg is conducting an elaborate experiment in disaster-proof underground habitats. The economic premise being, in the very near future, people all over the world will hire her company to build bunkers to protect themselves from environmental catastrophes. Tensions being what they are between a number of countries, Isenberg is also banking on selling her models to governments wanting to protect their leaders from terrorist attacks and the like.

"Isenberg has developed cutting-edge technology to build them quickly and economically—for a huge profit, of course," Pope added.

"I had a feeling about this," said Triton. "It's all about making more money for that rich bitch."

"Consequently, we have curtailed surveillance of her compound," said Pope. "And the kidnap order for her daughter and grandchildren is now off the table."

Triton said they should go ahead and kidnap her family, anyway, "just to put a scare into the bitch. See if that organic deodorant one of her companies makes will keep her from sweating over this one."

"I would advise against proceeding with the kidnap, Mr. President," said Pope. "We have much bigger fish to fry."

"Come on, Daddy, let go of this one. Don't punish innocent children over your spite for Isenberg," Olivia pleaded. "It's *OK* for a woman to have more money than you ... we talked about this."

"How is it that my own kid doesn't know when I'm joking," Triton laughed. It was a laugh that seemed as put-on as the makeup on his face.

General Pope's cellphone rang. He looked at the caller I.D. and said, "If you'll excuse me for a moment, Mr. President, it's my assistant. He knows not to disturb me when I am in a meeting with you—it must be urgent."

"You have two minutes," said Triton. "I have a tight afternoon schedule, flight leaves very soon. Already some of my friends are waiting on the South Lawn."

"Thank you, sir."

The general's eyes looked ready to jump from his face during the conversation. He listened intently, throwing in an "I see," or a "copy that," at various points.

"Mr. President, I have more news from the Isenberg camp. There has been a defection by one of her senior people, my assistant reports. At this point, all we have is that the man is very angry, wants to rat on his former boss, claims the whole of Isenberg's management team has gone stark raving mad. Says they told him their true mission began years ago, when they were visited by an alien in their dreams."

Olivia Triton's face froze.

"Can you … repeat that … general?"

Her voice was so low, no one took notice.

"We do know aliens have been visiting Earth, we have proof," said Probert.

"What?" said Triton. "Aliens have been to Earth—and we have proof?"

"Sir, the Pentagon's file on extra-terrestrial activity was in the dossier I presented to you, just a few days into your presidency," said Pope.

"I don't have time to read dossiers, general. My days are very busy. You were supposed to give me a breakdown of everything I needed to know—what happened?"

"Sir, if you will recall, I was about to do that, when your manicurist and make-up artist arrived."

"I had to prepare for an interview on DOX news, surely you see how important that is, general."

The President looked around the room and said, "Hands up everyone who knew about the alien thing."

Every hand went up.

"How are we able to keep this so top-secret, general?" said Triton. "Seems like *everybody* knows about it."

"Nobody wants to be labelled a conspiracy nut," said Pope. "Which is what happens to those that try and convince the world aliens exist. Whenever the military or NASA is asked about alien visits to Earth, we lie, sir. Plain and simple.

"Before you became President, Intelligence was working on an indoctrination program to prepare the public for NASA's announcement about alien life, but too many world leaders don't think it wise to tell people what we know about alien visits to Earth. They keep to the dogma that it would blow people's minds."

"I happen to agree with that," said Triton. "Can you imagine the chaos if people knew this … suicides, nervous breakdowns, the fall of religion—Christ, I would likely go bankrupt."

"I disagree, father," said Olivia, her voice growing stronger. "Humanity *is* ready for this kind of news. You are not giving people enough credit …"

"Nonsense," Salter jumped in. "I am the communication specialist and let me tell you, the President is right—chaos, ruin and more chaos. The world as we know it would cease to exist."

I need to end this dialogue of idiots, Pope said to himself. He looked over at Olivia, still sitting next to him on the couch. Her lips were mouthing a message to him. "Call me later. Urgent," she appeared to be saying. Pope nodded. Message received.

"Mr. President," said the general, "this defector, Jack Holt, if I remember correctly, will be meeting with my staff forthwith. We will know more about this crazy story, soon.

"Moving forward, I have news from our scientists that will most please you, sir."

"You threatened to whip them, and they liked the idea?"

"Daddy!"

"There was no need for threats, Mr. President. Fact is, the operation is ahead of schedule. We will be ready to test the wave bomb in less than a week."

"Hallelujah!" said Triton. He jumped around the Oval Office like his shoes were spring-loaded, giving up high-fives to his disciples.

"They want to test it at Point Nemo," Pope continued, "smack dab in the middle of the South Pacific. With your authorization, of course, sir."

"And it's called 'Point Nemo' after Captain Nemo. He's the submarine captain in the Jules Verne's' novel *Twenty Thousand Leagues Under the Sea*," Salter explained, reacting to the quizzical look on Triton's face.

"How far is that from Easter Island, general?" Olivia wanted to know.

"Close enough that some pretty powerful waves will strike the island," said Pope, checking his note. "And there's a strong possibility the statues near the coast will be toppled, perhaps washed out to sea."

Olivia jumped up, pleading, "We can't do this, daddy. Those artifacts are precious, world-renowned treasures."

"Those hideous statues were made by heathen hands," said Triton. "Nobody gives a crap if they topple over. Trust me."

Triton ignored Olivia's continuing pleas, turning his eyes to Braddick, then asking if a plausible explanation for the potential devastation of Easter Island was up his sleeve.

Braddick looked up, almost immediately.

"Got one. How about this: American seismologists point to a rupture in the Earth's tectonic plate near Easter Island, as a reason for the destructive tidal wave?"

"Can't we just make the bomb less powerful?" said Olivia.

"We have no sure way of knowing the true force of the waves generated by the bomb until we complete the first test," Pope explained.

"Only then can our people establish parameters which enable the scientists to calibrate the residual forces. The science is very new and lab tests have been inconclusive."

"I love your idea, Braddick. Works for me," said Triton. "Salter, be ready to call a presser for the hacks after the first wave bomb is tested. Formulate an explanation for the destruction based on Braddick's brilliant idea."

"Of course, Mr. President," said Salter. "My only concern is that other seismologists around the world will surely dispute that finding. They will dig deep for the truth. Could be a mess for us to manage, given how much the mainstream media is gunning for you, sir."

"Let them," said Triton. "They will fail. The *truth*, people, is whatever I say it is."

CHAPTER 23

The heart, attacks

The pounding in Jimi's head wouldn't stop, even after he popped four of the extra-strength ones two hours ago. This was one hangover that refused treatment. The heavy punch to his head courtesy of Sanchez wasn't helping matters.

Sitting on a bench in the busy Departures zone at the Portela Airport while he waited for Delia and Sanchez, gave Jimi time to ponder the bizarre chain of events since he abandoned his carefree life in Las Vegas.

He'd met an extra-terrestrial with powers like a comic-book alien, risen from the dead like he was Jesus, fended off a notorious hit man, and been an accomplice in crimes ranging from car theft to murder.

Maybe he should have died back in the casino's parking garage. Better than facing life behind bars. No court would believe he was an unwitting participant in all of this. There had to be a way to get out of this mess …

Delia and Sanchez were retrieving the anti-gravity device from a locker on the other side of the airport. Delia saying that, now that she was blond, authorities would not spot her. Sanchez agreeing, noting it was fortunate he destroyed the security system when he arrived at Mr. Lam's property.

Getting the black box through customs was another concern they discussed. Delia insisting there were no scans humans had invented that could detect the device.

The three of them had spoken in hushed tones during the flight from Madeira. Sanchez admitted he was hired to kill Delia, but after watching her rise up with Jimi's body in her arms in the underground parking lot, he realized he'd witnessed a miracle. He also saw the Gravity Girl video online, and was the one in the BMW Delia claimed was following them on the way to Albufeira. But it was not until he eavesdropped on Jimi and Delia's conversation in their hotel room at the Nomar that Sanchez said he finally grasped who Delia really was.

Sanchez explained that his whole belief system was turned on its head. He now recoiled in horror at everything he used to believe in.

"Yes, I murdered people for money, but they were mostly evil ones. That was the only life I knew, and it was my way out from under the thumb of the drug cartels in Colombia," he told them with fat tears making his scraggly beard wet.

"I went to church and prayed, every Sunday. I always thought that God would understand. I always believed that God, in all his mercy, would forgive me of my sins. Now I see the light of true divinity."

This guy is a psycho killer, Jimi remembered thinking, a hit man with no conscience. How could Delia fall for his lies? Sanchez was not to be trusted.

Delia consoled Sanchez, told him he was a victim of circumstance.

"When wickedness usurps the purity of a single human soul, everyone suffers," she told him. "There will be forgiveness, and a new beginning. I promise."

Sanchez was nodding, like he understood what she was saying, which made Jimi feel even more uneasy; he didn't have a clue what Delia was on about.

Then the repentant killer asked if Delia was referring to Samantha Isenberg's sanctuary project, New Eden. Delia did not seem surprised he was aware of it. Jimi eyed her with a "What is he talking about?" look.

Sanchez explained he received a call from Isenberg, shortly after he'd listened in on their conversation at the Nomar.

"She had been calling me for days, but I had destroyed my old phone. How she was able to reach me on my new burner was a miracle, nobody had that number," said Sanchez.

"Ms. Isenberg told me I must cancel my contract to take you out. I agreed to become your protector, bring you safely to Isenberg's compound. That is what she asked me to do."

"I don't know how long I can stay at New Eden, Sanchez. I must return to my home world to regenerate. My vessel was damaged when I arrived on Earth. The little black box is an anti-gravity device that a man stole from me in 1918.

"At the time, I inhabited the body of a young woman named Agnes Scuffs, who was near death after being shot by a Russian spy who was aiming for her father, a member of the Latvian underground during your First World War.

"Shortly after that, Agnes was killed during heavy shelling by Russian tanks. I left her body just in time. But I had to return to my home world to regenerate."

"You have not answered my question about New Eden," said Jimi.

"All in good time, Jimi."

Remembering the conversation on the plane to Lisbon only added to Jimi's anxiety.

"You could really use a drink right now," kept echoing in his head.

Then he recalled something he read in a book by a psychologist: "All it takes is one bad day to reduce the sanest man alive to lunacy." Was he experiencing a descent into lunacy? Jimi shuddered. With all he'd experienced over the last few days, it certainly seemed like he'd entered the lunatic fringe.

Jimi struggled to keep it together, telling himself there was a purpose to all that had happened. He left the Departure area and went for a walk around the airport. When he came upon one of the "Living Spots," a place with comfy chairs and power outlets for travelers to recharge electronic gear, he took a seat. Through the large windows, he could see the sun burning off shadows as it warmed up the city.

He overheard two passersby ask a security guard for directions to The Heineken Bar. Sounded close by. Jimi got up and followed them, hoping the bar had something stronger than German beer. The old Van Halen song popped into his head. "Might as well *drink*," he sang out loud as he shuffled along, repeating the chorus. People dashing by gave him the "guy's a moron" look.

He lost track of the couple he was following to the bar, found himself in a line of travelers headed for the ticket booths. That's when the idea struck him, like a wrecking ball through a brick wall. He spotted American Airlines and headed straight for the wickets.

"Any flights to Las Vegas?" he asked a young clerk at the counter.

"Yes. We have one scheduled for 6:00 tomorrow evening, sir."

"What have you got for anywhere on the West Coast, that leaves soon, like real soon?"

"Let's see … there is a flight leaving in two hours for Los Angeles, sir. There are a few seats available."

"Book it, one seat, one-way," said Jimi.

"Window or isle, sir?"

"Window seat, easier to snooze with something to lean against."

Jimi had just enough euros left to pay for the ticket. Going home was the right thing to do, he thought as he headed for the Departure gates. He had feelings for Delia, feelings that terrified him. His heart felt like it was wrapped in cellophane, struggling to beat its way free. He was afraid of what might happen next.

The lyrics from David Bowie's *Scary Monsters (and Super Creeps)* suddenly played loud in his head. The words triggered haunting memories from his childhood: His monstrous father standing over him with his leather belt raised high, lashing his backside until his skin ran red.

Then he started worrying about what would happen to Delia when Mother was done with her. It was too much. Not even a bottle could help him. He had to get away. More than this, Jimi was beginning to feel homesick. He missed his friends, especially Hugo. He even missed being bossed around by the domineering Cross-eyed Mary. He missed his bed. He missed his music.

From L.A., he would get back home to Vegas. Tell everyone at the casino that he left due to a family emergency, had to visit his dying mother in New York. Fact is, he didn't even know if his mother was still alive.

Everything would work out, he just needed to get away from the psycho killer and the alien. Maybe the law would never catch up to him. Did the United States have an extradition agreement with Portugal, he wondered? Even if they did, the authorities would have to find him first. If he had to, he could lose himself in Mexico or maybe Canada. One of his old friends from Little Havana was now living in Toronto. Jimi knew he would help out.

As he approached his gate, he started to feel better about his decision to return home. While he waited for the boarding call, a strong hand tightened around his arm, spinning him on his heels.

"Where do you think you are going, my friend?"

It was a scary voice, one Jimi hoped never to hear again. Crisco, the coca-leaf-chewing assassin. He turned towards Sanchez, glaring at him with all the anger his eyes could show.

"I am going home. If you try to stop me, I will holler for airport security—tell them who you are."

"Jimi, please, let's talk about this," said Delia as she approached. Sanchez held tight. Jimi could feel the hammer-strength grip pressing into his bones.

"You have to let me go. I am of no use to you. And, I would put you in danger because I don't want anything to do with you, him, or whatever crazy scheme you are up to."

"Sanchez, let go of him, leave him be."

Sanchez let go of Jimi's arm reluctantly and stepped a few feet back. Jimi felt the blood flowing in his arm again.

"You are right, we don't need you to help us the rest of the way," said Delia. "But, I, me—Delia, I want you to stay, Jimi. Won't you stay, for me?"

"But I'm scared, Delia, afraid for my life, afraid that when the authorities catch up to us, I am either going to be killed or spend the rest of my days rotting in a cell somewhere. I can think of a hundred other reasons why I should go."

"You are right, Jimi, you have a hundred reasons to go, and I can only think of one for you to stay."

"Look, my heart is not in this, I just want to go home. You *must* let me go."

"But *my* heart *is* in this, Jimi. I need you. Don't go. You belong here," said Delia, placing a hand over her heart and gently patting it.

Delia stepped into Jimi and wrapped her arms around him, pulling him into her, tighter and tighter. Jimi dropped his bag to the floor and hugged her back. She felt so warm.

She kissed him gently on the cheek. Her lips felt like silk against the whiskers of his unshaven skin. He felt her breath blowing softly over the back of his neck, making his spine tingle.

Jimi's senses overwhelmed him. Should he stay? Was she worth the risk?

Jimi released Delia just enough so that he could look at her eyes. The answer came to him instantly.

CHAPTER 24
Rocky rumble

North from the White House is Meridian Hill Park, so-named because it was built on the exact longitude of the original District of Columbia milestone marker, planted in 1791.

A popular spot for couples who visit the park is the sprawling, 13-tiered cascading fountain that spills into a large reflecting pool. But there were no lovers in sight on this cool, wet evening.

Two men draped in trench coats to ward off the chilling rain approached each other from opposite sides of the reflecting pool.

"Jellybean, good to see you after all these years," said General Isadore Pope, reaching out to shake Deon Carter's outstretched hand.

"Been a while, General Pope. You know, in my office I have a picture of the two of us during my college football days."

"Those were some good times, weren't they? You were a powerhouse linebacker, Jellybean, you could've made pro. I had you all set up for the draft—the scouts loved you.

"All we had to do was train you to be quicker on your feet. It was as doable as ordering a double-bacon cheeseburger which, sadly, you were far too fond of doing."

Carter didn't much appreciate the General's comments, but he remained pokerfaced. He remembered his college years well enough. Coach Pope riding his tail during practices, making snide remarks about his "cheeseburger-built belly" slowing him down.

It was coach Pope that also poked fun at Carter's habit of chewing handfuls of jellybeans on the bench during games.

When his teammates took up the cry and started calling him "Jellybean," Carter loathed the nick name. Especially after the coach stopped calling him by his first name and loved hollering out, "Jellybean, time to roll," when he wanted him on the field.

It wasn't until his colleagues in the Secret Service started using that nickname as a measure of respect that Carter got beyond the derogatory slant to it. Until the coach said it again just now …

"I like my knees and back just the way they are, sir. The pounding those guys take in the pros, not worth the millions if you're a cripple later in life."

"Don't talk wussy to me, Jellybean. Football is the arena of warriors. You had the force of a true gladiator at your fingertips, but you wilted on me like a thirsty petunia. Fact is, son, you were my biggest disappointment as a coach. The scouts I brought to the games to see you …"

"Well, sir, my apologies for not enabling you to get your share of that fat signing bonus."

General Pope put his hand up, like he was ready to smack Carter in the face. Carter stepped back, shaking his head and looking down on the half-foot-shorter Pope with "Go ahead, try me" in his eyes.

Much as he would love to flatten the general for old times' sake, he understood it was a different man standing before him. The king of the military, America's highest-ranking soldier.

If he was so inclined, the general could have him taken out. All he had to do was signal the two soldiers standing guard at the top of the hill above the reflecting pool. They may have thought they were one with the tree trunks they hid behind, but Carter had a good look around when he arrived.

A soldier of Pope's rank never went anywhere without muscle.

Carter was on edge about seeing Pope. Why this secret meeting in a deserted park on a rainy evening? And why was he ordered to come alone and make sure no one was following him? Carter's radar was giving off warning bleeps. He wouldn't let the general control the scenario.

"Sir, if it wasn't for those two sentinels you posted at the top of the hill, I'd let you *try* to hurt me … such as it is, let's just get to the reason why you called me here. You said this was a matter most urgent?"

"Where is your cellphone?"

"In my coat pocket, sir. Don't worry, I turned it off."

"It can still be accessed, let me see it."

Carter handed his phone to the general, who placed a small piece of clear tape over its microphone.

"There, now even if someone tries to listen in on us, the voices will be too muffled. I have already taped mine."

That only served to make Carter even more anxious, but deadpan he stayed. Who would want to listen in on their conversation? Then he remembered his chat with Bonnie Best during his drive to Meridian Hill Park. She had updated him on Samantha Isenberg.

Her chief engineer had deserted the project and was now talking to Pope's people about why he left. Bonnie had listened in on the conversation. Apparently, the engineer was adamant that Isenberg and her associates had lost their minds. He went on about aliens and a big flood coming, a really bizarre story. Carter was not sure what to make of it.

Bonnie also asked him some odd questions about his personal life. He thought this was totally uncalled for, and answered her questions with measured indifference.

"That's a great little trick, I'll have to remember it," said Carter, placing the phone back in his pocket.

"So. Why did you ask to see me, sir?"

"You were in Portugal, hunting down the redhead, she eluded you?"

"It's not that simple, sir, and you *do* know her name is Delia Cassavetes?"

"Of course, but before we ID'd her we referred to her as the 'redhead' and the name stuck."

The general wanted to know about Carter's connection to the redhead and Isenberg, but refused to answer Carter's query about how the military knew he was involved.

"Most importantly, Carter, you need to tell me why the redhead broke into my office—what was she after? Who sent her?"

"I know nothing about that, general. If I did, why would I tell you?"

Pope spat on the ground, just missing Carter's feet.

"Unfortunate *accidents* just seem to happen to people who are less than cooperative," said Pope, furrowing his brow as his dark eyes aimed up at Carter. "You copy?"

Carter didn't need a translation. Pope would as soon spit on him as have him done away with. While in the Secret Service, Carter was privy to information that documented suspicious accidents or strange disappearances in the political realm. Some of these cases were linked to Pope. None of those particular incidents was ever investigated.

Carter was intrigued by assassins and their methods. He kept a file on them, even after leaving the Service. He named the file: "50 Ways to Kill Your Brother," courtesy of his fixation with an old Paul Simon song.

In the wired world, extortion was a popular way to neuter a target. No messy crime scenes, no bodies to make disappear, no hitman to pay off. Secrets could no longer be buried. And everyone had skeletons they wanted to keep in their closets. Exploiting them, was easier than ever.

But the new-age assassin continues to learn new tricks. Killing with impunity took a new turn with the advent of self-driving vehicles. A savvy slayer could gain control of the vehicle and orchestrate a deadly crash. The hacker then 'fries' the vehicle's control module, erasing any trace of the hack.

It was as clean a hit as a kill could be.

When Carter first heard of this, he vowed never to buy a self-driving car, or any vehicle that was 'smarter' than it needed to be. What most concerned him, however, was the potential for terrorists to gain control of a self-driving smart truck filled with fuel, or a self-driving bus filled with passengers …

"I have heard nothing about a break-in at your office but, let me tell you what I do know," said Carter, figuring it was best to play it the general's way.

Carter told him about the woman who gave him "a big pile of cash" to find the redhead then turn her over to Isenberg's people, and how events unfolded, up to his return to the U.S.

The only part he left out was knocking Delia over the railing at the hotel in Lisbon.

"What the hell does Isenberg want with her?" said Pope, his eyes as demanding as the question.

"Maybe it's because she's one of *your* space-age super soldiers, sir? I have seen that video of her parachuting down the side of the hotel using a towel, then landing softly on her feet, so don't toy with me. She's not a regular human—you've amped her up, she's bionic, isn't she?"

The general thought for a minute, his eyes twitching.

"Nonsense! We *may* have what you call 'super soldiers,' but she is *not* one of them. My people analyzed that footage of her dropping to the ground. So far, they are stumped as to how she pulled off such a death-defying feat."

"Look, general, can we jump right to why I am here," said Carter, checking the time on his watch. "I am meeting some old friends from the Service for drinks—been a long time since I was in town—and I don't want to be late."

"Do I look like I give a crap if you're late?"

"No sir."

"Good. Now that we have dispensed with the insults, which I can understand, perhaps I was a *little* unfair with my comments about your abilities on the field …"

"Perhaps …"

The friendlier tone to the general's manner had Carter's internal lie detector doing cartwheels.

"Tell me, Carter, what do you think of our President, Douglas Triton?"

"Do you want bullshit, or an honest answer, sir?"

"I think President Triton is a complete moron. Does that answer your question?"

Carter was not surprised by Pope's reply. On the streets of America, it was a widely held opinion of the Commander in Chief. But why was the President's top military man saying that to him?

"Well sir, he *has* led our country down the road to economic Armageddon. China is fast becoming the economic powerhouse we once were, Christ they own half our country.

"Not to mention that Triton looks like a clown with all that girly makeup he wears. So yeah, I would not quibble with the term 'moron.' But we're stuck with the chump, at least until the next election. And who knows, he may just win again—he fooled us all last time."

"What if I told you there may be a way to 'neutralize' Triton … for good?"

"Say what, sir?"

"Oh, come on Carter. You're *far* sharper than that. I am in need of a man like you. I'm offering you a job, a well-paying job. I have an assignment perfectly tailored to your skills, right here in the Capital of the Free World."

"Sir, I have to respectfully decline. My home is in L.A. now, I will never work in Washington again."

"Did you not hear from Linda Kozlowski on your way here?"

"Linda *who*? I don't know that name, sir."

"I guess she never told you her real name. You know her as Bonnie Best. She works for me."

Carter always wondered who the higher power Bonnie answered to was … now he knew. "Shit," he said in his head.

"That means you failed the test, son."

"What test?" said Carter, cursing himself for having strapped his Smith & Wesson so low on his inside left leg.

"I asked her to test you, see if you could be trusted. If you passed, she was going to tell you her real name. I don't know how you failed, but I am certain she will fill me in later."

"Now I remember, yes, Linda Kozlowski … she did tell me that, it just slipped my mind."

Before Carter finished talking, the general waved his left hand in the air as his right hand pulled a Beretta from his coat pocket. The two guards started galloping like horses gone wild down the hill towards them.

Carter knew military guards have a habit of shooting first, funeral later. He recognized the bigger man, Johnny Merriweather, a former armed forces boxing champion.

He had one move before it was too late.

Carter took a quick step to his left and snatched the general's gun from his hand. Then he pivoted on one foot to get behind him and executed a one-armed bear hug. He put the barrel to the general's head, challenging the on-coming guards with, "Stop right there, or the general gets it!"

"Jellybean, they are not going to harm you, put that gun away."

The general saying it like he was a lion facing down a field mouse. The guards positioned themselves on each side of Carter, then started circling around him.

One of the guards drew his gun from its holster and urged Carter to back down.

"I am a deadeye shot, fat man," said the guard. "Release General Pope immediately, or even your momma won't recognize your face."

Now you've done it, Carter was thinking. A standoff with the king of the military. Where did the other guard go?

He felt cold steel against the back of his neck. The other guard had snuck up behind him like a silent stalker. Carter let go of the general and dropped his gun.

"Show him who's boss, but don't put him in the hospital—I don't want to speak to the cops or have this written up in any reports," Pope said to the guards.

"Just give him a taste of 'These boots are made for walking,' military style."

Before the general finished talking, the guard behind Carter swung a heavy leg into the back of his right knee, collapsing his colossal frame to the ground with a heavy thud.

Carter knew he was in for a beating, but not without getting in a few licks himself. This wasn't his first rumble in a park.

The general saw Carter's phone had fallen from his pocket. He crushed it with a heavy stomp, threw it into the reflecting pool, then removed the tape from his own phone. As he walked away, the echoes of boots striking ribs sounded like Rocky Balboa sparring with sides of beef hanging in a meat cooler.

As the general exited the park, he noticed a message on his phone and one missed call. His cellphone rang as he was about to retrieve the message. He stopped moving to answer the call.

"General, it's Olivia Triton, are you secure?"

"Was that you that left me a message?"

"My message said it was my father who wanted to talk to you, but that was a ploy to get your immediate attention."

"What makes you think I wouldn't respond to a call from the President's daughter?"

"Forgive me … I am feeling a little out of sorts, general. We need to meet. I need some clarification on matters of a personal nature."

"Personal? I fail to see how I can help. Can you be more specific, Olivia?"

"No, not on the phone. Are you familiar with the Oxon Run Park, on Livingston Road?"

"Why yes, in the Highlands."

"Meet me there, 8:30 tonight."

"Lot of trouble in that area. Not even the cops want to go there after dark," said Pope.

"Precisely. Don't be late."

As General Pope continued on his way to the vehicle waiting for him, there was a loud splash, like a body falling into water.

"Jesus … sounds like my boys are having some fun with Carter."

CHAPTER 25
Old habits die hard

The young girl opened her eyes and looked to her left. Her mother was still sleeping. She unbuckled her seatbelt and adjusted her pillow, then lay her head back down, just below the window. She looked out at the twinkling lights on the airplane's wing. She pulled her cellphone from her pocket and took a picture. The pillow slipped from its perch as she jumped in her seat.

"Mommy, mommy, wake up. There's something out there."

When her mother didn't respond, the young girl placed her phone against the window and took another shot.

"What are you doing, sweetie?" said a passing steward.

"There is a spaceship flying beside our airplane. Look, do you see it?"

"What's going on?" said the girl's waking mother.

"There's a spaceship outside our window, mommy. Do you see it?"

"Your daughter has a vivid imagination," the steward smiled.

"There's nothing out there, honey. You were just dreaming."

"But I took pictures, mommy. See …."

The mother took the cell phone from her daughter and had a look.

"I just see the airplane wing."

"Look closer, mommy. Past the wing tip … do you see it?"

"Let me have a look," said the steward.

"I do see an unusual cloud, shaped like a long cigar. Is that what you thought was a spaceship, little lady?"

"Oh, it's a cloud. OK, sorry."

***

Inside the 'cloud' the young girl spotted were Salvatore Two and Salvatore Six. Through the translucent hull of their ship, they could see the airplane trailing behind them now.

"It's fortunate we slowed to one quarter impulse when we entered the atmosphere," said Salvatore Two. "Gave us a chance to scan the vessel we passed."

"It's full of *homo sapiens*, packed together like a school of fish," said Salvatore Six. "Strange way to travel."

"Everything about this race is odd. That's why we are here."

"At this rate of velocity, we will arrive early for our meeting with Xeno," said Salvatore Six.

"Gives us an opportunity to do a little sight-seeing before we land. Since it's our first time visiting this planet, we should determine for ourselves what it is that Mother finds so fascinating about Urantia," said Salvatore Two.

"Agreed. In her reports, Mother described Urantia in glowing terms, everything from a 'magnificent little blue planet,' to 'one of the great beauties in the cosmos.' It *is* a lovely, colorful little world, but after witnessing the singular splendor of Saturn on our way here, with its striking 82 moons and its glorious rings, I dare say what the humans call Earth pales considerably in comparison."

"Indeed," said Salvatore Six. "I see nothing particularly unique or remarkable here. Which makes me wonder what else Mother has been embellishing in her reports."

"The bias Mother displays for Earth is clear," said Salvatore Two. "Xeno can tell us more when we rendezvous with him."

"When we meet, we must remember his motives," warned Salvatore Six. "Xeno despises the humans. He has proven to be deceitful."

"Agreed," said Salvatore Two. "Any Deus who betrays another cannot be trusted. We will board his ship. I have an idea."

Salvatore Six eyed a glowing instrument panel.

"We are being followed. Two vessels, shaped like little black birds, armed with weapons that may harm our ship."

"If these vessels are any indication, it appears humans have significantly advanced their technology in the last 20 years," said Salvatore Two.

"Yes, far more rapidly than other species Mother has introduced on other worlds. The rate of their technological progress begs some questions. I believe Mother has facilitated their advancement. A notion widely shared by the other Salvatores.

"All the more reason to make sure our extinction strategy is realized."

Salvatore Two began to glow a brighter blue; a sign he was anxious.

"I say once more, I am not comfortable with this plan. Destroying a civilization is contrary to our Prime Directives," he said.

"The Salvatores are the only Deus who will ever know the *real* reason for their demise. The others will accept that the humans annihilated themselves again, just like they did on Mars. The precedent has already been set."

"I will not go against the rest of the Salvatores over this decision, but I tell you, this will haunt me," said Salvatore Two.

"All things must pass. The Salvatores will prevail. Ease your conscience. Consider again the dire circumstances our unwavering analysis and countless simulations have predicted," said Salvatore Six.

"If the humans are allowed to continue advancing their technology at such an alarming rate, they will branch out from their solar system in 100 years. Much sooner, if they discover the power of dark energy. Within 200 years, they will be conquering constellations, and challenging the Deus as the ultimate authority in the Cosmos.

"As the Salvatores, it is our duty to safeguard the Universe and the Deus supremacy."

"I understand our obligations," said Salvatore Two. "My issue is not with our responsibilities. I have reviewed the simulations and read the reports. What I still have difficulty with is the overriding assumption that humans will *never* evolve from their primeval austerity as time passes—how can it be that a race does not progress ethically and morally, in step with their advancing scientific aptitude?"

"It is not an 'overriding assumption,'" Salvatore Six countered.

"It's justifiably based on the imperfection in Mother's DNA sequencing, an error she made at the very beginning of the process. There is no way to repair it."

Salvatore Six was eager to continue the dialogue but was distracted by an alert from the ship's AI.

"The human ships are picking up speed. Shall we find out how fast their vessels can travel these days?"

"Yes, let's advance at intervals of point zero three in quarter time. See how long the human vessels can keep up."

***

"Beta 3 to base. The unidentified aerial phenomena is picking up speed. I won't be able to keep pace much longer. Already pushing Mach 7. Over."

"Roger that. I have patched in General Graff on his direct line. Over to you, general."

"Beta 3, how long before the UAP is out of missile range?"

"Within 30 seconds, sir. At top speed, my targeting instruments are about three percent less accurate. Over."

"Then shoot it down—now. Those are your orders."

"Roger that, general."

Within seconds, the jet fired an AGM Maverick at the UAP.

"General, sir, the missile literally bounced off the ship without detonating."

"Fire your whole damn payload—now!"

The pilot followed the general's order.

"General, sir, the missiles seemed to bump the UAP slightly off course, but no detonation. Over."

"Follow it for as long as you can."

"Sir, my instruments are no longer reading the UAP. It disappeared in the blink of an eye."

***

It was nearing midnight when Viktor Kozlov arrived at the predetermined meeting site near the base of Glastenbury Mountain, deep in the green woods of southwestern Vermont. He had journeyed for hours by dirt bike on the Long Trail, a popular hiking route in the Green Mountains.

The sky was cloudy with no Moon in sight, making it pitch black in the woods, but the Deus do not see darkness, even when they are within a human host.

Kozlov turned his motorcycle off and approached the ship, which had become the color of its surrounding, blending in with the woods like it was just another thicket of trees.

Two glowing blue orbs emerged from the ship, passing through its hull like sunlight through a window, and moved toward Kozlov like soap bubbles carried by a gentle wind.

It was Salvatore Two and Salvatore Six, but to Kozlov or any other Deus, they were known as Consul Prime and Consul Duo, respectfully, two of the highest-ranking members of the Imperitus Council.

"Welcome to Earth, Consuls," said Kozlov as he removed his biker helmet.

The Deus stopped moving and hovered about three feet off the rocky ground.

"Xeno?" said Salvatore Two. "You look so small as a human. It must feel so incredibly confining to be stuck inside a rigid carbon shell."

"You get used to it, Consul. Movement is slow and extremely limited, and this body feels horrible pain when I forget my place, but it won't be for much longer."

"You are the first human we have ever seen in person. You don't appear scary …"

Salvatore Six interrupted, saying: "What's *frightening* about the humans is the savagery of their minds, Consul. Physically, they are a puny species, and fragile as the spirit flowers on the garden world of Antheia."

"I agree with your assessment, Consul," said Xeno. "Their diminutive stature belies what their violent minds are capable of."

"Open your mouth, Xeno. I want to see your teeth," said Salvatore Two.

"My teeth?"

Despite the odd request, Xeno complied.

"Tell me, how is it the humans eat each other's flesh and bone with such small teeth?"

"Ah, I understand your reference, Consul. Humans being cannibals is based on a very old report from the Angelus, when they surveyed a primitive area of Earth called the Amazon jungle.

"Modern-day humans are *not* cannibals, although there are numerous accounts of humans resorting to eating other humans when trapped in extreme circumstances with no food or water. But that is their primordial survival instinct kicking in."

"On the contrary," said Salvatore Six. "The information we reference is very recent. It's based on a religious group that numbers in the hundreds of millions called Catholics. They partake in a ritual called 'Holy Communion,' where they eagerly consume the 'body and blood' of one of their fallen heroes named Jesus Christ."

"Although symbolic in nature, that is indeed cannibalism by definition, Consuls," Xeno observed. "However, millions of humans only consume plant life. The others satiate their desire for flesh by eating other species on this planet. Certain animals are raised, then butchered, specifically for human consumption."

"I'll bet this animal flesh tastes similar to human flesh," said Salvatore Six. "Old habits are hard to break for this race of barbarians."

"Enough of this talk," said Salvatore Two. "It's making me ill."

"Agreed," said Salvatore Six. "What do they call you here on Earth, Xeno?"

"I am Viktor Kozlov, an ambassador from a country called Russia. I am currently working in a city called Washington, the center of political power for the country called the United States of America."

"Viktor Kozlov. That's an odd name, we will call you by your Deus name," Salvatore Six insisted.

"As you wish, Consuls."

"What is that contraption behind you, some sort of weapon?" said Salvatore Two.

"No, Consul, it's a vehicle for travelling in rough terrain called a BMW 1200 GS Adventure, more commonly known by the humans as the 'Cadillac of dirt bikes.'

"Consuls, how was your journey?"

"Swift and smooth, until we had a bumpy encounter with an Earth air ship while passing through the atmosphere," said Salvatore Two.

"It fired weapons that looked like spears at us, bumped our vessel off course for a second," said Salvatore Six.

"We had no idea human technology had advanced to that point. I was beaming blue all over our vessel."

"I can understand that would make you nervous, Consul. Mother and I were attacked in the same manner when we arrived on Earth."

"Consul Prime worries for not, Xeno. There are no Earth weapons that can penetrate our hull—are there?"

"No, not yet, but Earth scientists are even *more* ingenious than we previously understood, I have learned. Ever since the giant corporations that make war weapons started offering huge bonuses—in the form of 'money,' what the humans use to accumulate gigantic dwellings, servants and lucrative leisure items—the advances in weaponry have accelerated like comets in the Oblivion system. Each more deadly and sophisticated than the last."

"It would seem the predictions made by our simulations of future human endeavor were correct," said Salvatore Six. "Greed has become the driver of all human enterprise."

"I do not wish to deter from the accuracy of your academic simulations, Consuls," said Xeno. "However, in my estimation, given that I have spent much time living among humans, the desire for *power* over others is also a significant part of their motivation equation."

"The two behaviors walk hand-in-hand, nurturing immoral deeds and fostering malevolence," said Salvatore Six.

"The Universe will be a better place when the humans become the departed."

"No quibbling with that prognosis," said Xeno.

"We also had some time to review the most current reports about human customs on our way to Earth," said Salvatore Six.

"We are appalled at the violent nature of their civilizations and their irrational ceremonies, in particular, a celebration called Remembrance Day that we just read about. Very disturbing ritual, makes no sense whatsoever. Can you enlighten us?"

"Of all the strange human customs you could ask about, why has this one so intrigued you, Consul?"

"It seems an oxymoron to us, Xeno, to celebrate death and destruction with such honorary aplomb."

"Agreed, Consul. Remembrance Day, yes, I have experienced that phenomenon many times here on Earth," said Xeno.

"There is a moment of silence called around the planet that the humans say is to honor the millions of souls that were purged during mortal combat, in the 'noble' pursuit of peace and freedom. The grave ceremonies are immersed in such splendor and pomposity that, in reality, I believe this is how humans celebrate war and glorify murder, by stoking the notion of individual sacrifice for the greater good."

"Preposterous," Salvatore Two declared. "The failure of discourse among competing sides should *always* be viewed as an appalling disaster, a time of great shame, especially if lives are lost as a consequence. There can be no fathomable moral virtue that comes from the murder of a sentient being."

"These humans, they have a different view," said Xeno. "They claim that to take a life or risk their own lives for a cause they believe in, *is* morally justifiable."

"Xeno, I find that a bewildering contradiction," said Salvatore Six. "Our records show that the humans are *always* at war with each other somewhere on this planet, there has *never* been a time of lasting peace on Earth that we can identify."

"From what I have been able to determine, Consul, having spent some time engaged with government officials of various countries, peace—and their goal of achieving it—is a myth, a dream they dangle before the ill-informed masses to give them hope, while sanctioning their military as being of noble purpose."

"You mean to say they promote the pursuit of peace to motivate humans to slay their own kind?" said Salvatore Two.

"Is there anything more fraudulent and reprehensible in all the Universe? If the other members of the Deus Federation were aware of these vile tactics, there would be an unequivocal demand to revamp our Prime Directives, so as to authorize the elimination of species like the humans."

"What you say cannot be true, Xeno," said Salvatore Six. "Surely your logic is flawed—how can war beget peace? The two principles are diametrically opposed. Clearly the humans know this, having been engaged in violent, murderous skirmishes since the beginning of their time."

"I would not assign such a heavy burden of guilt upon the common human, Consuls, they are the victims, the ones who suffer the consequences of war. It is their leaders who seek to venerate conflict and chaos as a means to an end. They believe it is their solemn duty. If there were no wars, there would be no need for soldiers.

"That is why cunning military leaders will never permit lasting peace, their power and privilege would cease to exist. Strategies for propagating war are treated like a science by the human military. There is always an 'enemy' to confront. When there isn't, they create one, and the cycle is perpetuated."

"That's appalling, Xeno. Don't humans understand the cost of war is outrageous?" said Salvatore Six.

"On the contrary, Consul, war is the most profitable enterprise on Earth for corporations that supply the military with weapons. Everything from building their big battleships, rifles and bombs to crafting the combat boots and helmets their soldier's wear. The making of war supplies and killing machines is the biggest manufacturing unit on this planet. Nothing else comes close.

"If there were no wars, there would be no need for weapons. The makers of killing machines and instruments of death fear peace, because so much of this planet's economy is dependent on the manufacture of weapons and its associated industries. Selling those armaments and supplies has become their most profitable enterprise."

"You are describing Economies of Death, Xeno," said Salvatore Two. "Making profit from the killing and maiming of their own kind ... I am feeling ill at the very thought of that."

"Your condemnation is warranted, Consul, but it is worse than that," Xeno continued.

"It's the humans struggling to get by who pay for the cost of war through a system called taxes they are obliged to pay to their rulers, not to mention the loss of their loved ones killed in the bloodbaths. Then they pay more taxes to help rebuild destroyed cities and feed the displaced humans, while the makers of the weapons employed to wreak the destruction walk away wealthier than ever after each battle. This has been happening for thousands of years.

"So you see, Consuls, this is why the cycle of war has become self-perpetuating for humans. Their leaders continue to expend vast resources for war. In comparison, little to no effort is made to pursue peace.

"For these, and many other reasons, I firmly believe the species will never evolve beyond the primitive. Never," Kozlov concluded.

"What about all of these 'peace movements' I read about in some reports, led by enlightened humans like Gandhi, the Dalai Lama, Jesus Christ, Martin Luther King Jr., John Lennon, a massive group of young people called hippies, and many others I could name. Why were they unsuccessful?" Salvatore Two wanted to know.

"For many of the same reasons I mentioned earlier, Consul. You need to maintain context with what we already know to be symptomatic of this species. Humans truly seeking peace are openly mocked, discredited or killed by the powers that seek to uphold the status quo. The 'love is all you need' hippies, for example, were branded as lazy, long-haired, drug-crazed sex maniacs and low-life criminals."

"But surely the human populace understands how they are being manipulated?" said Salvatore Six.

"Indeed, some do, and there have been notable literary works that address this very condition. Again, these academics are mocked and discredited, the authorities label them as communists, anarchists and radicals, a threat to stability.

"Sadly, the vast majority of humans do not take these progressive thinkers seriously enough to stimulate change in their societies. Governments everywhere go to great lengths to keep potentially dissenting minds distracted."

"How do they manage such 'distractions?'" asked Salvatore Six.

"In very clever ways, Consul. It used to be that religion was the opiate of the masses, as a famous human scholar once declared. Today, with religious institutions falling out of favor with many humans, authorities make sure the masses are kept busy watching sports, developing addictions to video games and social media, while playing lotteries that offer deceptive dreams of a better life, to name just a few tactics.

"The most tangible tragedy of humanity is this, Consuls: The planet is bountiful, but its riches are horded by the few. The vast majority reap so little. The ones who suffer most are the ones so preoccupied with acquiring the basic necessities for life, they are too fatigued to find a way out of the madness."

The three Deus stopped sharing thoughts, at the same time. It was a silence of the minds. Xeno understood why. The visit by the Consuls was initiated by uncertainty. They sought confirmation their decision to deceive the humans, resulting in their annihilation, was based on irrevocable evidence. He knew they questioned his judgement. He also knew they were mindful of his own objective: Bringing Mother back to him.

The eerie silence was finally broken when Salvatore 6 said to Xeno, "What if we met with Earth's leaders and ordered them to make peace with one another? Surely, they would listen to superior beings like us."

"Consul, they attacked you the minute you arrived on Earth. They would find a way to kill you, of that I am certain."

The two Salvatores shared their thoughts for a few minutes. Xeno was excluded from their conversation.

"We accept the reality of what must be done, Xeno," said Salvatore Two.

"I acknowledge your divine wisdom, as always, Consuls."

"Earlier you mentioned you were also attacked entering Earth's atmosphere," said Salvatore Six.

"Yes, and like you, we had no prior knowledge that human weapons had advanced so much since our last visit. Their flying battleships ambushed us shortly after we slowed down upon entering the atmosphere. We did not know they could detect our arrival—they never had in the past. We let them follow us for a few minutes, not realizing we were in danger.

"Suddenly, the ships fired missiles at us, bombarding the same spot on our vessel in a rapid-fire pattern before we eluded them. When we landed, sensors warned that, with all the heavy banging against the hull as the missiles struck, the vibrations damaged the gyroscope on the main drive, which is positioned under the same section of the hull that was repeatedly struck.

"Mother has retrieved an anti-gravity device that was taken from her during a previous Earth visit. It will provide just enough lift for our ship to break Earth's orbit. We will return to Caelum, using the Hyper Vortex corridor just beyond Uranus."

"Are you quite certain that your departure will occur on time, as intended?" said Salvatore Six.

"There will be no delays, Consul. Mother is on her way here right now."

"She knows nothing of our plan?" asked Salvatore Two.

"No, she does not."

"Are you aware, Xeno, that Mother may be capable of masking her true thoughts from any probe we Deus can administer?" said Salvatore Six.

"I understand that only a handful of Deus have those abilities. I have no reason to believe she is one of them."

The Salvatores exchanged thoughts between themselves again.

"Before we depart, we will pass through your vessel, Xeno," said Salvatore Six.

"Might I ask why this is necessary? I have described the damage to you, and our remedy."

"We need to confirm a few particulars, for the report we must submit to the Imperitus Council upon our return to Caelum. They are sticklers for details."

"As you wish, Consuls."

"Splendid. Just one more item of discussion before we take our leave," said Salvatore Two. "How is it that you were able to get the American humans to go along with developing, then using, the wave bomb so effortlessly?"

"The answer is simple, Consul, and again relies heavily on what we have already discussed as basic human failings."

"We want to hear the story, Xeno," Salvatore Six insisted.

"Of course. First, you have to grasp the economic reality in the country called America at this present time. The American humans elected a leader who promised to bring economic prosperity, at a time when the country was losing its standing as an economic powerhouse, while their so-called enemies were experiencing huge economic growth.

"Have I lost you?" said Kozlov, sensing confusion from the others.

"On the contrary, Xeno. Courtesy of the comprehensive Angelus reports, we have a basic grasp of human economic theory, free-market enterprise *and* the machinations of politics," said Salvatore Six. "We may not comprehend fully what you express, but we *will* understand the gist of your narrative. Please continue."

"It turns out that their President was more of a fraud than an economic redeemer. He implemented flawed policy measures that plunged the American economy into freefall. When I approached the top American military leader with an idea for a secret new weapon that would result in a massive economic recovery, he took it to the President. Their interest was ravenous."

"What made them so eager to learn more about this new weapon, how did you say it could be used?" asked Salvatore Six.

"I told them they could create tidal waves that would target specific coastlines of their economic rivals and that the cause of these waves would appear to be of natural origin—no one could pin the deed on them."

Kozlov explained the rest of story, how the scientists involved in the secret project were skeptical, how they worried about the testing.

"But it was the President that endorsed the wave bomb wholeheartedly. He plans to send tidal waves to cripple their biggest competitor, a country called China. Manufacturing—the creation of trinkets that end up in huge caverns in the ground because they need to constantly be replaced to maintain the cycle of production—would be rejuvenated in his country. As such, he would win another term as President."

"If I understand you, correctly, Xeno," said Salvatore Two, "humans create products they bury in the ground when they are done with them, then they have to buy replacements ... this is what they call a 'good' economy?"

"Why don't they just make products that last for much longer?" asked Salvatore Six.

"The humans are always inventing new products, that is why they make goods with a short lifespan, designed to break down or erode in quick order. Then the products must be replaced with so-called more advanced models."

"And this makes their lives better, constantly updating and replacing their products?" said Salvatore Six.

"On the contrary, Consul. From what I have observed, mental illness and other afflictions associated with technology addiction and the desire for bigger and better everything, have led to a massive increase in social malfunction disorders.

"Humans are so stressed they seek relief in all manner of ways, including the abuse of drugs, especially the most popular drug by far, alcohol. One expert on human psychology that I spoke with defined modern humans as a society riddled with 'nervous ninnies,' due to their many compulsions, especially those addicted to their hand-held communication machines."

"Why do their leaders allow this to happen to their race?" said Salvatore Six.

"Their leaders are also victims. Humans are so preoccupied, they don't realize they are at the mercy of corporations that manipulate their lives with subversive intent. The corporations call it 'marketing.' We know it better as 'behavior control.'"

"This is all very disturbing, Xeno," said Salvatore Six. "We have heard enough of this sickly species. They do not belong in our Universe."

Salvatore Two agreed, adding that this trip to Earth brought with it a great sadness, one that he may never fully overcome.

"Consuls, before you return home, I need confirmation that, as a result of my work here on Earth at your behest, you will uphold our agreement. Mother will never learn of my betrayal, and you will not reprimand her for breaching the Prime Directives."

"We are the most honorable of Deus, Xeno," said Salvatore Six. "We also need you to keep your end of our bargain. We must remain the only three Deus to ever know we had a role in the decimation of this species.

"Mother will be allowed to continue her work of establishing civilizations on other planets. But, when you both return to Caelum, she must agree *never* to come back to this dreadful planet."

"That will be a difficult request. Mother adores the humans, believes in their goodness, says they are capable of such beauty, the likes of which the Universe has never seen."

"Utter nonsense," countered Salvatore Six. "What humans are most adept at is creating chaos and fomenting violence, like the Universe has never seen."

CHAPTER 26

Avarice and arrogance

Olivia Triton was puffing on a cigarette, something she hadn't done since finishing school. She blew the smoke out the window of her Bugatti Chiron, but she knew the smell would linger for weeks. The Bugatti was a gift from daddy for her 35th birthday. She made a mental note to pick up some air purifier on the way home.

She lit another smoke before the first one was spent and heaved the still-burning butt out the window, smacking her 10-carat diamond ring against the black glass. The ring was also a gift from daddy, to replace the one she flushed down the toilet after her last divorce.

She pulled down the vanity mirror and checked her makeup and hair for a third time since arriving. Then she adjusted the way her long, strawberry blond hair fell upon her thin shoulders.

With her free hand, she cupped one breast at a time, adjusting its upward angle inside her bra until just the right amount of cleavage surfaced above the lacy cut of her blouse.

As she sucked another long drag, she watched in the mirror as her plump lips formed a circle to let the smoke escape her lungs. She checked the time again and shook her head, her face looking like it was holding back a scream, her lips mouthing the two words her mother taught her *never* to say out loud, unless she was in the throes of passionate love-making.

A hard tap on the car window startled her, knocking cigarette ash onto her lap. She turned to see who it was, as her hand quickly brushed the ash off, in case an ember was hot enough to leave mark.

"Sorry I am so late, Olivia. Had a prior meeting, took longer than I anticipated."

"General Pope, I have been waiting here for almost an hour—do you have any idea what it's like to have every man that walks by give you the once over?"

"Don't flatter yourself, it's the stunning car they are dropping their tongues for. A Bugatti, not very common, especially in *this* neighborhood. Stands out like a unicorn at a dog show."

"Not very common in *any* neighborhood, general. Get in."

General Isadore Pope had barely closed the door behind him when Olivia roared the Bugatti onto Livingston Road, tires squealing like a banshee chasing its prey.

"What's the hurry, lead foot?"

"They claim the Chiron goes 0-60 in under three seconds. Every once in a while, I like to prove them right."

"This is why you wanted to meet where the cops don't come after dark, to take me for a joy ride in your over-priced hot rod?"

The general looked far from pleased, gripping onto the safety handle like it was a life preserver.

Olivia ignored him, weaving in and out of traffic like the Bugatti was a hurtling pinball, pinging off obstacles in an arcade game with stealthy precision.

When she snapped the steering wheel hard left to make a turn, barely squeezing between two oncoming cars, the general lost it, squealing like a little boy feeling the first cut of a circumcizor's scalpel.

"You maniac—Stop! Let me out!"

The general's beefy neck snapped back against the headrest as Olivia brought the Bugatti to a dead stop, pulling to the curb on a darkened side street, where kids had taken out a number of streetlights with slingshots last year. The city had yet to repair them.

"They also say this car can stop on a dime," said Olivia. "They were half right."

"Why ... stop ... here?" heaved the general, between breaths as big as sails.

"I scouted this spot out on my way here. Dark, quiet ..."

"In this neighborhood, I'll give you five minutes before we get car-jacked," the general jumped in, one hand pushing down over where his heart was still pounding.

"Let them come. This car is bullet proof and bomb proof, the frame is triple-reinforced steel."

"Good god, it's a bloody tank on rubber wheels."

Olivia looked over at the riled up, red-cheeked general and concluded that her plan to throw him off his usually stoic guard was working. The time to strike was now.

"What do you know about Jack Holt, general?"

"What? Who?"

"Don't stall me, general ... you brought up his name at the last White House meeting. Jack Holt, he's been working on a secret project for Samantha Isenberg. Tell me what he told your people about what's *really* going on at Isenberg's compound in Colorado."

The general gave her his best surprised-as-hell look, eyes wide open and aimed at hers, bushy eyebrows to the sky.

"I thought you wanted to talk about something 'personal,' Olivia. What the hell is this?"

"Look at me, general ... NO, I mean *really* look at me. What do you know about what Jack Holt told your people?"

"And you need to know this because ..."

"Like I said, it's personal."

The general unbuckled his seat belt to help him breathe easier.

"Are you thirsty, general? Your lips look parched. I don't have any water, but I can offer you a mint."

"Yes, thank you, that will help ... Jack Holt has turned on Sam Isenberg, he is at HQ for debrief, as we speak."

"That much, I'm already aware of. I need to know more."

"What the hell more do you want, that you don't already know?"

"I want to know what Holt said about aliens visiting Isenberg and her associates in their dreams, when they were young."

"Christ, that intelligence has not been verified ... the debrief is still ongoing."

"I'm sure they keep you up to speed regularly, it's how you operate. Tell me specifically about that, what did Holt say about their visions, the aliens visiting them?"

"If I tell you, you will mark it down as the words of crazy people with god complexes, as Intelligence already has. Word is Holt is making all this up to discredit his former boss, with whom he had a major falling out. Intelligence is not taking him seriously, but we are debriefing him because your father despises Isenberg, and any dirty nugget we can dig up will please him."

"I will be the judge of what Holt's motives are."

"Suit yourself."

General Pope recounted the Intelligence report he had read just hours ago. Holt continually referred to Isenberg and her merry cast as deranged lunatics. Everyone in Isenberg's inner circle claimed that during their youth, in various countries around the world, they all had the same visions: An alien presence that called itself 'Mother' came to them in their dreams, offering guidance and direction as to the career path they should choose and what the future held for them.

Olivia put a hand in front of her eyes, hiding them from the general.

There is a 'Mother,' I was not insane, I was *not* crazy, she said to herself. All those psychiatrists and mental health freaks my father made me go to when I was young, all those drugs they made me take—but I WAS NOT CRAZY!

Mother said I had been chosen by her, she told me I was to lead humanity down a new path. I must contact Samantha Isenberg right away ...

"Why are you crying, Olivia?"

"I, um ... find your story very moving," she replied. No way she would tell him they were actually tears of joy.

The general's phone rang.

"Goddammit, thanks to your imitation of a Formula 1 driver, I forgot to disable my phone before we started this conversation. Did you take precautions, Olivia?"

"I turned mine off, it's OK, general."

"Not OK! Someone had ears on our conversation, believe me."

He looked at the caller ID.

"It's your father, I have to take this."

"Oh my god, do you think it was *him* listening in?"

"Your father may be a moron, Olivia, but he's a man with a mission, and that make's him dangerous. To all of us.

"Yes, Mr. President ... My apologies sir, my phone was on the charger ... Of course, sir, I will return to the White House immediately ... Yes, sir, copy that."

"What does he want? I am coming with you—have us there in 15 minutes."

"He said it would just be me and him. You cannot attend this meeting, he specifically said not to bring you."

"Then he knows I am with you. What will you tell him?"

"I will lie."

CHAPTER 27
Lady Stardust

Jimi, Delia and Sanchez were on a flight from Lisbon to Burlington International Airport in Vermont. From there, the plan was to rent an all-terrain vehicle and drive deep into the Green Mountains, to meet Viktor Kozlov.

Midway across the Atlantic, all three were sleeping soundly. Jimi sat between Delia and Sanchez, whose shrill snoring would have disturbed the dead, were it not for the overriding din of the jet engines.

Jimi was resting comfortably against Delia's shoulder, dreaming about his life in Vegas. It was his day off, the maid had already cleaned up, so he was listening to music, loud as his burly amp could pump, and drinking his favorite bourbon to pass the afternoon. This is how Jimi liked his chill time.

The bottle was near-empty by the time he pouted his way through the 28 tracks on the Smashing Pumpkins' *Mellon Collie and the Infinite Sadness*. He was indeed feeling melancholy and searched his collection for a record that would cheer him up, take his thoughts somewhere far, far away.

He put on his favorite David Bowie record, *The Rise and Fall of Ziggy Stardust and the Spiders from Mars*, first released in 1972, but Jimi's version was a remastered pressing, issued in 2016, the year Bowie passed away.

As the record spun on his turntable, Jimi felt the elation that seeped into his thoughts every time he listened to that album. He stripped down to his briefs and started prancing around his living room, like Tom Cruise in *Risky Business*. By the time the needle reached *Starman*, he was singing out loud, trying to mimic Bowie's one-off vocal style.

"I love that song," he heard a voice say. "I helped him with it."

Jimi stopped singing. He shook his head, told himself it must be the whack of the bourbon.

"Jimi, I am here with you, in your dream."

Jimi's glass fell from his fingers, landing on his right foot, but he didn't feel a thing.

"Who the hell are you?"

"It's Mother. Don't be alarmed, Jimi. I sensed the music playing in your dream. When I heard Bowie, it brought back so many memories. I didn't mean to startle you."

"So, I *am* dreaming? And what's happening, right this minute, this is not real?"

"It *is* real, in the metaphysical realm."

"What? ...You lost me."

Jimi listened as Mother explained. When humans are in a dream state, their subconscious mind takes control. Only during that time, when the mind lets go of the physical world and enters the metaphysical realm of the subconscious brain, can the Deus interact with humans.

The subconscious mind is far more open to outside influences, infinitely superior in terms of creativity and problem solving, than is the heavily filtered, highly regimented conscious mind, she told Jimi.

"Dreams are like stories that try and tell you what you could be, what you can become. Surely, you've had the experience where you go to sleep with a problem that seems impossible, yet when you awake the next morning, the answer is there, in your head, ready for you to engage?"

"I usually just wake up with a hangover."

"You would not consume alcohol to such excess if you knew love, embraced it as a virtue above all other passions, made it the core of your existence."

"Yeah, all you need is love, who are you, John Lennon?"

"I helped him and Paul write that song, too."

"Oh yeah? ... You say make love the 'core of your existence,' that's for 'fairies who wear boots'—like Ozzy Osbourne sang. I got all the 'love' I need right here—look at the size of this. A real dude's dick. Gets me all the lovin' I want." Jimi looking smug, pulling it out for her to see.

"Jimi, the drink is doing the talking for you. ... Allow me to *illuminate*, in another manner."

Jimi felt his skin heating up, like he'd stepped from the shadow of a towering oak and exposed himself to searing summer sunshine. A strange sensation caressed him. It felt like he was sliding into a bathtub filled with warm, gooey chocolate.

He sensed a calmness he'd never felt before. His body felt like a feather drifting in a soft breeze.

"I have revealed myself to you. Do you see me now?"

"Yes ... you are a beautiful blue light ... how did you do that?"

"I unlocked your mind, Jimi, freed you from yourself."

"Everything looks so different to me now. Why?"

"You have been trained since early childhood to believe only what your eyes can see. The human eye, Jimi, can only 'see' a fraction of what is really all around it."

"You are warm. You smell like candy."

Mother's blue light flickered briefly, like a glowing candle kissed by a gust.

"You know me now, don't you?"

"You are peace, you are wisdom, you are love … You are Mother."

"And, I am everything you love."

Mother's outline changed, until it was shaped like a human body, with a head, arms and legs. A face formed. It was Delia's.

"Why don't you flip the record over and place the needle on the first track, Jimi. We can listen to it while we talk."

"*Lady Stardust*? Why? Is that what Bowie used to call you?"

"Sometimes, very perceptive, Jimi, but the song is not specifically about me. More like a stage persona he envisioned for himself, after meeting me."

"Yes, that makes sense to me now. So, you came to him, in his dreams, just like you are here with me in mine."

Jimi held the vinyl by its edges with the palms of his hands, never letting his fingertips smudge the grooves as he rolled it over and placed it gently back on the turntable.

When the song began, Jimi started singing again. Mother joined right in.

"You *do* know this song."

"I told you, I helped him write it. In the morning, he woke up and scribbled out the lyrics in minutes."

"What was he really like? I know at that point in his career 'wild and crazy guy' doesn't begin to tell the story."

"I first met him when he was a young man named David Jones. Incredibly shy but disarmingly charming. Super intelligent—an awareness that was off the human scale. He had such a beautiful soul, he loved the darkness of space and always wondered who was out there. He loved people who were not 'robots' and, he loved his drugs."

"What's a virtuoso without a vice?" Jimi smiled, pouring himself another drink.

"Well, he was an original. There will never be another like him. Do you have *Diamond Dogs*?"

"With Bowie dolled up, his head fused to a dog's body, draped across the double cover, and a bleak *1984* theme—totally brilliant, totally Bowie. Of course, I have it."

"Let's spin that next. It's quintessential Bowie. His music was ethereal and yet so visceral. Even his more complex works retained a quality that connected with the primitive.

"I have seen many of Bowie's live shows, Jimi, but the second performance of the *Diamond Dogs* tour in Toronto, in June of 1974, was his finest ever. Bowie magnificently merged magical theatrical scenes with spirited rock 'n roll spectacle. I think he was inspired by the enchanted theatrics of Pink Floyd's *Dark Side of the Moon* tour the previous year," said Mother matter-of-factly.

There was something as wonderful as it was peculiar going on, Jimi thought. Here he was, with an alien unlike any he had ever heard of in the annals of science fiction. Yet, he felt like he was having a simple chat with a fellow music enthusiast. Then he remembered he was dreaming. Dreaming is good. Nothing can hurt you in your dreams.

"Wow, you really know your music. Are all the Deus music lovers?"

"We do not have music to brighten our endless existence. Ours is a dour, joyless reality, personified by duty, always seeking out order and balance ..."

"So, you *are* like the Vulcans from *Star Trek*. We talked about that before."

"In some ways, yes. I used to dream with Gene Roddenberry. He understood what I wanted the human race to become, and tried to help get that message out through his work."

"The original *Star Trek*, and series of spinoffs that followed, I saw them all on that channel that used to program nothing but old Sci-fi TV shows," said Jimi. "They were so important to me growing up. The idea that humanity could visit so many amazing planets just blew my mind—I could not wait for the future to happen.

"I do find it very strange, however, that you do not have music. How did this happen? You are such an advanced race," said Jimi.

"We have become a species smothered by our own complacency. Creativity has been stifled as a result of this smugness. Nothing 'new' or 'unique' has occurred or been conceived for a hundred million years on my world. 'Same old, same old,' as you humans say.

"There is no longer any such thing as beauty or art in the Deus world. We have no paintbrushes or instruments. There are no violins, pianos or accordions. Humans are one of the few species in all the universe that create music, but remain the only ones that understand its joy and its ability to enhance life. More importantly, music is Earth's universal language, a force for unity like no other.

"It is my hope that, one day, humans can bring the sense of joy only found through music and the arts to the Deus. I hope you teach us about happiness, to help us experience the feeling of unbridled ecstasy."

"So, there is no art, you don't make movies, you don't dance?"

"Sadly, no."

"Then, in my estimation, Mother, the Deus are *not* as advanced as they think they are …"

"As I have heard humans say to one another, Jimi: 'You get me.'"

Jimi smiled as he poured the last drop of bourbon into his glass. For some reason, he no longer felt the effects of alcohol, despite the empty bottle.

"So, tell me, who else have you visited while they were dreaming?"

"More than I could say in a single day, and you probably would not believe me, Jimi."

"Try me. I remember reading about famous people who claimed their ground-breaking ideas came to them in a dream."

"Such as?"

"For one, I remember Albert Einstein said the theory of relativity originated in a dream he had as a young boy."

"That is true. I visited him many times in his dreams."

"Bob Dylan has also said he composed music that originated in his dreams."

"True again. There are thousands of others, from Socrates to Benjamin Franklin, the one you call William Shakespeare to Johann Sebastian Bach, Joan of Arc …"

"Who would you say was the most remarkable human that ever lived?"

"That would have to be Leonardo."

"Leonardo da Vinci?"

"Yes. A truly fascinating human. He came to understand that the Universe is like a circle; there is no beginning, there is no end.

"He also had the remarkable ability to ignite, then unite, every partition in his mind. He did not see boundaries or limits to knowledge. He did not think in terms of categories like astronomy, the arts or mathematics. He had the ability to let his mind wander and explore, with no inhibitions or preconceived notions, and it took him places no one had been before."

"So, thinking is the best way to travel?"

"Indeed, 'no luggage required,' very clever."

"It's a line from a Moody Blues song, not my own," Jimi smiled.

"You know, I've noticed a big difference from when you talk to me as Mother, and when you talk to me as Delia. As Mother, you sound like a university professor answering questions after a complicated lecture..."

"You are correct, Jimi, there is a quantifiable difference. Right now, I am with you in your dreams, so it is just Mother talking. In reality, the voice is a combination of our two personalities, as it were. For example: Delia has a keen sense of humor, but in the Deus world, we do not appreciate the notion of 'making a joke.'"

"But how does it work, when do I know for sure if it's just Delia talking or just you talking? Based on what you told me, if it's something amusing then it must be Delia?"

"How it works is simple. Delia and I share the same physical space but we are of two minds. However, her body is as fragile as any other human, which is why I need to remember to let her lead when it comes to physical movement, things like running or even walking.

"In terms of our journey to retrieve the anti-gravity device, I have been leading the way. In terms of feelings, whether it is pain, hunger or passion, that is Delia's domain. I share my thoughts with her, to a point."

"So, what it's like to be an entity in someone else's body? As a Deus, you are unlimited in movement—you can even fly, right? Don't you feel trapped inside a human form that will snap in two if you push it too hard?"

"Sometimes damage is done to the body, but I can repair it. The drawback to that is the energy I expend doing those repairs."

"How do you get 're-energized?'"

"Human beings are fueled by ingesting biomass, food. Deus must be on their home world, where our blue star gives us life. Right now, I am growing weak. You could say I am running on reserve power. I must return to Caelum, very soon."

"What happens to Delia when you leave her body?"

Mother did not immediately respond. Jimi asked again.

"You need to understand, when I merged with Delia, she was in a San Francisco hospital, seconds from death."

"That's crazy ... What are you really saying to me, Mother?"

Jimi felt a heavy grip on his shoulder, then the hand shook him back and forth like he was a baby's rattle.

"Wake up, fool," said Sanchez. "The plane has landed. We have arrived."

CHAPTER 28

Up in smoke

General Isadore Pope was in his spacious office at the Pentagon, enjoying a tall snifter of cognac and a Cohiba with his oldest military friend, Colonel Sam Davis. It was barely 2:00 on a cloudy afternoon.

Davis and Pope had been friends for 30 years. They belonged to the same church, their families vacationed together, and they confided in each other like blood brothers. Then Douglas Triton became President. Things changed dramatically when Triton made Pope his top military advisor. It wasn't long before Pope started ignoring Colonel Davis's calls and messages. Pope could no longer share intel with Davis, thought it best to let the friendship wither, even though he missed the candid conversations he used to have with the Colonel about all things military.

"It's been a really long day, Davis. Thanks for dropping by with the Cohibas, it's like you read my mind."

"Nothing better to chase away the dregs of a long day, Pope. It's been a while since we did this."

"Yes, it has. … How are the wife and kids, Davis?" The general making small talk, least he could do for the pleasure of a fine cigar.

"Doing well. Sam Junior has been accepted at West Point, going to be a fine officer someday. My daughter wants to get involved in environmental studies, obviously I'm strongly discouraging that."

"As you should be, Davis. The only 'green' this country needs more of is fried green tomato recipes."

Davis chuckled as hard as the general, then said, "Yes, and I prefer she take to the skillet more than the science. Make a good soldier a fine wife someday."

"Where did you pick up the Cohibas, Davis? A rare treat these days, they never make enough of them."

"I have meetings once a month with the Border Patrol chiefs. The cigars were part of a huge bust. Smugglers had them stashed with a legit shipment of avocados coming in from Mexico. Sniffer dogs went wild, guards ripped open the boxes, found a case of cigars at the bottom of every one."

"Ah, the perks of being inside the Border Patrol's circle. They never send *anything* my way."

"That doesn't compare to the perks a soldier of your privilege experiences every day—when was the last time you actually paid for *anything* out of your own pocket, Pope?"

The general feigned a "thinking long and hard" look, even put a finger to his chin. "Hmm, I'd have to say it was the $10,000 I paid one of my son's coaches years ago, to guarantee him a spot on the football team. Hard to get that one past the four-eyed military accountants."

"You should have just taken it from the slush fund, like the rest of us," Davis laughed.

"How do you think I paid for my wife's Cartier necklace," Pope laughed back.

"I'm taking the family to Hawaii again for Christmas. Won't cost me a dime, tying it in with an official visit to Pearl Harbor, representing Triton. He would rather make an appointment with his manicurist than tend to such formalities."

The two soldiers traded a few more tales of extravagance for zero of their own dollars before Pope decided he was done with small talk.

"What do you really want from me, Davis?"

"It is nice to catch up, Pope, but I *am* here for another reason … or two."

"Like I didn't know. Have not talked to you in months, you show up out of the blue with some fine cigars. What's on your mind? Lay it on me."

Colonel Davis asked Pope if he'd been getting phone calls and emails from someone named Rudy Olsen, claiming to be president of the B612 Foundation.

"I have indeed. Had the guy checked out. He's a nutbar, like all those other astronomy kooks."

Pope continued to warm the snifter of cognac with the palm of his hand as he watched Davis pull a thick document from his briefcase.

"Did he send you *this* report?" said Davis, placing the document on Pope's desk, then relighting his Cohiba.

"I heard he sent that report to everybody—NASA, FBI, NSA, CIA—*everybody*. No one is taking him seriously. I didn't even print mine out."

"Hmmm … maybe you should have, Pope. One of my contacts at NASA, son of a cousin of mine, new on the job, forwarded it to me, saying the report was being dumped on and nobody was even reading it. He did. So did I."

"OK, but why should I care, and who is this guy and his B612 Foundation? Sounds like a vitamin company."

"I'll tell you what I know, Pope. The B612 Foundation is a non-profit headed up by former astronauts, retired physicists, mathematicians and space geeks from the likes of Stanford. In 2017, they launched a super high-tech asteroid-finding space telescope called the Sentinel, all with private money, because the government had slashed what was left of the funding for this kind of venture."

"Government did the right thing, cutting funding for those kooks, when what we really need are more bombers and missiles to protect our great nation from the terrorists and crazies of this world."

"Wait till you hear what they found, Pope. If this report is the real thing, more bombers and missiles will prove irrelevant."

"OK, I'm listening."

"B612 has been tracking a mysterious unnamed planet that orbits the Sun, beyond the tiny ice world of Pluto. They say it's the fabled Planet Nibiru, what NASA calls Planet X ..."

"Nonsense, that Planet X thing is a hoax perpetrated by sniveling conspiracy kooks," Pope broke in. "It's what they do for a living. Glad I did not bother to read this horse crap from these spaced-out lunatics. Christ, I'll bet LSD is popular with that lot again."

"Pope, they are *not* kooks. Hear me out.

"Apparently, NASA is well aware of the planet Nibiru, published a paper on it, way back in 1988. It has an extreme orbital period, something around 3,600 years, compared to our one year around the Sun. B612 believes NASA was ordered to bury the research on Nibiru— somewhere really deep—on account of the discovery that Nibiru is the forbearer of 'A major apocalyptic event that will forever change life on Earth.'"

"Good Lord, will the Doomsday Dogs ever stop barking?" Pope bellowed. "Bloody 'end-of-the-world' heretics should be rounded up and burned at the stake, like the old days. Only God can proclaim Judgement Day."

"Pope, please read the B612 document, or at least have one of your trusted people suss it out. What have you got to lose? If there is something to the report's claim that, 'Planet Nibiru has already disrupted the orbits of outlying planets in the solar system and has entered a disruptive passage into the inner solar system,' you should call NASA out on this."

"I will do no such thing. You can stop the pretense ... had you made from the start, Davis. Now, why are you *really* here?"

Pope was well aware of Colonel Davis's network of highly placed contacts, hell, he helped Davis set them up years ago, when they were military brothers.

Davis knew something, Pope could smell it on him. He was as crafty as anyone Pope knew. What was he hiding? Right then Pope decided that Davis was not leaving his office until he was satisfied the colonel had all his cards turned face up.

Davis urged the general to take him seriously, this was not a diversionary tactic to veil a hidden agenda for his unannounced visit. All he got in return was a big cloud of cigar smoke in his face.

As he used a bony hand to wave the smoke from his teary eyes, Davis said, "Why do you think billionaire Samantha Isenberg is building a massive underground bunker? This is no coincidence ..."

"You know about Isenberg's bunker?"

"It's not a big secret, Pope. Every government agency knows about the bunker, what is not known, is *why* she is building it. You can't keep a lid on anything these days, Pope. Hell, I even know about your secret project with the President."

The general almost choked on his cognac. His eyes stabbed at Davis and his mug grew smug. Friendship flew out the window quick as a pigeon released from its cage.

"Who's the leaker?" said Pope, leaning steadily forward, sucking hard on the stub of his Cohiba, again blowing the exhaust into the Colonel's twice-thin face.

Davis fanned the air, then said: "My source says it's one of the scientists you and Triton have locked away on a submarine in the Pacific that leaked about it. Calls it the 'wave bomb' project, right?"

Pope's mouth opened wide, his Cohiba stub dangled from his bottom lip on a strand of sticky saliva.

"So, there is *indeed* a covert operation, your reaction confirms it. I got you, Pope."

"I confirm nothing ...what do you *think* you know?"

Davis dipped his long nose into the snifter, then blew in some Cohiba smoke to warm it some more. He savored a large sampling by rolling it around on his tongue, then smacked his lips like a bad kisser.

Pope started rattling his fingers on his desk, like he was playing air piano. The two men stared each other down. Eye upon eye, neither giving in to a blink.

"Now, Davis, I want answers NOW," said Pope.

Colonel Davis rose from his chair, still giving Pope the deadeye, and said: "I believe we are done general. I have everything I came here for."

"Guards!" General Pope screamed at the closed door to his office as Davis prepared to leave.

The same two good soldiers that accompanied the general everywhere he went came storming into the room.

"Take the colonel into custody, he has been relieved of duty," said Pope.

Before Davis could finish pleading, "You can't do this, Pope ..." the guards pounced on him like vultures on roadkill.

"You won't get away with this Pope—I am not the only one who knows about your plan!"

Davis started screaming for help as the soldiers dragged him out the door.

"Don't be afraid to knock his teeth into his throat if he doesn't shut up, boys. Lock him up in one of the dark cells. No one talks to him or sees him without my express authority—understood?"

"As you command, general," said one of the guards, twisting Davis's arm behind his back and forcefully bending his bony body forward with ease.

"In fact, nobody is to know he's here, nobody has seen him. I will inform the staff he is *persona non-grata*, have any surveillance footage with him in it erased, and his name deleted from the visitor logs."

"You want us to interrogate him, sir?"

"No, that's a job for Mr. Needles. I'll give him a call, right now."

CHAPTER 29
The letter

President Douglas Triton adjusted the lighting on the full-length mirror he had installed in the Oval Office the day he moved in, setting it to "evening glow." He tweaked the knot of his hand-made silk tie, then adjusted how it draped down his chest, ending an inch below his vintage leather belt.

A little dab of Clive Christian 1872 on the neck below each ear, followed by a tiny splash on both wrists, and the Triton Look was perfected.

"You're so handsome, I could kiss you," he cooed.

The President was having dinner with a woman who was an activist from Chicago, lobbying to reinstate a program that gave free breakfasts to underprivileged children when they arrived for school, after Triton slashed federal funding to the Feed the Kids organization.

He had instructed his aides to use social media and check out what she looked like, after the request for a meeting was received by his staff.

"If she's hot, tell her I will meet her for dinner, if she's a skank, one of you give her five minutes of your time," he told his aides. Apparently, she met Triton's standard for hot.

Triton was fussing with how his bangs swung across his sloping forehead when his private cellphone began vibrating.

"People always call me when I'm busy."

It was General Isadore Pope.

"Pope, got a super-important meeting coming up that I am prepping for—call me tomorrow."

"This can't wait, Mr. President, we have a big problem …"

"Whatever it is, fix it, then call me tomorrow. I am seriously busy right now."

"Sir, this is critical, I will be brief."

"You have five seconds, Pope."

"Due to matters that just came to my attention, we must move up the test date for the wave bomb. Time has become a huge factor, sir."

"So, what's the problem—that's what I wanted all along, Pope. Get it done."

Triton ended the call while Pope was still talking. It vibrated again, so he turned it off. He took one last look in the mirror, smiled big at himself, then headed for the door.

He stopped before opening the door and bent over to pick up an envelope that was half inside the room.

He flipped the envelope over. One word was written on the front: *Father.* Why didn't she just phone him, as she usually did? And why did the Secret Service guards allow her to slide the envelope under the door, without notifying him? He would have them reprimanded for this.

Triton ripped open the envelope and unfolded the letter.

Father, do you remember all those nightmares I had when I was young, about a bright, shiny ghost, that came to visit me? Well, I have never forgotten.

You insisted I was losing my mind, possessed by demons. You made all those psychiatric specialists do painful tests on me, told them they had to fix me.

I was subjected to shock therapy and forced to take an assortment of debilitating anti-psychotic drugs for years.

The experience was devastating. It changed me. I lost my way.

You were wrong, Father. So wrong. My nightmares were actually dreams and visions of my future.

They were real. I was never crazy or possessed, like you said I was. I have gone to fulfill my destiny.

I am never coming back, father. My place is not with you.

Don't send your people to find me. They won't.

Fare thee well,

Olivia

"Hmmph, she'll be back in no time," Triton snorted. "She'll be back."

He was about to rip the letter up when he noticed there was writing on the flip side of the page.

No, I won't.

CHAPTER 30
Goodbye girl

When a weary Delia, an uptight Sanchez and a groggy Jimi landed at Burlington International Airport in Vermont, Jimi said he had to make a bathroom run.

"That *food* they served on the airplane—chicken something or other—did a number on me," he explained.

"Please hurry, Jimi," said Delia. "We have a long drive ahead of us."

Jimi nodded and walked off, turning his head every few seconds to see if the other two were watching him.

In the meantime, Delia asked around for a place to rent an off-road vehicle. Sanchez took his coca leaf bag from where he'd stashed it for the flight, tucked inside a smelly pair of rolled-up socks in his suitcase. He shook his head in dismay, after seeing how low his supply was.

Jimi returned 20 minutes later, to the ire of a not-enough-coca-leaf-for-me-today Sanchez.

"That long on the toilet, huh? You have the stomach of a candy-assed *jabrony*."

Delia stepped closer to Jimi, placing herself between the two men.

"Jimi, you smell like liquor," said Delia.

"Must be what I had on the plane."

"You were asleep during the flight."

"When you drink a lot, you stink a lot," Sanchez spat.

"Well, better to smell like a good bourbon than to have the stench of dead bodies wafting from your murdering mouth," Jimi spat back.

"*Que puto maricon*—I will crush your puny head with my arm pit!"

"This is no place for a pissing match," Delia whispered. "Jimi, you *have* been drinking. You went to the bar at the airport, that's why you took so long.

"And Sanchez, stop behaving like a baby needing his soother to suck on. You can do without your coca leaf fix for a short while, can you not?

"Now, *gentlemen*, heads up. We've gotten the attention of those two security guards by the exit doors. Tread quietly as we leave."

The twitchy trio waltzed their way past the security guards, Delia flashing a smile, making sure her sexy sway was all their eyes were interested in. Sanchez nodded politely, one hand pressed against the pocket holding the illicit coca leaves. Jimi followed behind Sanchez, bloodshot eyes to the floor.

They hailed the nearest cab. Delia stumbled as she was getting inside. Said she was tired. Jimi offered to drive the rental when they picked it up, but Delia reminded him he'd been drinking. Sanchez will drive, she insisted.

The cab dropped them at a rental joint in South Burlington, where they selected a Jeep, the so-called Hard Rock Edition. Delia was told by a clerk that spoke with a waggish southern drawl that this particular Jeep could clear the roughest terrain, its axles were designed for "slow-speed crawlin'."

When she answered the curious clerk's question as to where they were headed, he immediately started in on the "Mystery of Glastenbury Mountain" tale.

"That's bullshit," was Sanchez's reaction to the story.

"Don't count on it, fella. Look 'er up online," said the clerk. "Lotsa folk gone missing 'round there. Some say man-eating rocks swallowed 'em up. Some say the Bigfoot took 'em."

Just as Sanchez moved toward the clerk with an "I am going to slap you silly" look in his eyes, Delia pointed to the Jeep and ordered him to start loading their bags. Sanchez bowed his head and did as she asked.

"You look like fine folks," said the clerk. "Honest with y'all now, I don't pay no attention to the weird things going on up there, Glastenbury's just an old logging camp. Nothing to be feared of, lessen' you believe in ghosts," he snickered, showing teeth that would give an orthodontist nightmares.

Delia went to the Jeep, saying she was tired and needed to rest. Jimi responded to the clerk's "Hey, buddy, come over here for a sec," request.

"You look like the kinda fella that could use a good snort. Got me the finest 'shine, sell yah one for $20, two for $35. Hunerd proof, gets you higher than a kite goes. Here, have a little taste."

Jimi looked at the clerk sporting a "Triton stands for America" T-shirt, then at the bottle being offered to his lips. He smacked it from the clerk's hands.

"Screw off, you freak. I got some Eagle Rare at the airport. You can keep your backwoods gut rot."

The clerk introduced Jimi's cheek to his clenched fist. Jimi hit the dirt like an unhinged mannequin. Sanchez came hurtling across the parking lot, grabbed the clerk by his long brown mane, snapped his head back and threw him to the ground. He slammed the clerk's neck down with his boot and pressed hard on his wind pipe.

Delia got out of the Jeep and ordered Sanchez to stop the violence, asked Jimi if he was alright, then put a hand out to the clerk as he got back to his feet.

"My apologies for the trouble. Please accept this as a token of my regret."

Delia handed him a Benjamin Franklin. He stuffed it in his shirt pocket.

"Least you can do for the hundred bucks is give us directions," said Sanchez.

"Sure, Monkey Man—just stay away from me. President Triton was right about wanting to keep your kind outta our country," the clerk said as he gently rubbed his throat.

Sanchez glared at him, but restrained his fists.

"You want directions … Alrighty then. Take the harbor road in Bennington, the old rail line to Glastenbury. Don't take this baby onto the Appalachian Trail, it's too narrow in spots for city folks.

"Cut across the road to the fire tower, Fire Road 71 from Route 9, then follow Fire Road 325. Quick hike to the ruins of Glastenbury from there."

"Sounds complicated," said Sanchez. "Can you repeat that?"

Delia said that wouldn't be necessary, and shooed the clerk away.

"You're driving, Sanchez. I will give you directions."

With Sanchez at the wheel, Jimi got into the back seat with Delia. She smiled at him, then rested her head on his shoulder. Jimi was thinking her eyes had lost their sparkle.

He recalled asking Mother what would happen to Delia after she left her body. Sanchez cut his dream short. Jimi didn't get an answer. What if Delia died when Mother left? His heart fluttered at the thought of that.

He was overwhelmed by emotions as he looked at Delia. For the first time in his life, there was a woman he really cared about. With love, comes pain. Jimi did not like to hurt.

The cocky Vegas lady's man, was being upstaged by the frightened little boy hiding inside him.

He could hear the bourbon calling out to him, like a seductive Siren, promising instant relief, at least until tomorrow. The half-full bottle he stashed in his carry-on was right next to him. He was reaching for it when Delia turned her head. She looked at him, blue eyes gone dark.

"Why do you look so sad, Jimi?"

"You're going to die when Mother leaves, aren't you?"

"I don't know."

"I can't bear the thought of something happening to you."

"Come what may ... your heart will go on, Jimi."

Her eyes closed, as her head sank back into his shoulder.

Jimi started stroking Delia's forehead. He ran his fingers down the middle of her nose, then gently over her lips, as he tried to make sense of all the thoughts making his head spin.

Fate had wagged its fickle finger at him. Payback for a life sadly lived. The sum of his life was less than zero. He had accomplished nothing. Who would miss him when he was gone? Jimi tried to bring some names forward.

"No one, there is no one that would miss me ..."

He let his head drop as his body collapsed into itself, hoping all those scary thoughts would fly away. His eyes closed.

***

Jimi was roused by the sound of a voice he'd never heard before. He wondered how long he'd been asleep.

"I have to take her to our ship. We must leave immediately."

Sanchez stood back and let the man enter the Jeep. He pushed Jimi away from Delia and hoisted her up into his arms, sliding her out of the Jeep with care.

Delia's eyes opened.

"Xeno, the anti-gravity device is in the back of the Jeep ..."

"Save your energy, Mother. I have already installed the device. It will give us just enough lift to break orbit."

"Put me down, Xeno. I must speak to my friends before we leave."

He set her down gently, her legs wobbled for a second but held firm. Sanchez approached her, then dropped to his knees, his head bowed, his hands making the sign of the cross.

"You are Deus," he said. "Please forgive me my sins, Mother. I promise to be a good man, a kind man. I plead for your forgiveness."

"Arise, Sanchez. Never bow to anyone again."

Sanchez reached for Mother's hand, and kissed it.

"It is time," said Xeno, looking intently at Mother. She turned away from Sanchez and headed for the vessel. Xeno followed her through a portal that closed as quickly as it opened.

"That's it—she's not going to say goodbye to me?" said Jimi, coming out from the Jeep.

"I don't think they are coming back out," said Sanchez.

"But she can't just leave like that. And who the hell is that guy?"

"From what I figured out, while your lazy ass was sleeping, he is a Deus named Xeno, works with Mother, right now living in the body of a man named Viktor Kozlov."

"He's here to take her back to her home world?"

"That's what he said. But, wow, who knew ..."

"Knew what, Sanchez?"

"Who knew that God was actually a woman.

"Jimi ... why are you crying?"

CHAPTER 31
Pieces falling into place

"I have to give you credit, Mother. I had my doubts about your plan to retrieve the anti-gravity device. But it worked. We can leave this miserable little planet behind us."

"Don't be too quick to write the ending, Xeno. This story has many chapters still to play out."

Xeno paused, like he was pondering Mother's words, before saying, "We need to be partners again, like we used to be. I am pleased, aren't you?"

Mother did not respond. She had proceeded to a medical station in the vessel's main chamber, used to assess the vitality of a life form.

"Mother?"

"Keep talking, Xeno, I'm listening."

Mother waved her hand to boot up the laboratory she brought from Caelum, then used her eyes to transmit data to its matrix.

"You seem rather energetic for someone who is 'dying.' Minutes ago, I was carrying you in my arms."

"It was a performance for the humans."

"This whole journey has been a 'performance' by you, hasn't it? Clearly, you neglected to inform me of some particulars, Mother."

"I will inform you, now."

Xeno was aware of how the portable lab Mother was using functioned. He helped her create the specs for it, but she never explained its ultimate purpose. When he saw the analysis displayed on the translucent screen, he said, "There is a malfunction, Mother. It's only showing one life form."

"The readings are correct, Xeno."

"That's not possible ... not possible. Please explain."

"I have merged with Delia; the transformation began weeks ago. This kind of fusion merge has never been attempted, until now. Long ago I modified the lab, for the purpose of expediting the last binary connection for the conversion process.

"The transformation cannot be stopped now."

Xeno looked as confused as a Deus can be confused. His human face arched its thick eyebrows as its eyes asked for answers.

"But how will *you* still exist, Mother?"

"We may share the same body, but we will remain two separate minds. I will know everything she knows and she will know my thoughts, when I choose to share them. I will draw energy organically, by tapping synergistically into her carbon-based life force."

"What have you done? Have you forgotten … humans *expire*."

"We will live long enough to achieve the next phase of my plan, much longer than a normal human, since I will continue to heal this body as it ages."

"This is madness, you have been corrupted by all that is despicable about humans—don't you see this? How will you cope with the realization that you will no longer be immortal?"

"I will be researching ways to prolong our life. If I fail, I will perish with her. I have made my peace with it."

"That is what humans say, Mother."

"I am no longer pure Deus, Xeno. And I am not going back to Caelum with you."

"But you are my partner. We have always been together … we are meant to be together for all time."

Mother started to breathe deeply every few seconds, deeper with each breath. Goosebumps pickled her skin, like something inside Delia's body was changing. Rapidly. The goosebumps disappeared as quickly as they surfaced. Her breathing became normal. Her eyes were shining brighter.

"The transformation is complete."

"No … I will not let you go. We must remain partners."

"I was your partner in the Deus realm, Xeno. What we had, as with all Deus unions, was friendship. We were companions. I need more than that, now. I want to experience human emotions … hate, pleasure, rage, and love."

"Love? That's just a quaint human fantasy. Don't you see that such emotional magnitude is what doomed your human experiment from the start?"

"This is where you are supposed to remind me, *failure is not an option*, remember?"

"I can't do that, Mother. You *have* failed."

"You're wrong, Xeno. And love is what makes humans formidable, a force the Deus have yet to define. Love is power."

"No, what you are really saying is *you love power.*"

Mother stepped closer to Xeno. From her left pocket she removed a small black cylinder with a shiny silver tip.

"You will never understand, Xeno. Don't torture yourself."

She was right next to him now. His eyes were downcast.

"As is the custom for humans, you must give me a hug before we part company."

Xeno did not move.

Mother embraced him, wrapping one arm around the small of his back, then placing the hand holding the small cylinder on his neck, where the brain connects with the spinal cord. She plunged the cylinder into his neck, until beads of blood formed around its edges. Xeno froze. The look in his eyes defined disbelief.

When she pulled away and released him, his body crashed to the floor.

"What have you done to me ... I feel so weak."

Xeno struggled to raise himself up on his hands. He looked up at Mother, his eyes a blank stare.

"I can't see. Everything is black."

"I have siphoned your life force from Kozlov's body."

"I am Deus. You cannot do that to me."

"Yet, you are expiring."

"That's not possible ... how ... tell me how?"

A device I created, a very long time ago. Your energy has been transferred to this cylinder," she said, holding it up to show him.

"But I am still here, in this body."

"Fragments of you are still active in Kozlov's brain, but your life force has been converted back to pure energy. It's trapped in here now. I will be able to draw from it to sustain my own life force, here on Earth."

"So, that's how you will live longer than a normal human? Leaching from the life you stole from me?"

"The sacrifice is necessary. The future of the humans is all that matters."

"What future? Your dreams are finished, Mother. The Earth will be ravaged by massive tidal waves. All life will perish. I have seen to that.

"The joke is on you, as the humans say."

"Do you really believe I did not know about the wave bomb? Or your betrayal of me?"

"You knew ... all along? But how, who told you?"

"No one *told* me. I have my ways."

"You have devised a plan to save the humans again, haven't you? That's why you are doing this."

"Not just any humans, Xeno. Only the best and the brightest, as selected by me. We will survive the coming floods in a large underground habitat, the construction of which is almost complete."

"This is why you sent me to Russia, the other side of this planet, when we arrived, isn't it? So you could carry out your plan, build your underground habitat, without my knowledge.

"Who betrayed whom, Mother?"

"You left me no choice. The humans are everything now."

"But you will fail, like you failed on Mars. You may think you are superior to the rest of your race, but your precious humans will be the bane of your existence. They will be your undoing."

"I have recalibrated. Nothing has been left to chance."

"You have betrayed the Deus. And, you have murdered me, Mother."

"Every triumph comes with a cost."

"You have become a cold-blooded killer, just like your humans. You dare call this a 'triumph?' I must know why."

Tears squeezed out from the blinded eyes of Kozlov.

"You have little time left before Kozlov's brain gives out, so tell me where the lifeboats are. You moved them, didn't you, Xeno? Navicula will not tell me where they are."

"I don't know where the lifeboats are, or why Navicula is silent. Its function is to safeguard our vessel. Clearly, it sees you as a threat."

"You know something, Xeno. Tell me."

"Maybe the Consuls had something to do with this. They were on our vessel, insisted on doing so, before they returned to Caelum."

Mother rushed to Navicula's sensory display.

"Navicula *has* been tampered with, Xeno. I don't have time to sort this out, but I do have a sure-fire solution.

"Wait—you must tell me what I need to know. I will not exist long enough to inform our kind about what you have done. You must grant a dying man's last wish, Kozlov is saying."

Mother agreed. Besides, what did it matter now? She quickly gave Xeno an overview of her intentions.

"This was your vision from the beginning, since you first created the *homo sapiens*, was it not? You deceived and manipulated *all* of us. You even managed to get the Imperitus Council to do your bidding—without their knowledge. Or mine.

"It all makes sense now. The wave bomb … this was your idea, wasn't it? Wipe out the humans you don't want, save the few who meet your genetic dynamic. The survivors will see you as their god. That's what you desire, isn't it?"

"I don't have time for this."

"Don't deny me, Mother. Grant me peace before I depart. You owe me."

"I owe you nothing. You are still assigning Deus logic to the mechanisms of ulterior motive, Xeno. Have you learned nothing from living with humans?"

"Yes. I have learned to despise them. They are ravenous beasts that gorge on self-gratification and self-indulgence. You will regret your decision to champion them."

"Don't be a fool, Xeno. How do you think I was able to achieve my objectives, while keeping my true motives hidden?"

"You are the most advanced of Deus. That is clear to me now."

"You are mistaken. It all came from the humans, master manipulators like Mao, Hitler, Stalin and Trump. I observed their kind … I learned how they used fear to their advantage against more powerful adversaries, how they planted the seeds of false narratives that quickly grew to become truths.

"There is not a life form in the universe as cunning and manipulative as a human with a mission."

"I see your plan, for what it really is, Mother. I read your secret notes. I know about your dream to create a race that will one day challenge our kind.

"The Deus will despise you, excommunicate you. You are a traitor."

"They will eventually come to see me as a savior, Xeno."

"*Never*. You have opened a portal to the unknown. Don't be so certain of the outcome."

Xeno's voice was sounding fainter with each word.

"Like I said, Xeno, there are many chapters yet to be written."

The Deus devised their interstellar vessels to be living singularities, conscious and aware. Mother knew Navicula would respond to any action that threatened its existence and the safety of its passengers, despite what the trespassing Consuls may have overwritten in Navicula's programming.

She manually reset Navicula's destination headings for the heart of the Sun and deleted all possible override scenarios, giving herself two minutes to leave the craft before takeoff. All she had to do was say "engage," and the clock would start ticking on Navicula's demise.

"Give me the lifeboats, Navicula. I won't ask again."

Navicula remained silent, but complied. Instantly, the bottom drawer of a stacked compartment in the far corner of the control room lurched open. Mother gathered up three of the five orbs and put them in her pocket.

"Engage," she said.

The vessel must never return to Caelum. Navicula could recall everything and provide evidence of what Mother had done. The Sun in the Earth system burned just hot enough to reduce Navicula and the vessel to fumes.

Mother went back to Xeno and bid him a quick "Farewell, Xeno." His body was dead limp, but his mouth started moving.

"There is no death more agonizing. I must know, Mother, why … *why* do you love the humans so?"

"Humans are the future. They have their faults, but it is those faults that make them extraordinary. You could never understand this, Xeno. One day, they will lead the Universe, achieving a greatness the Deus never realized was theirs for the taking."

Xeno's eyes went dead. Mother didn't bother checking for vitals.

As she neared the portal to exit the vessel, Navicula finally spoke.

"You killed Xeno … You betrayed the Deus … You are the darkness."

Mother exited the vessel, Navicula's last words echoing in her head.

When Jimi saw Delia emerging from the ship, he quickly wiped his tear-streaked face with his shirt. Sanchez got back on his knees and made the sign of the cross, three times in succession. She walked slowly towards them, smiling. Behind her, the Deus vessel rose to the height of trees, then vanished into the night skies, like it was never there.

"That was amazing," said Sanchez, his eyes fixed to the sky. "The ship made no noise, not a single sound. And there was no smoke, like when the rockets lift off from Cape Canaveral. I have seen the vessel of God."

Jimi was more interested in Delia, looking at her reignited blue eyes with disbelief as she approached him.

"Are you Delia, or Mother?"

"I am Delia. Mother left for Caelum with Xeno."

"But I thought you would die when Mother detached herself from you—how are you still alive?"

"Mother gave me life, at her own expense. She did not want me to die, she wanted us to be together, Jimi.

"Now, everyone back in the Jeep, we have to leave, immediately."

"What, again? It never stops with you," said Jimi. "Where are we going now?"

"Home, to San Francisco. I must pick up my daughter."

CHAPTER 32

Pick your poison

Samantha Isenberg didn't know a petunia from a geranium. Her world was one of Commerce, and the only things she was interested in 'growing' were profit margins. She had never worked the soil with her fingers. Making that primal connection with nature held as much value for her as last week's stock market report.

So, it was with some annoyance that she agreed to join an afternoon meeting with the staff in charge of all things flora for the New Eden project. Apparently, there was much bickering going on over choices regarding the selection of seeds to be placed in cold storage for future use.

It's as if they knew there really was a mass extinction event coming and their choices meant something, she thought, as she witnessed the heated discussion for herself. But only her inner circle knew. The staff's disposition was one of well-intentioned rationality, not the anxiousness of necessity.

"Look people, for the last time, the *ricinus communis* is one of the most poisonous naturally occurring substances on Earth. Surely, it's not a plant we want to save," one of the botanist staff was arguing.

"Its beauty alone—big, tropical-looking leaves swaying in the breeze—is reason enough to keep *ricinus* on the seed list," another staffer countered. She then picked up her laptop and went over to where Isenberg was sitting.

"Here, look, Sam. This is a photo of the castor bean plant, *ricinus communis*. This is my favorite variety, with red leaves and branches. Don't you think it's gorgeous?"

"But the seeds are poisonous—to humans and wildlife," said the opposing botanist.

"Sam, it's up to you to cast the deciding vote. As you can see, we are deadlocked," said chief botanist Nancy Pelligrino.

Isenberg had heard enough already, there were more important matters to attend to. Looking at pictures of plants was a waste of her precious time.

"If it's poisonous, it's off the list," she said firmly.

"Not fair, what about *atropa lilium*?" said another staffer. "It made the list for its unbridled beauty, yet it's also extremely poisonous. Plus, Nancy has a live one in her office."

"Wrong," said Pelligrino. "The belladonna lily, we all agreed, made the list because of its potential medicinal value."

"Well, we make castor oil from *ricinus* ..."

"Enough!" said Isenberg. "Here is my ruling, then I *must* attend to more pertinent matters. If there is room in the chamber for the seeds in question, they make the list. If we are running low on space, dump the potentially poisonous plants first. Clear to one and all?"

The six heads in the room seemed to bobble in unison.

"While we have you here, Sam," said Pelligrino, "I would like to appeal a decision previously made regarding *habenaria radiata*, the white egret orchid. It's the most beautiful flower nature has ever created. It was excluded because we cannot provide the exacting habitat for a live specimen, and saving the tender corms for future cultivation is also challenging, given its requirements to survive periods of dormancy."

Pelligrino showed Isenberg a photo of the orchid.

"Absolutely stunning," Isenberg beamed. "It looks just like a graceful white egret in flight. Find a way, people. This flower is a keeper."

The six heads bobbled in unison again.

Isenberg got up to leave, Pelligrino followed her out of the room. There was one more matter for her to rule on, that is best kept between the two of them, Pelligrino said.

"There was a request made for *erythroxylum*—live specimens, not seeds, Sam. We need all available space in the cultivation area for food production. With your approval, I would like to turn that request down."

"What the hell is *erythroxylum*?"

"It's the coca plant, Sam, what cocaine is made from. Surely, this is one crop we can do without, although I don't have a problem with keeping it on the seed list."

"Ah, yes, the coca plant. Consider that a priority, Nancy."

Isenberg knew where that request came from. Christo Sanchez. It was one of two things the assassin demanded when she was negotiating with him to switch from killing Delia to protecting her. Sanchez flatly refused to explain how he learned about New Eden, but it was clear he knew. Isenberg lost patience with the stubborn Sanchez and gave in to his demands, largely on the premise that he would protect Delia with his life.

One of the demands was that he be allowed to join New Eden, the other was a fresh supply of coca leaves. She was well aware of Sanchez's predilection for violence, and she understood his addiction. Providing him with a daily ration of coca leaves seemed the best way to ensure his cooperation, by keeping him happy and relatively sedated.

"That's just plain crazy, Sam. Plus, we'll have to go all the way to South America to pick up live specimens. We don't have the time for such undertakings," said Pelligrino.

"Like I said, make it a priority. Send someone to Colombia in my private jet, bring back two live coca plants. Let me know the minute arrangements have been made."

Pelligrino whipped up her argument against the coca plants, and demanded to know why they were a priority. Isenberg's walkie-talkie clicked on. She told Pelligrino to follow her orders then answered the call.

It was Isenberg's security chief. He said a helicopter was approaching the compound's perimeter and a passenger on board was demanding to meet with her.

"Have you checked the helicopter out—is it military?"

"It's a private service out of Denver, mam, no military affiliation that we can see."

Do we know who is on board, wanting to see me?"

"Affirmative, mam. Claims she is President Triton's daughter, Olivia."

"Under no circumstances is that woman to land anywhere near us."

"She said you would say that, mam. Told me to respond with, 'It seems we have the same mother.'"

Isenberg's eyes stayed open.

"Mam? … are you there? What are your instructions?"

Isenberg juggled the cellphone from one hand to the other as she lit a cigarette and dragged deeply, twice, before replying.

"When she lands, first confirm it is indeed Olivia Triton, then bring her to the house."

"Do you have reason to believe she may be an imposter, mam?"

"None whatsoever. Just do it. Put her through all the standard screening procedures, before bringing her to the house. And don't be in any hurry, no matter how much she whines, understood? … I will be in my office, waiting."

Isenberg was buying time. If the reason why Olivia came to the compound was what she suspected, hell was about to freeze over.

CHAPTER 33
The last supper

Olivia Triton and Samantha Isenberg dispensed with the necessary pleasantries, quickly.

"Your security team is certainly thorough, Sam. They kept me waiting for 30 minutes while they confirmed my identity. I thought for sure up next was a lie detector test."

"Well, that's only because I asked them to dispense with all the usual checks for unannounced visitors."

"Uh-huh, I'm sure you did."

"Please, take a seat, Olivia."

The two women inspected one other from opposite sides of Isenberg's large mahogany desk. Olivia crossed her lean legs and assumed her power pose; a piercing stare, elbows out, chin angled up.

Isenberg countered by straightening her back to make herself look taller and leaning forward, claiming as much territory as possible.

She took note of Olivia's outfit: A mid-grey skirt with matching blazer, over a lacy black blouse that gave her front-forward breasts ample space to make themselves known. Her shoes were open-toed with gunmetal heels.

She figured she could buy a car for what Olivia spent on her precious outfit. And those breasts of hers, so shamelessly intrusive. She and Olivia could never be BFF's.

Isenberg was dressed in plain skinny jeans and a plaid shirt, with well-worn runners. Despite her wealth, she never spent more than $40 for a pair of jeans.

"Everybody knows I'm filthy rich, why rub it in their faces," was the logic she drew on to explain her bargain-basement attitude toward fashion. In reality, she had been to the posh designer boutiques, even tried on a few $10,000 ensembles. But when she looked in the mirror, her eyes said she looked like a boy in women's clothing.

Olivia uncrossed her legs, put both arms on the desk and said, "You know why I am here, don't you, Sam?"

"Spying for your father, no doubt."

"Please, Sam, I did not come here to engage in a cat fight ..."

"Look, I know your father has been snooping around—unsuccessfully, I might add."

"That has nothing to do with me, not any more. I have left Washington behind. I am never going back. I had the dreams growing up, Sam. Mother visited me regularly. She foretold my destiny. I have come to claim it."

Isenberg's worst fears were realized with Olivia's last six words. She quickly lit a cigarette.

"I haven't the faintest idea what you're talking about," Isenberg stalled, exhaling a long drag deliberately in Olivia's direction.

"Mother must have told you about me. I am to be the leader of New Eden. This is Mother's design."

Olivia was right. Mother *was* specific about the roles of those she selected for New Eden. She had asked Isenberg to spearhead the operation until the true leader arrived.

"She has been temporarily lost to us, but she will find her way to New Eden before the high waters come," Mother told her years ago.

Isenberg also remembered Mother's more recent instruction, for when the 'true leader' made it to New Eden. Still, she could not help the mounting urge to smack her big-boobed adversary senseless. Olivia was the new chick in Isenberg's henhouse. Blood will be spilled before she would hand over control.

"Where were you when *I* was getting New Eden off the ground, Olivia? You think you can just breeze in here with your designer duffs and start telling me what to do? I have invested billions in this project—how much have you contributed, bitch?"

"You dare call me a *bitch*?"

Olivia got up quickly, her left leg rising over a black wire dangling under Isenberg's desk and snapping it from its jack as she stood. She glared down at the still-sitting Isenberg, her nostrils flaring, an inborn trait her father bestowed upon her.

"Why you pipsqueak, I'll kick your ass—if I can find it."

"You want my butt, here it is, come get it," Isenberg said as she slid from her chair, a flying middle finger pointed at her rear end.

Olivia cranked her neck left and right, then back again.

"Still not seeing that butt. Maybe because your body is like a broomstick, with two cherries glued to the handle."

Isenberg picked up the letter opener on her desk and aimed it at Olivia. She had never felt such rage. She wanted to stab Olivia, over and over. Once Olivia fell to the ground, her eyes would get it first, then her Botox-built lips could use some *piercing*.

Both women started circling the big desk like strutting roosters in a cock fight, sizing up their opponent, waiting for the perfect time to strike.

"You think that letter opener will do you any good against me, Sam? I have more than a foot and 40 pounds on you."

"You're on stiletto stilts, and we'll see how much you weigh after I drain all that silicone from your cowgirl tits."

There was a polite knock at Isenberg's office door. Olivia turned to face the sound, just as Isenberg jumped over the desk and thrashed the air with the letter opener, catching an edge of the lace on Olivia's blouse. A small blood line formed quickly across her chest.

The door opened in the middle of Olivia's scream.

"Um, ah, sorry to disturb your meeting, *ladies*," said Nancy Pelligrino.

The faces of Isenberg and Olivia flushed with red. Isenberg put the letter opener back on her desk, Olivia adjusted her blouse so the scratch didn't show.

"You asked me to let you know the minute arrangements were made to pick up the plants you asked for, Sam. I tried to call you on your direct line but it appears to be out of order."

Isenberg bent over to check her phone and noticed the line was unplugged.

"I must have accidentally kicked the line out from its jack. My apologies, Sam."

The smile on Olivia's face was returned by Isenberg.

"No apologies, necessary, Olivia. We use a line-based internal phone system; nothing is wireless here, to keep hackers at bay.

"There, plugged it back in … working fine now."

"Will there be anything else, Sam?" said Pelligrino.

"I could use a first-aid kit, if you have one handy," said Olivia.

Pelligrino said there should be one in Isenberg's bottom right drawer, then left the office, closing the door behind her.

Muffled giggles were heard from the other side of the closed door. Olivia and Isenberg looked at each other. Mad laughter erupted between them.

"Can you believe … what clowns … we have been, Sam?"

"Did you see Pelligrino's face when she walked through that door and saw us clawing at each other like rabid schoolgirls," Isenberg chortled.

"Priceless," Olivia hooted. "Too bad there was no one here to record our little 'dance'—million online views, first minute alone."

"I record all my meetings in this office," said Isenberg, pointing to the top right corner of the room, where a security camera was flashing red for 'active.'

The laughter suddenly stopped, like both women realized the same thing.

"I will personally delete that footage," said Isenberg.

Olivia nodded in agreement.

"Now, where were we?"

"We need to clear the air about something first, Sam"

"The silly fracas is over. It's a clean slate, Olivia, we don't need to bring any of that up ..."

"Alright, except for one thing that requires a correction, Sam. My boobs are *real*. There is no silicone in them."

Isenberg wanted to tell Olivia she was full of it. Spent enough time looking at the size of other women's breasts to know a real boob from a counterfeit. Instead, she bit her tongue, hard.

"Let's begin with bringing you up to speed on New Eden, Olivia."

Isenberg went back to her seat behind the desk and sat down, then lit another cigarette.

"Do you have to smoke?"

"Yes, I do."

"OK, screw it, give me one of those."

"Spoken like a true leader," Isenberg snickered, as she pushed the cigarette pack in Olivia's direction.

"I'm quitting soon," said Isenberg. "The day we go inside, is the day I give up the cancer sticks. There's a no smoking rule in New Eden and I intend to honor it."

The two women chain-smoked their way through an hour's conversation about everything New Eden, including the recent visit from two FBI agents, posing as inspectors for the firm that manufactured the giant batteries to power the underground colony.

"I heard about that when I was in the Oval Office, Sam. They called it a real coup for *their* side. How did you pull that off, fool the agents so easily?"

"Their visit was predicted by Mother. It was a simple bait and switch operation. We installed dummy servers with 'convenient' access points for the spying 'inspectors.' On those servers were fake files about the New Eden project, basically telling them it was a prototype for future doomsday bunkers that one of my firms was contracted to build for antsy world leaders and gonzo billionaires."

"Incredible. Mother is so perceptive, it's like she can predict the future."

"She does not *predict* the future, Olivia ... she shapes it.

"What have you heard in Washington about my former chief engineer, Jack Holt?"

"Don't tell me Mother had a hand in that, too? His coming to the authorities with his wild story is how I became aware of my role here in New Eden. Holt went on about you and your people talking to aliens in your dreams. Needless to say, they agreed with Holt's contention that you're all lunatics, part of a doomsday cult."

"I can't say for certain it was Mother's design things happened that way but, here you are, just as she said you would be. What else did Holt tell the stuffed shirts in Washington about us?"

"I did learn more about Holt. Just before I left, I managed to eavesdrop on my father's conversation with General Isadore Pope in the Oval Office."

"You *bugged* the Oval Office?"

"Not exactly, they have detectors at every entry and that whole complex gets swept for foreign devices morning and night. What I did was place a bug *inside* Pope, just before he left me to meet with my father."

"*Inside* of him?"

"Sam, it's a new bug I got from a friend in the CIA. He gave me some samples … we, um, had a thing going for a while, after my second divorce. He wanted to impress me, so I let him try," Olivia smiled.

"The bug was secretly developed by the agency's tech staff. It's ingenious. Encased in mint candy is a microscopic, organic-based transmitter. As the target sucks on the mint, the tiny transmitter finds its way into the stomach, where the digestive juices eventually dissolve it completely. It usually transmits for about three hours, but the best part is the target will never know about the bug. No evidence, no trace."

"Very clever of you, Olivia."

"*Me clever*? Look at what *you* have accomplished, Sam. I have always admired you and stood up for you, despite my father's repeated attempts to knock you flat every chance he could.

"Um … no pun intended, Sam."

"None taken. That's a trifle compared to what I've put up with since grade school. You must tell me what else Holt said."

"Holt held out at first—he wanted money before he told the rest of his story. Got smart, realized he no longer had a paycheck coming in. Apparently, my father agreed, a suitcase full of cash was delivered to his hotel room within hours. What they got from Holt, other than the crazy alien stories, were profanity-laced proclamations about what a bunch of lunatics you and your staff are. In short, we should have no concerns about my father regarding New Eden. He's written you off as a bunch of crazies."

"Works for me," said Isenberg. "Seems like everything is going smoothly, just as Mother said it would."

"Do you have anything on Christo Sanchez, Sam? My father and General Pope think he may still be after Mother."

"Sanchez is with *us* now, out there protecting Mother from your father's henchman. He's also joining us here at New Eden, that's what Pelligrino was just in here for, to tell me the live coca plants he insisted on as part of the bargain I struck with him were en route."

"He is coming to New Eden? Does Mother know about this?"

"You know what, I now believe he was also part of her plan. He's actually as crafty as they come, and that denotes intelligence, of a different kind. He certainly hoodwinked me, had to throw in the coca plants as part of our deal on account of his trickery."

"We both know that if he out-maneuvered *you*, Sam, he's far and above the Neanderthal assassin Pope and my father see him as."

"That's for sure. In fact, the more things come together, the more I suspect Mother has kept all of us on a need-to-know leash about New Eden. There was a time when she needed $5 million and I could easily have given it to her, and more. But she headed off to Vegas to win the money she needed instead, and broke off contact with me. I had to hire a specialist that was recommended by my mole in Washington to track her down."

"If what you suspect is true," said Olivia, "then doesn't it also make sense Mother's plan included that side trip to Vegas?"

"That's entirely plausible, yes. She met Jimi James there, and he is still with her. Sanchez also came into the picture in Vegas. Hmmm … and he has also become part of her entourage. Which makes me wonder about that former Secret Service agent named Carter that I hired."

"Former Secret Service agent, and his name was Carter?"

"Why yes, Deon Carter. Why do you say *was,* Olivia?"

"His name was mentioned by General Pope when he was meeting with my father. He's dead. They both laughed about it."

"No wonder we can't get in touch with him. How did he die?"

"His body was found in the reflecting pool at Meridian Hill Park. He was beaten to a pulp, drowned in his own blood—before he was thrown in the pool."

"I doubt his death was part of Mother's plan, Olivia, but the more we piece together … let's just say nothing would surprise me anymore."

Isenberg continued to inform Olivia about what Mother had in mind for New Eden, including the basic blueprint for building a new society on Earth. She also confided specific details about the colony, that Mother only shared with her.

"But surely the Deus will hear about New Eden. Won't they be angry that Mother deceived them?" said Olivia.

"Not going to happen. The Deus are a benevolent, peaceful species. They have no spine when it comes to confrontations, they abhor violence, and they have no weapons that could hurt us. Most importantly, Mother told me she fixed it so the Angelus won't be able to send their ships to Earth on scouting missions, for a long time."

"The Angelus?"

"I only know what Mother told me about them. They are from the closest blue star to Earth called Rigel, in the Orion Constellation. They look a little like humans, but are much smaller and have wings, so they can fly …"

"Angelus is Latin for angels."

"I hadn't thought of them in those terms before, Olivia. Mother also told me the Angelus use a unique breathing apparatus when they visit Earth because oxygen is lethal to them. She described it as looking like a halo over their heads."

"Sounds to me like the Angelus *are* the 'angels' of myth and folklore."

"You may be right, Olivia. Anyway, the Angelus have been reporting to the Deus about Earth for thousands of years, so Mother downloaded a virus she concocted into their broadcasting infrastructure. They can't communicate with the Deus, or even leave their home world, since the navigation systems on their inter-planetary vessels are malfunctioning as a result of the virus."

"How long will it take the Angelus to restore their systems, Sam?"

"Mother says it's a perpetual virus. It replicates itself. It can't be eradicated because it 'lays eggs' that go undetected. Every time they wipe the virus from their system, the 'eggs' hatch and the cycle begins again. She said it will take the Angelus years to decipher her virus, perhaps longer."

"Sounds as if Mother has left nothing to chance."

"It would seem that way, Olivia. Even the construction of New Eden, despite my chief engineer's resignation, is pretty close to schedule, and let me tell you, construction of anything rarely hits the completion target."

"That could not have happened without you, Sam."

Isenberg was pleased that Olivia seemed genuinely impressed. She lit another smoke and passed one to her.

"All this smoking is making my stomach growl, Sam. I haven' had a bite since I arrived in Denver this morning."

"Feeling pretty famished myself. I can have my chef whip up something fast, Olivia. How does tomato and cucumber slices on quinoa bread with a coleslaw vinaigrette side sound to you?"

"Yuck—no thanks. I have a craving for fried chicken, mmmm ... with garlic-mashed potatoes and gravy."

"Better get used to cucumbers, Olivia, along with tomatoes, peppers, kale and a few herbs, it's one of the few fresh foods our people will be able to grow once we move underground."

Olivia said she was less than thrilled about that.

"Throw in a fat dill pickle and I'll manage," she laughed.

Isenberg called the kitchen to place the order, saying she also needed another pack of cigarettes.

"Bottle of Cabernet Sauvignon, as well," Olivia shouted into the phone before Isenberg could hang up. "And make it a Screaming Eagle cab, if you have some."

"We have wine, but nothing in that stratosphere," Isenberg said. "You'll have to settle for a modest California Cabernet."

When the food arrived, the chef handed Isenberg a pack of cigarettes saying, "Your supply is very low, Ms. Isenberg. Would you like me to grab a carton from your quarters in the bunker?"

Isenberg's eyes nearly popped from their sockets.

"Ida, who told you about the cigarettes in my quarters?"

The chef seemed hesitant to answer, placing forks, knives and wine glasses in their place, avoiding eye contact.

"Ida ..."

"Begging your pardon, Ms. Isenberg," Ida finally said, her hands fidgeting nervously. "Your pledge to quit smoking when you move underground is the reigning joke amongst the kitchen staff, Ms. ... We all know about the cartons of cigarettes you had secretly transported to your quarters last week."

Isenberg lost it.

"You make sure NO ONE goes near my quarters—those cigarettes are not to be touched!"

Ida turned tail and quickly left the room.

"That seemed a little harsh, Sam. Why are you so upset that people know about your secret smoke stash? Hell, I plan on bumming some from you myself."

Isenberg thought for a minute, wondering if the President's daughter, an adversary until this past hour, could be entrusted with the cigarette secret. She concluded full disclosure would reveal more about Olivia's character than any part of their conversation so far. It's what Mother would want her to do.

"There are no cigarettes in those cartons."

"Oh? What are you really telling me, Sam?"

"Mother gave me something for safekeeping, until she arrives. Inside the cases are vials of a formula she created. We are to distribute daily doses to New Eden's people, from the first day of habitation. I opened one of them, couldn't help myself."

"Please tell me it's vitamins, designed to get us through all those months of no meat and no sunshine?"

Isenberg nodded in the negative.

"Some kind of antibiotic, to keep us from getting sick? … Come on Sam, you have to tell me, and you know it."

"Mother says the formula will help us advance, very, very quickly. A thousand years of evolution in three generations is how she framed it. The 90 percent of our brain we really don't use right now …"

"Yes, I'm aware of that."

"Well, that's going to change, Olivia. Mother says the human brain is already capable of sending and receiving telepathic messages. Some of us do it, without knowing, the others just need to be taught. She will teach us."

"I have heard of studies that suggest we have telepathic abilities. Tell me more, Sam. I have to know these things."

"Mother says our level of intelligence will eventually rival that of any species in the Universe. Including the Deus."

"This is fascinating … But why would Mother entrust *you* with all this?"

"She said it was in case something happened to her."

A moment of silence ensued, broken only by lungs breathing, hearts beating and stomachs churning. Olivia's eyes blinked rapidly, like she had an eyelash rubbing against her pupil. Her right hand moved under her chin to prop it up as her head dropped to her shoulders.

"I find these revelations difficult to sift through, Sam. … Did you have the formula analyzed?"

"Indeed, by my own inner circle, no one else could know."

"What did your analysis determine?"

"We could not identify any specific elements. They are unknown to us. But we did determine that, structurally, the elements are arranged like our own DNA helix. Our genetic blueprint has a group of genes whose purpose is still being studied—we don't know what they do, or are capable of doing. Our theory is that Mother's formula will 'release' those genes. For what eventual purpose, only Mother knows."

"Surely you ran some tests …"

"Not on humans. The thinking was that anything conclusive would have taken years of research, Olivia. We tested it on rats, instead. Added small amounts to their drinking water. Within weeks, their entire genome—their complete set of DNA—began some sort of transformation. Physically, they looked the same, except their eyes and tails started turning blue. Their behavior, however, changed dramatically."

"That's incredible. Did the rats survive?"

"We don't know ... the rats escaped from their cages somehow and were never seen again."

"That's so bizarre."

"I find the whole scenario a little scary, Olivia. I've had many a sleepless night trying to come to terms with this shadowy future Mother has in store for us. I don't know if it's right, or if it's wrong. I am at a moral and ethical crossroads, with no clear path ahead."

"For me, the path is *very* clear, Sam. It's horribly wrong to interfere with humanity's natural course of evolution. Bad things will happen, if Mother does this to us. It's too much, too fast. We are not built for a fast-tracked genetic makeover."

"I understand your position, Olivia, it makes sense from a Darwinian perspective. But perhaps we need to keep in mind that Mother *is* our creator ... and maybe that alone gives her the right to alter our genetic destiny so dramatically."

"Humans have free will, Sam. As our creator, she gave us that, it's what sets us apart from other life on Earth. Are we to stand idly by as she takes that away from us?"

"But what if the transformation of humanity turns out to be a wonderful thing, Olivia? What if this was our destiny all along, to evolve into the greatest species in the Universe?"

"I like us as we are. We may have our flaws, but in time we will resolve them. I have faith."

"Well, maybe that's the key here, Olivia ... 'faith.' In the Bible, Genesis 1:27, it's written that God created man in his own image. What if Mother isn't done yet? What if this is the transformation that makes us into beings in *her* own image? What if she is just fulfilling that prophecy?"

"You are a dreamer, Sam. The Bible is full of falsehoods, written by small-minded men who did not understand the true meaning of spirituality. Not to mention all the changes that have been made to it over the centuries by 'holy men' with pompous agendas.

"No, what Mother has in mind doesn't ring true for me," Olivia continued. "I am suspicious of her motives. I mean, she is a Deus—do you really believe the foremost species in the Universe is going to be thrilled when humans rise to challenge their dominance?"

"I have to admit, that prospect *is* chilling. I doubt the Deus will welcome us with open arms."

"Chilling isn't the word here, Sam. I was thinking more along the lines of horribly terrifying. If you like biblical references, ask yourself, what if Mother is Satan, not God? Because, for me, what Mother has in mind for us is pure evil."

"But she is saving us—at least a few of us—from the calamity that will extinguish sentient life on our planet when the Big Waters come. That has to count for something."

"Perhaps. And there is an element of 'rebirth' to this. Water cleanses everything. But ask yourself, Sam, what proof do we have that a catastrophic flood is coming? Why have our scientific experts not detected this?"

Olivia's eyes flew open, like something suddenly made sense to her. Isenberg took note.

"Olivia, you know something, don't you?"

"Maybe. It's a secret project my father is up to his ears in. It might be related ... but, no, it couldn't be."

"Out with it, Olivia."

"I am so sorry, Sam. With the barrage of information I've had to process, it didn't click until just now."

"What didn't click?"

"My father is testing a revolutionary new weapon called a wave bomb, soon, very soon. The detonation is expected to generate a massive tidal wave."

"Do you really think I didn't know about the wave bomb?"

"*You know*? ... Is that what is going to destroy the planet?"

"Yes. Mother predicted it."

"I can't let that happen. I must stop him."

"You will do no such thing."

"I can and I will, Sam. Billions of people will die, needlessly. Don't you see how horribly wrong this is? How could Mother be so evil?"

Olivia slumped forward, then took another one of Isenberg's cigarettes and lit it.

Isenberg watched her, intently. Olivia's eyes told her everything. Isenberg knew what had to be done. In seconds, she had a plan

"I think your concerns may have some merit, Olivia. How could an alien with Mother's powers simply accept that billions of us must die? Could she not have found a way to save more of us or even prevent the flooding? Why save but a select few? It does not sound honorable."

"I don't think I can go through with this plan to transform humanity, Sam. And keeping it all a big secret? The anxiety alone would put me in a very bad place. I don't think I can cope ... I don't think I am capable."

Those last words gave Isenberg pause. Her ploy to draw out the real Olivia was working.

"You only say that because you are tired and hungry, Olivia. You've barely touched your sandwich, and your long journey here must really be catching up to you. Why don't you go get some rest and we can talk about this again when you are refreshed?"

"OK," said Olivia, suddenly looking as fatigued as Isenberg suggested.

"You know what? The kitchen staff are culling the chickens I have on my compound to provide fresh eggs, since we cannot take any livestock with us underground. You wanted fried chicken and mashed with gravy? I can have some made for you by the time you wake up. How is that, feel better?"

"Yeah, sure. Fried chicken. OK."

"Go see Ida in the kitchen. She will show you to your room on the third floor. The one at the back of the house. It's quieter there."

As soon as Olivia left her office, Isenberg made a phone call.

"Nancy, come see me. Now."

Pelligrino arrived within the minute.

"You have been loyal to me and the project, Nancy, and I know I can trust you with anything."

"I will always have your back, Sam. If you brought me here to affront me with useless platitudes—I have more pressing matters to tend to."

"Easy, girl. ... Earlier today, we had the meeting about plants, and some were very poisonous, yes?"

"Not to worry, Sam, I am disposing of the most poisonous ones."

"No—wait. Can a mixture be made from these plants or their seeds that would be strong enough to kill a human?"

"Don't mess with me, Sam. If you want me to concoct something up just say so. ... I saw how you looked at that bimbo. I don't like her being here, either."

"It's not about that, Nancy. It's a duty I must honor."

"It's your duty to end the bimbo's life? Explain, please."

"She is far from being a 'bimbo,' Nancy. Don't be fooled by her physical appearance. But she is not who we thought she was, or could be. Thanks to her outlandish father, she cannot be one of us. Her soul has been corrupted by money, fame..."

"Oh? Are you claiming that money and fame have had no impact on you, Sam? What is this really about?"

"Simple. She knows too much, wants to go back to her daddy. If that happens, expect a military assault on New Eden within hours. I do not trust her to stay quiet."

Pelligrino took a few seconds, then said, "I can do as you ask. The safety of New Eden comes first."

"How soon can you have this concoction ready?"

"When do you need it by?"

"Tonight, before dinner. And it has to taste and look like gravy, chicken gravy."

"Done. We have some chicken bouillon in the pantry. I will find a way to increase the toxic alkaloids without making them taste nasty. The symptoms will be similar to someone having a heart attack.

"Now, Sam, aren't you pleased you attended that plant meeting, after all?"

"Put that smile away, Nancy. And get to work. Keep this 'Last Supper' thing between us."

"As always. You're the boss."

Shortly after Pelligrino left, Isenberg called up Ida in the kitchen.

"Olivia said she likes the room … She's asleep already? Good, very good. Now, I need you to make one serving of fried chicken, with garlic-mashed potatoes. … No need, Nancy is making the gravy."

CHAPTER 34
Stranger things

President Douglas Triton was in the Oval Office, on the phone with the Secret Service agent tasked with finding his daughter, Olivia, and bringing her back to him. He was informed she was still in Samantha Isenberg's compound. All attempts to make contact with her failed.

"Keep trying, agent Wickersham, let me know the minute you have anything. Remember, this stays between us."

Triton was confident Olivia would return, once she realized she was associating with lunatics in an alien-worshipping doomsday cult. What he did not understand was why she went to Isenberg's compound in the first place. Was there a clue in her goodbye letter that he'd missed? No, he would have caught it, he assured himself.

He knew Olivia would miss the perks of their privileged life in Washington, hell who wouldn't. The lavish parties where no expense was spared, the 24-hour concierge and Secret Service protection, flying everywhere first-class, posh golfing weekends with their affluent friends, not to mention the generous clothing budget. If nothing else, Olivia would miss the weekly fashion runs to her favorite shops, Maxfield in West Hollywood, Armani and Oscar de la Renta in New York City. Triton understood Olivia's addiction, it was a rush like no other. For him, it was a new tailored suit once a week to rub shoulders with.

All the better when it's someone else's money. Triton prided himself on not having spent a nickel of his own since he took office.

"If you can't be treated like royalty, what's the point of being president," Triton told his aides when their eyebrows arched over the bills that came pouring in after he took office. Behind his back, the White House accountants used to quip that Triton's personal extravagances alone would bankrupt the government.

President Triton had another busy day ahead. Two work-related meetings, one with his merry band of advisors, the other with General

Isadore Pope, plus the usual make-up, hair and manicure appointments. In the late afternoon he had booked a reading with Michelle Cayce, a popular psychic with the Bentley and beluga elite, who claims to be a descendant of a renowned American mystic.

"Michelle is amazing, she will blow your mind with the accuracy of her predictions," a well-heeled golfing buddy told him when recommending the psychic.

"Why, she even predicted my fourth marriage, said she would be 20 years younger and a blond with hot legs. You've met Bianca. Michelle was bang on. She wants to do a reading for you, Douglas, even said she would dispense with her usual fee. You'd be a fool not to see her."

Triton was looking forward to his session with the psychic. Maybe she could tell him about his next wife. The one he had now was close to her expiry date. He had a few in mind, perhaps she could help him whittle down the candidates.

"Sir, Messrs. Probert, Braddick and Salter are here to see you," one of his aides announced over the intercom.

"Show them in, and bring us the usual hors d'oeuvres, half a dozen Kobe steak sandwiches and some of that donkey milk cheese ... yeah Pule cheese, that's the one. Scottie loves that stuff. ... No, I still have plenty of scotch and bourbon but getting a little low on the Hennessy. Better bring a couple more bottles.

"Make yourselves at home, gentlemen," said Triton, as his staff came through the door.

"Nibbles have been ordered, you know where the refreshments are—more Hennessy is on its way. Olivia will not be joining us for a few days or so. Silly girl ran off to Paris to meet an old boyfriend. You do your best as a father, but you have to let go at some point."

"Paris is wonderful this time of year," said Chief of Staff Adam Probert.

"Paris is wonderful *any* time of year," said Scott Salter, Triton's press secretary.

"Pour me a little more of that single malt, will yah, Scottie," said Probert. "Thirsty as a desert rat today."

"Speaking of rats," said Salter, "I gotta tell you guys this story one of the White House press hacks told me the other day."

"What, his rat is bigger than your rat," laughed Probert.

"No, seriously, hear this, it will blow your mind."

Salter proceeded to spin the tale about a woman who lived on a ranch, came down to the kitchen in the middle of the night and was spooked by a gang of rats with blue eyes and blue tails raiding her refrigerator.

"She called the cops, told them the rats could talk to each other, were organized as shit, and managed to get in through her front door, after disarming the burglar alarm."

"Yeah, I heard about that, lot of people were chatting about it online last week," said Stan Braddick, Triton's chief strategist. "Crazy story. People are saying they must be alien rats from another planet."

"What's crazier is that the rat raids have been reported all over that part of Colorado. Same every time, talking rats raiding the kitchen fridge," Salter said.

After fixing their drinks, the feckless four sat down on the facing couches in the Oval Office.

"First order of business," said Salter, "is sad news. I put a few feelers out to the White House hacks. The press party we wanted to have at Stan's place in the Hamptons is not going to happen. The basic response was they felt it would be a conflict of interest to attend a party exclusively for them and hosted by the President. Many of them also said that if the women were not invited, they weren't going either."

"Since when do journalists have scruples, that is *sooo* yesterday," said Braddick.

"I'm surprised," said Triton, "none of this was going to cost them a plug nickel. Didn't you tell them we were bringing in girls, Scottie?"

"No sir, did not seem appropriate, given the initial responses."

"Idiot. That would have been a deal-maker, count on it."

"Apologies, sir ... can we move on to the next order of business?"

Triton remained obsessed with the press' refusal to attend his party, muttering to himself as the others read the meeting's agenda.

"Next item is mine," said Probert.

"I have the latest economic figures, from the meeting this morning, Mr. President, the downturn continues unabated."

"What meeting, why wasn't I told?"

"Sir, you never go to these meetings, they give you a 'headache.' This is why I attend in your stead."

"Right that one, where they give you all these crazy numbers and expect them to make sense. Break it down for me, just the important parts."

"Of course, sir. To begin with, the top economic indicators are in a downward spiral," said Probert, looking at his notes. "The GDP has dropped seven percent in the last quarter alone. Unemployment levels are still rising, up a whopping 4.3 percent in the last quarter. PCE is down a staggering 13 percent over the same period, the Consumer Sentiment Index has dropped 19 percent. The Fed says inflation is ..."

"Enough already," Triton cried out, putting a hand up like it was a STOP sign. "So, things are bad, the economy is in trouble—that's all you had to tell me. I can take it from there."

"Of course, sir."

"I keep telling you people, the economy will be going great guns, firing on all cylinders, before re-election time even comes around. I have a plan, it's a no-fail plan. Count on it."

"But what do we say to Congress, and what do we tell the American people, about your 'plan?'" said Salter. "Everyone comes to me for answers, especially during the White House briefings where the press is like a pack of hungry wolves going after the same carcass."

The President looked each of his advisors in the face, with eyes meant to remind them who the boss was.

"The American people elected me because they trust me. I never gave them specifics during the campaign, and they bought in. No need to give them anything specific now, either. You just tell them—tell everyone—details will be forthcoming, once some crucial outcomes are fully evaluated."

"Sir, that is the same line you give us to deliver to the press about everything. The House and the Senate are clamoring for *real* specifics. We can only stall them for so long."

"You will stall them for as long as I tell you to stall them," warned Triton. "Do your job and stop whining. Plenty more where you came from."

"Of course, Mr. President."

The intercom beeped again. Triton's aide announced that General Pope had arrived.

"He's *early*. Alright, show him in. ... Gentlemen, I am afraid our meeting must come to an abrupt end. The general and me have important military matters to discuss, none of it for your ears."

"But sir, we still have much to get through," said a dismayed Braddick, flashing the agenda in the air right near Triton's face.

"You heard me. All of you—*out*."

As the three men left the Oval Office with their heads down, the general breezed past them without saying a word.

"Heard anything from Wickersham about Olivia, Mr. President?" Pope asked, after the door closed behind him.

"Nothing new. By the way, anybody asks, you tell them she left for Paris to meet up with an old flame. Be back in a few days."

"Are you sure that's wise, sir—what if she never returns?"

"You questioning my judgement, Pope? You're damn right she's coming back. She will miss me; she will miss all the pretty things I give her."

"Of course, she will, sir."

The general sat down after declining Triton's offer to help himself at the bar.

"You should at least have one of the Kobe steak sandwiches, Pope. Goes down in two chews. Shame to give my leftovers to the bloody staff again. Stuff is too good for them."

The general said he already had lunch at The Lafayette, seared veal loin with hand-cut frites, before heading to the White House. Triton said "suit yourself," then helped himself to one, taking big bites with his little mouth, barely chewing before swallowing.

"First, Mr. President, I want to thank you again for helping out in the Deon Carter case. My boys are good soldiers, they just got a little carried away. If Carter had not fought back like the beast that he is, the boys would've just given him a few bruises to remember them by, instead of putting him down."

"You owe me one, Pope—you think it was easy to get three levels of law enforcement to back off this thing? The local cops were the worst to convince, state troopers backed off when I ordered the Military cops to bury the investigation."

"I do owe you, sir. How unfortunate that a teenager was jogging in the park and witnessed the fight."

"Your boys should not have run off, they should have taken out the witness, would have made it easier to make this whole thing go away."

"Yes, sir. My boys also wanted me to pass along how grateful they are for your help. The press is still doing some digging, even called *me* up, but so far, we are in the clear."

"They won't find anything that will merit charges being laid," said Triton. "My people have made sure of that."

"Sorry to see your people can't seem to do much to help your own situation, sir."

"What are you referring to?"

"It's everywhere in the media, sir. 'U.S. economy has worst quarter since Great Depression,' was the last headline I saw this morning. Every report I have read or heard points the finger at you for the poor economic numbers. Your detractors are having a field day with this, at your expense, sir."

"Being President is not a popularity contest, Pope. All the more reason to move ahead as quickly as possible with the wave bomb, now that your *friend* Colonel Sam Davis has let it spill that others know about our plan to test the device. Good thing you used Mr. Needles, or we might never have got the truth from that traitor.

"Once we knock out the whole Chinese coastline, where so much of their industry is headquartered, our economic problems are over. So, let's not fret over today's headlines. The economy will surge in America again. Count on it."

"We are good to go in five days, sir, maybe sooner," said Pope. "Talked to the scientists this morning. They assured me that, even though this will be the first test outside of the lab, they are confident in their scale projections for the wave's impact. If their calculations are a little off, worst that can happen is we lose Easter Island."

"An acceptable loss, as we already discussed, general. How are you going to be sure none of our ships or aircraft will be in the area at the time of the test?"

"Only way to do that and be certain about it, sir, is to let the Navy and Air Force know we are indeed conducting a secret test in that area of the Pacific. I am doing so in a meeting with the joint chiefs this very evening, sir. They will ask what is going on, of course, but I will make sure they understand it's highly classified. They won't buy it, but I will stick to my guns, sir."

"Any trouble, you tell them the order comes straight from me."

"As you wish, sir."

"What's more, have you followed through on my orders regarding the scientists we believe to be the leakers?"

"Indeed, I have sir. Their final payments are being withheld pending the success of the mission. They have also been told, in no uncertain terms, that if anything else leaks out about the operation, their wives and children will suffer the consequences. I have our special team ready to enact a series of bogus home invasions. Their orders are clear; take no prisoners."

"Excellent, that's why I hand-picked you to lead the operation, Pope. America *will* be the greatest nation on Earth again, thanks to loyal patriots like you."

For the next hour, Triton and Pope went over every detail of the operation in hushed tones, like nervous spies hoping like hell no one was listening. Everything hinged on the test working as expected. There was no Plan B.

For anyone outside the very small circle of conspirators, the wave bomb was being described as a test for a new Top Secret underwater guided missile system. There was no payload installed for the testing, so there was no chance of explosion, the participating military personnel were told.

The scientists needed just a few hours to make adjustments to the wave bomb after the Pacific test, Pope said. Triton would make a big speech shortly after, telling the world that the unfortunate tsunami was the result of shifting tectonic plates in the area that resulted in a powerful undersea earthquake.

Triton would credit American scientists as the source of his information. He would not name any specific scientists. He would also allude to some kind of climate change angle. That would be enough to keep everyone confused for some time, before any real analysis surfaced.

The China payload would be unleashed the very next morning by a new Ohio-class nuclear submarine, the one Triton insisted be christened in his name. The wave bomb will be programmed to detonate once it approached mainland China.

Triton would give another great speech after the tidal wave devastated China, pledging his support for the Chinese and offering to help in any way possible.

"Everyone involved in the mission was assigned very specific tasks with no details provided, over and above what they need to know to carry out their orders," said Pope. "No one person will be able to connect the dots."

"A strong strategy, but still, I need your absolute assurance, general, that other than our little group there is no one else who knows about our true mission."

Pope nodded in the affirmative and had opened his mouth to say something when there was a knock on the Oval Office door.

"Hold on general, it must be important."

"Sir, there is a strange woman being held by White House security. She insists you are expecting her," the Secret Service agent said.

"Get her on the phone."

"Yes, sir, right away, sir."

"Hello Michelle … you are here, already? My apologies, I forget to tell security you were coming to see me. Give me a minute."

***

Michelle Cayce had deep-set eyes as black as her pupils. Puffy circles made them look even darker. She wore no make-up, her shoulder-length hair was white-grey, and her hollow cheeks were a spooky shade of pale. A crinkled trench coat covered her from neck to knees. Low-wedge black shoes completed her attire.

Triton was expecting a stylish woman, one who was comfortable with the glamor and glitz that defined the lifestyles of her rich and famous clients, and looked the part.

"My apologies for my appearance, Mr. President. I have not been well."

"You do look um … tired, Michelle, and it must be such a long drive from where you live, somewhere in Vermont, right?"

"Yes, a small town called Shaftsbury near Glastenbury Mountain. I moved there recently, after I detected a very strong presence in the area. I have a driver, that is not why I am so fatigued.

"Mr. President, for months now, I have been having visions. Disturbing visions. Death, destruction, water everywhere ... I have never felt anything so strongly before. I have not slept well for weeks."

President Triton was pacing in front of Cayce as he listened. Her black eyes were fixed on him, following his path as he crisscrossed the Oval Office. They never blinked. The only part of her that moved was her mouth when she spoke, exposing nicotine-stained teeth behind thin lips.

"There is a darkness coming, Mr. President. I am searching for the source of this darkness. In my visions, I see Glastenbury Mountain. I see glowing blue lights at the base of the mountain. I see faces swirling within the coming darkness, like they are drowning in its shadows. Yours is the only face I recognize."

Triton's eyes stopped dead. He wanted to pull away from her as she stepped toward him, but his feet would not lift. She reached forward and seized both his hands with hers. Triton tried to shake her off, but his hands went numb when he felt the icy touch of her fingers.

"The darkness *is* with you ... but you are *not* its source."

Triton felt his hands being released. Michelle Cayce turned away from him and headed for the door.

"*Guards*—GUARDS—arrest this witch!"

CHAPTER 35
As high as the Sun

At the San Francisco International Airport, Delia and Jimi wished Sanchez a safe journey, just before he boarded his flight for Denver. For Jimi, his "See you later, alligator" goodbye was meant to be taken literally. He did not like the man, and he knew the feeling was mutual, despite Sanchez playing nice with him when others were around. They had been in the city loved by fog less than 12 hours. In that time, Sanchez had threatened to smash his "pretty little face" to smithereens, every time Delia was out of earshot.

Sanchez was upset that he was being sent away, claiming Delia was still vulnerable even though Mother was gone. He also reminded Delia of his sworn duty to protect her. She brushed off the threat of danger and insisted Sanchez had to go, even booked his flight when he refused. Jimi knew she did it for his sake.

Delia told Jimi they could stay in the Golden Gate city for five days, then they must also head to their final destination.

"You will love it here, Jimi. It's my home town, I know all the best places."

Jimi wanted to spend his last days of "normal life" partying like it was the year Prince immortalized in song. Delia reeled in the Vegas party boy, even forbade him his favorite elixir. When he barked about the ban like the sea lions frolicking in the water while they were lunching at Pier 39, she caved.

"You can be incredibly annoying, Jimi. OK, you can have a few drinks, but nothing until after dinner. No booze after midnight. When we pick up my daughter, the drinking stops."

Jimi reluctantly agreed, after being told booze was forbidden in New Eden. He may as well get used to the dry life. He had one demand of his own, however: They had to book a suite at the Highmont Hotel for the remainder of their stay.

"I really want to experience the Royal Suite, Delia. I read that's where famous celebrities and legendary musicians have spent the night—imagine the karma."

"I know the Highmont. Isn't that also where greasy politicians shagged their dirty little secrets and nasty gangsters planned bloody mob hits? Imagine the stench."

"But if it's the Highmont you want, come on, it's not far from here. We'll jump on the cable car at California Street, take us up to Nob Hill, where the Highmont is."

The Royal Suite was not available. The stiff-collared clerk explained it was booked by a high-ranking government official for the next two weeks. They did manage to snag the Dynasty Suite, two bedrooms, two bathrooms and a comfortable sitting area. Delia saying it was perfect because her daughter would have her own room.

They had electrifying sex the first night. Twice in the shower, in between taking turns to lather each up with the silky gel provided by the hotel.

Jimi told Delia he would never desire another woman. Delia smiled when he said that, but did not return the sentiment.

By midnight, the scent of their lovemaking filled the room. They lay in each other's arms, hot, sweaty bodies sticking to each other like human glue.

Jimi wanted to say "I love you, Delia," but held back. There was something frightening about that phrase. He did not remember ever having said those words before, and actually meaning them. He did come close to telling her, but couldn't get past the fear that, if he didn't say the words with conviction, 'I love you' would drop from his mouth like a dreaded cliché.

Jimi asked Delia about growing up in San Francisco. She only talked about her four-year-old daughter and how nervous she was going to be when they picked her up.

"I have not seen Audrey in almost a year, Jimi. My parents kept her shielded from me, and refused to let me see her."

"But she's your kid, how can they do that to you?"

"I guess I'll have to tell you what happened. My parents are good people, they were protecting Audrey … from me and my, um, problems."

"OK, you've piqued my curiosity …"

"Five years ago, my professional life was in the ditch. Then I met a man, really smart, owned a little start-up tech company here in the Tenderloin, close to where some of the tech giants were headquartered. He did well. We had planned to marry. I got pregnant. Then he was offered $500 million for his little company by a tech firm that craved an app he just developed. He sold out, became addicted to the high life—there were drugs stashed everywhere in our bay-front condo. He was so strung out he failed to see our lives were going nowhere. Fast.

"When I was seven months into the pregnancy, I came home early one day. Found him in bed with another woman. I went to live with my parents, it was finished between us.

"Just before Audrey was born, he came to my parents' house, wanting me back, and promising to be a good father. He was still using. He couldn't hide it from me. My parents freaked out, urged me to keep him away from the baby.

"I gave birth at home, with the help of my father's friend who was a doctor, and Audrey was registered as my mother's daughter. We filled the form out online. One day the guy came around again, but my parents told him I'd moved to L.A. and warned him never to come back. My parents moved to Pacific Heights shortly after, where they still live today."

Jimi listened like he was a priest taking confession.

"I was a total wreck, Jimi. The birth was traumatic and I suffered from severe post-partum depression. I was crying all the time, I couldn't sleep. It wasn't long before antidepressants and mood stabilizers ruled my life. I was a drug addict, but it was legit because doctors prescribed them.

"I tried to kick the drugs cold turkey and became totally psychotic. The mood swings were unbearable for my parents, they could not handle the drama. Said I was ruining Audrey's life before she even had a chance to grow up. Eventually, things came to a head. They kicked me out and took Audrey from me, threatening to call social services if I dared try to take her back."

Delia went on to tell Jimi she had nowhere to go, and she had no money. She got busted for stealing some expensive clothes for Audrey, with the intention of impressing her parents when she visited at Christmas. They vowed that Delia would never see Audrey again after her conviction.

She hooked up with some old friends who were rich, raving party people. They offered her a room in their seven-bedroom mansion. It wasn't long after that she was in hospital, on her deathbed as the result of a heroin overdose.

"That's when Mother saved me, Jimi, otherwise I would be ashes in an urn on my parents' mantle."

"It's incredible you survived all of that," said Jimi, pulling her in closer and tightening his arms around her.

Jimi sensed there was more to the story than Delia was telling. But he was high on the moment, so he let things slide. Except for one nagging little detail.

"About Mother, you are sure she is gone, right?"

Delia offered no reply.

"Mother is gone for good, Delia? I need to know …"

"Yes … she is gone."

Jimi believed her. Because he wanted desperately to believe her. If she was lying to him, he knew it would kill him. They did not speak for some time. Delia rolled over and turned her back on him, mumbling something about her arm falling asleep and she had to change positions.

"What will life be like in New Eden?" Jimi finally said. "How will people deal with being the only ones left on the planet? The whole idea scares the crap out of me."

Delia turned back around to face him, her eyes spicy. She pressed against him, her hand reaching down between his legs.

Jimi forgot all his troubles, forgot all his cares.

Delia's eyes opened early the next day. The gap between the curtains let the morning light come streaming across her face; nature's wake-up call. She rolled on top of sleeping Jimi, two darts dangling above his mouth. He woke up slowly, but a smile came quickly.

After slippery sex in the shower again, Delia said they would spend the day sightseeing, before picking up Audrey in the evening. Jimi said he was on edge about meeting her parents. She told him not to worry, they knew nothing about him. He was to wait around the corner in a cab, while she went inside to get Audrey.

"My parents gave me permission to see Audrey, and I had to plead with them just for that. But she is not going back to them. We are taking her with us to New Eden. Audrey must live."

The thought of sharing Delia with her daughter gave Jimi the willies. What if Audrey didn't like him? He decided to wait before beating himself up over something that hadn't happened. It may just turn out OK.

As he was getting cleaned up before they went out, Jimi noticed his penis had developed a bluish tint on its head, like he'd been poking it into a can of blue paint.

"What the hell?" he said, as he tried to rub it off, again and again. He scrubbed it hard with a soapy towel, but the color would not come off.

Delia came barging into the bathroom.

"Aren't you ready yet?"

"Look, my dick is turning blue. I should see a doctor."

Delia grasped his penis, then turned it from one side to the other.

"It looks like bruising to me, Jimi. You're an animal in the bedroom."

After passing on Alcatraz, Jimi saying just looking at the fabled penitentiary gave him the creeps, Delia gave him a quick tour around town. Fisherman's Wharf, the Presidio and Baker Beach, lunch in Chinatown, followed by a leisurely stroll along Land's End, watching the Pacific pounding the rocks like it was furious they were in its path.

Then they rented Segways, barreling down Lombard, "the crookedest street in the world," like snowboarders carving through fresh powder. Jimi lost control of his scooter on the last of the eight hairpin turns, trying to catch up with Delia. His body flipped sideways off the two-wheeler. The Segway stayed on the road and came to a dead stop. He landed in a garden filled with lush hydrangeas to soften the blow. He got up laughing, saying the ride was a blast.

Jimi was still picking pieces of the hydrangea bushes from his clothing as he waited in a cab near Delia's parents' home later that day. He assumed he would be waiting for an hour or more, what with all the questions and demands her parents must have. He hoped that was enough time to quell the jitters he was feeling again. Minutes later, he saw Delia walking his way, holding hands with a little girl.

They got into the back seat with him.

"Jimi, this is Audrey."

"Hi Audrey, very nice to meet you."

"Nice to meet you, too. My mommy says you are a very special man."

Audrey had long, reddish-brown hair and dazzling blue eyes. She was tall for her age, and looked like a princess when she smiled, Jimi thought.

"Well, I'm glad your mom thinks I'm special. I think you're special, too."

Jimi liked the girl. Things were going to work out just fine.

The sun was quick to chase the fog from the Golden Gate on their last day in San Francisco. By the afternoon, it was 78 F, balmy for early May on that part of the California coast.

When Audrey was asked what she would like to do, she chose to visit her favorite place, Golden Gate Park.

"They have everything there, amazing slides, an aquarium with big fish, a fun playground and a fun carousel ride!"

"It's a beautiful park, Jimi, we *must* go. We can have dinner at the Cliff House, you will love the view."

"OK, I'm sold. Sounds like it's going to be a wonderful day."

The trio got out of their cab on Fulton Avenue, walked down 8th Avenue, then trekked the rest of the way on John F. Kennedy Drive until they reached the playground. Audrey walked in the middle, holding Jimi and Delia by the hand. Just like a real family, Jimi was thinking. It felt good, it felt right.

Audrey and Jimi went together on the big slides, then he pushed her on the swings, as high as the chains would allow. Delia watched them, smiling, quickly brushing her bangs from her face when the wind tussled them over her eyes, like she didn't want to miss a second of Jimi and Audrey.

The sound of organ music playing grew louder as they neared the carousel. Audrey was excited and couldn't wait for their turn. Jimi straddled a reindeer, Audrey got on a white horse and Delia hopped onto a dragon.

Audrey and Jimi laughed their way through the ride. When it was over, Jimi rushed over to the ticket wicket and bought another round. Audrey said, "Thank you, daddy." Jimi's heart was on fire. He could not believe this was happening to him.

As they walked toward the entrance to Steinhart Aquarium, Audrey let go of their hands and started running with another bunch of children eager to get inside. She was the cheeriest child in the bunch.

Delia turned to Jimi and said, "Are you happy?" Jimi wanted to say yes, he had never known such joy. Instead, tiny tears streamed down his face as he looked at her.

The view from their table at the Cliff House had Jimi reaching for superlatives to describe what he was seeing. To the north was the gleaming orange outline of the Golden Gate, a steady stream of cars and trucks snaking their way across its sturdy frame. Down below he could see the whitecaps riding the waves as they attacked the cliff.

"This is the third version of the Cliff House," Delia explained, in response to Jimi's question about the restaurant's history.

"The original burned down in 1894, but the owner, Adolph Sutro was his name, built a huge Victorian palace—right on the cliff-top here. I've seen the old photographs. It was a sight to behold. The palace survived the big earthquake in 1906, but a fire the following year destroyed most of the building. After Sutro died, his daughter rebuilt the Cliff House we are eating in today."

Delia ordered the ocean beach sandwich, Audrey went for the fish and chips, while Jimi declared the hefty half-pound burger with garlic fries was a "must try."

When the waitress asked what he would like to drink, Jimi ordered the same as Delia, sparkling water. He didn't even feel like wine or a cocktail. His heart was content, free from the sorrow that consumed him since the day he was born. His mind was at peace, he saw a purpose ahead for his life. He wanted to be with Delia and Audrey for the rest of his days.

After dinner, they joined the crowd atop the cliffs near the restaurant for a stroll. Jimi and Delia were discussing whether it was getting too late to take Audrey to see a movie.

Audrey pointed out to sea and said, "Look mommy, the water is as high as the Sun."

Others noticed the fast-approaching wall of water and the air filled with blood-curdling shrieks. Some people froze, watching the giant wave with terror-filled eyes.

"We're all gonna die! … We're all gonna die!" a man kept screaming as he pushed his way through the madness, stepping on top of people that had been knocked over like they were part of the ground.

Jimi was one of the traumatized, his mouth open, wanting to scream. A mile out into the ocean, a wall of water as high and wide as he could see was headed right for the shore. Jimi's eyes rolled in their sockets. He dropped to the ground like he was already dead.

Delia calmly removed the three lifeboats from her pocket. She put one in Audrey's hand and helped her squeeze it. Instantly, a giant bubble formed around the shocked little girl, rising off the ground, then hovering about 20 feet in the air.

"Everything will be fine, sweetheart. Mommy and daddy will be right behind you."

Delia looked out to sea. The wall of water was about to sweep San Francisco into oblivion. Quickly, she bent over and placed a lifeboat in Jimi's lifeless hand and squeezed. His body was instantly engulfed by the same clear bubble. He floated upwards until he was right next to Audrey.

Just as the tidal wave breached the cliffs, Delia's bubble joined the other two. All three rose like rockets straight up in the air, until they were well above the surging seas. Beneath the billowing mist, there was nothing but ocean, for as far as the eye could see.

***

Reports of the oceans rising up all over the planet and flooding the continents took Samantha Isenberg and her people by surprise. When Isenberg's Washington mole arrived in New Eden, he said the tidal wave would not hit until the next day. Now they had less than 20 minutes to finish moving the last of the campers and supplies underground before the giant waves arrived.

Chaos overwhelmed New Eden. People screeched like crazed lemmings as they scurried to the bunker's entrance, discarding belongings that slowed them down along the way.

One man went totally berserk, chasing after Isenberg, yelling profanities and threatening to kill her. Christo Sanchez got to him just as he was about to grab Isenberg by the neck. Sanchez bent him backwards over his knee and snapped his spine in two.

Delia, Audrey and Jimi came floating down from the sky, landing amidst the mass of frenzied humanity, just as the rushing waters were minutes from submerging the whole area. Delia made the lifeboats disappear and with a now-awake Jimi and her daughter in tow, raced for the entrance to the underground habitat.

The airlocks closed shut just as the raging waters came thundering over the stone roof of New Eden like Niagara Falls on steroids. The chaos turned to eerie silence. People were holding onto each other, crying softly. Some were on their knees, their heads bowed, deep in prayer.

The sound of the pounding water was deafening. One nervous woman told others around her they were doomed, saying the whole mountain was going to wash away.

There was no fear in Delia's eyes. After moving Jimi and Audrey to a safe location, she asked them to stay put, there was something she needed to do. Audrey said she would be fine as long as Jimi stayed with her.

"Where is Olivia Triton?" was the first thing Delia said when she found Samantha Isenberg.

"She's no longer with us. The sins of a life burdened by avarice and arrogance broke her once-noble soul. She enjoyed her last supper."

"Why didn't you wait for my arrival, Sam?"

"She wanted to stop her father from testing the wave bomb. I had no choice."

"You could have easily prevented that from happening without taking her life."

"She was beyond repair, Mother."

CHAPTER 36
House of cards

President Douglas Triton was in the Oval Office with General Isadore Pope. They were in the mood for celebrating after giving the order to proceed with testing the wave bomb, a day ahead of schedule.

Their plan was unfolding as they envisioned. Both men had smiles on them that would befit drunks in a strip joint offering free lap dances.

"History will remember us as true American patriots, perhaps the greatest ever, if I have a say in it," said Triton.

"It's a glorious day, Mr. President. We are *men of history.*"

"Damn right we are, Pope. And to think some crazy loon calls herself a psychic told me I was part the darkness … *'part of the darkness,'*" said Triton, doing his best imitation of the Wicked Witch of the West in the *Wizard of Oz.*

"This calls for Hennessey and a fine cigar," said Pope as he went over to the bar by the window.

"I have a box of Cohibas here somewhere, Pope," said Triton as he fumbled through the drawers of his desk. "*Ahh.* Here they are, right next to my vintage Colt .45, still works like the day it was made."

Phone calls started coming in, but every time Pope or Triton answered, the calls went dead. Triton cursed that whomever was playing phone tag with them would have their fingernails extracted.

"What is that? … *Oh my god …*" said Pope, his snaky eyes breaking wide open as he stared out the big windows in the Oval Office.

President Triton dropped the Cohibas. He came up behind Pope, who was still staring out the window. Triton pulled the trigger on his Colt .45 and shot Pope in the back of the head. The general snapped forward as blood and brains splattered in all directions, his body falling into the table in front of the window, breaking it in half.

"You son of a bitch, this is all your …"

Before Triton could finish, a towering wall of seawater swept the White House from the face of the Earth like it was made of playing cards.

CHAPTER 37
The sermon

"Delia …"

"Yes, Mother…"

"The time has come, my child. Have a long, peaceful rest."

"You are the Divine One. You gave me life again after I destroyed it. You gave me back my daughter. Audrey will be your *greatest* disciple. I am ever so grateful … I ask only that Audrey, and Jimi, be looked after. Mother, I love them, I want them to be happy."

"Peace be with you, my child."

"Mother … may I come visit Audrey sometime, just for a little while? Will you let me come back?"

Mother's answer was swift.

"Have a long, peaceful rest, my child."

"I am yours. Take me."

Mother was alone. But then, she had *always* been alone. The most advanced being in the Universe was fated to solitary existence, one that harbored secrets she could *never* share.

Her plan took a million years to reach this point. Another 100 years and the humans would be ready. She had persevered, despite her miscalculations along the way. She was all-powerful, but not invincible.

She did what had to be done.

***

Mother surveyed the contents of the giant warehouse situated directly beneath New Eden. A cavern below a cavern. No one else knew of its existence. She built it more than 2,000 years ago, when the mountainous terrain was but occasionally traversed by roaming tribes of indigenous people. This is why she had Samantha Isenberg purchase the acreage from the ancestors of those who once called this land home. This is why she had New Eden built right over top of it.

For hundreds of years, she stocked the cavern with items the humans would need to build a new society. With the innovative materials, tools and instruments she collected from across the Universe, a functioning new village could be built in a matter of days. There would be unlimited power for all of their needs, sourced from dark energy. Mother also stored a replica of her laboratory from Caelum in the warehouse. She would need it to continue refining the genetic formula she would administer to the humans, as well as finding a way to extend her life force, indefinitely.

From her pocket, Mother took the small cylinder she used to collect the energy that once sustained Xeno's life force. She placed it on the back of her neck and absorbed a small amount. Her body began to rise off the ground. She moved forward without walking, heading for the secret tunnel that led to the center of the habitat above her, where the survivors had gathered.

The design for New Eden included a large central square to be used for distributing provisions, holding meetings and other social functions. Its standing-room capacity was just enough to fit the colony's residents. As Mother drifted up the vertical tunnel that led to the square, the sound of chaos echoed off the stone walls like a seething speed metal band in warp drive.

"I have a rebellion to quell," she sighed, as she reached the entrance and surveyed the bedlam.

Backed tightly into a corner of the crowded square were Samantha Isenberg and her four lieutenants. They looked like bandits about to be strung up by a lynch mob. Isenberg stood atop a makeshift podium of wooden crates, stacked high enough so that the tiny woman could see over top of the dissenters, waving her little hands in the air and shouting, "Listen to me people!"

"You lied to us you scheming little bitch!" "You will pay for what you have done!" "We're all going to die!!" were the loudest of the hollers reaching Mother.

A man waving a Bible got up on the crates with Isenberg, pushed her aside and shouted at the crowd, saying: "The Apocalypse is here! This is the end of days—the prophets were right!"

"Don't listen to him," Isenberg shouted back. "Apocalypse is ancient Greek for an uncovering, a revelation. What it really means is a new beginning—not the end of days."

A woman brandishing a knife yelled out, "She is a devil worshipper—off with her head!"

It's disturbing how quickly the brilliant human mind can descend into darkness when raw emotion crushes its intellect, Mother observed. That will soon change.

From her thoughts, she dispatched an energy wave to locate the cigarette cartons stashed in Isenberg's quarters. Cases of drinking glasses were found in the dry goods storeroom.

In the corner where Isenberg was holed up, the standoff got uglier. Isenberg began shouting overwrought slogans like, "I have seen the light—you can too!" "This is for your own good." "God works in mysterious ways!"

With that last declaration, the mob began throwing things at her, whatever they had on hand or in their pockets. Keys, lip sticks and coins poured like metallic rain over Isenberg and her people.

Barging his way toward the battered corner came Christo Sanchez, throwing kicks and landing punches on anyone who tried to hold him back. Just before he reached Isenberg, three men tackled him from behind and Sanchez crumbled to the floor beneath them. More bodies swamped over him until he was completely pinned down.

Mother took that as her cue.

Like an angel without wings, she ascended to the middle of the square's 30-foot ceiling. Her body circled slowly in place as she gazed down at the angry mob. A vivid blue light came streaming from her eyes, the glow becoming brighter as it spread throughout the cavern until the shadows vaporized.

The mob grew silent. Hands shielded tender eyes as the blue light became blinding.

"Our god is here!" Sanchez yelled, pointing a finger up at Mother's circling figure.

Mother smiled down at the humans, her radiance dimming considerably, as everyone stared up at her.

"She's not a god!" yelled a voice in the crowd. "It's another one of Isenberg's dirty tricks."

"This is a simulation, she's a freakin' hologram," said another angry voice.

Isenberg got on her makeshift podium again and shouted back.

"She is *not* the god of our bibles—*we* created that god. She is the Divine One, our Creator."

Some people started picking up the coins and other small items that were previously thrown at Isenberg and began hurling them at Mother. The flying objects passed right through her, bouncing from the ceiling then falling back down.

"She *must* be a hologram, stuff passed right through her. Let's find the projector, we can prove this is a hoax," rang the voice of a dissenter.

Mother's arms raised slowly from her side, palms turned up, like she had seen a Pope do during a holy mass in St. Peter's Square years ago. A softer blue light radiated from her.

The dissenting voices slowly died down. There was silence for a minute, then hushed prayers broke out, too low and too many to be distinguished.

"You are all my children, no harm shall come to you," Mother said, like a parent comforting a frightened child.

Jimi James had been watching the madness unfold from the safety of a recess in the square's chiseled walls, a trembling Audrey under his protective arm.

"Daddy, what's mommy doing?"

"That's not your mommy, Audrey."

"Where did my mommy go?"

"We will find her. We will bring her back to us."

"Are you still my daddy?"

"Yes, sweetheart. I will always be here for you."

Audrey snuggled tight against Jimi's leg. He put a hand over her eyes.

A determined Sanchez pushed his way to the center of the square until he was directly below Mother. He got on his knees, made the sign of the cross, then clasped his hands together in prayer.

Out of the blue light, glasses half-filled with water appeared above each person in the crowd. A shimmering, halo-like circle held each glass in place.

A woman reached up and took hold of the glass above her head.

"This is not a hologram," she said to those around her.

One by one the others reached for their glass, until everybody held one. With her arms, Mother signaled for them to come closer, until a massive human circle formed around her slowly spinning figure.

"Drink, my children. Drink of my essence. You will be born anew. You will find peace."

Jimi did not drink from his glass. He poured it on the floor, then did the same with Audrey's.

When they finished drinking the water, some of the people did as Sanchez had done. Within minutes, everyone in the square was kneeling. As if on cue, they held their empty glasses high in the air in Mother's direction, like good soldier's saluting their leader.

Mother's aura was spellbinding. She shone brightly once more. This time, no one raised a hand to shield their eyes. The kneeling souls were like receptors, absorbing Mother's glow like it was the light of life.

"My children. Behold your Creator. Join me for a new beginning, and let us dream as one. Together, we will reach the stars. Together, we will rule the heavens. Together, we shall claim the Universe as our own."

"Amen."

CHAPTER 38
'Valley of Ashes'

Jimi cared for Audrey like she was his own blood. The connection he felt when they first met in San Francisco grew stronger with each passing day. Every time Audrey called him "daddy," his eyes still got wet. He came to understand why Mother wanted him along for the journey, the real reason why she kept telling him she needed him.

Neither he nor Audrey drank the water ration passed around during breakfast in the colony's cafeteria, where everyone ate their meals except for Samantha Isenberg, her four lieutenants, and Mother. After the first month at New Eden, everyone developed a bluish tint to their eyes. A few weeks later, their skin began turning a pale shade of blue.

"The Blue Ones," Jimi called them. He realized it was only a matter of time before the Blues noticed his eyes were still brown, his skin still pale white—if they hadn't already. He worried about what would happen to him and Audrey if they were found out. Would they be snubbed by the others? Would they be punished?

Right the next day, Jimi was told by one of Isenberg's lieutenants he had to make himself useful, be a more productive member of the colony. She also asked him if he was drinking the daily water ration. He insisted he was, as she inspected his eyes and examined his skin color.

"I want to see you again in one week's time," Nancy Pelligrino told him. "Bring Audrey with you. We will run some tests."

Jimi and Audrey began drinking the water ration the next morning. Better Blue, than sorry.

Audrey was in school every day, as there were no longer such things as weekends, holidays or days off. Mother did not like the human pattern of time, as divided by days, weeks and months. The days became just numbers, but there were still 365 of them in the year.

In keeping with Pelligrino's directive, Jimi applied for a position on the kitchen staff. It was the only job posting he had a chance to qualify for. Other openings included assistant building engineer and health care provider.

A crash course on food preparation was arranged for Jimi. When he reported for duty the first day, there was music playing in the New Eden kitchen. A woman with long grey hair brushed back past her forehead, heavy in the hips and wearing a weathered white apron, was singing along.

"Just a slave like one of us …"

Jimi recognized the song instantly, *One of Us* by Joan Osborne. He found it odd the woman substituted the word "slave" for "slob," as it was sung in the original, then remembered that Prince also recorded a version using slave in place of slob on his *Emancipation* album.

"Hello, I'm Jimi, here for the cooking course."

"I was expecting you. My name is Ida."

"I see you are a *Prince* fan …"

"So, you know his version of the song? Yes, I always change the 'slob' to 'slave,' like Prince did. Being in this place, it has a ring of truth to it."

"I hear you, Ida. Why not play the Prince version, then?"

"I couldn't find it in the colony's music library. Music helps me pass the time while I work. Put this apron on, Jimi, let's get cracking. I think we are going to get along splendidly."

They did. Jimi discovered he had a flair for cooking. It became a creative outlet for him. He also enjoyed the music on the kitchen staff's playlist. Many were David Bowie fans and the cooks got into some great sing-alongs as they worked, especially during *Rebel Rebel,* making fist pumps with hands held high in-between chopping up vegetables.

With limited food supplies in New Eden until the homegrown crops reached maturity, the cooks had to improvise, rewriting recipes to reflect what was available. They were able to concoct interesting meals for the residents, utilizing grains like wheat and rice, root crops like carrots, potatoes and beets, and dried legumes like beans and peas.

"Garlic is a special food with unique nutrients, so preparation is key," Ida explained as part of Jimi's ongoing training.

"First, you have to crush the cloves to release the allicin compound, let it rest for 15 minutes so the allicin can kick in. Then you only add it to the last few minutes of cooking, so as to maintain the strength of the compound."

This particular vegetarian stew they were working on was going to be served to Samantha Isenberg and Mother, Ida informed him.

"You cook everything for Samantha and Mother?" Jimi wanted to know.

"Yes. In fact, I used to be Ms. Isenberg's personal chef. When we heard the tidal wave was approaching, all hell broke loose as people rushed to get underground. I got pushed along by a bunch of screaming maniacs into the airlock at the habitat's entrance. I'm not even sure I am supposed to be here. Ms. Isenberg was happy to see me anyway, put me in charge of the main kitchen. I cook everything for the leaders of New Eden."

"How is Mother, if I may ask?" said Jimi, as he cleaned some carrots before dicing them up.

"I hear the leaders talk, especially while I am serving them. They are so used to having me around because I also served them before we came to live underground. They say Mother is not well. Sometimes she doesn't come to eat for many days in a row. Ms. Isenberg takes food to her."

"Do you know where Mother is staying? No one has seen her for a long time."

"Some 'secret place,' people tell me."

"I have been everywhere in New Eden, through every passageway. My daughter Audrey likes to explore. Never found any 'secret' places."

"From what I've heard, the secret place has been here much longer than New Eden."

"That doesn't surprise me. Mother has many secrets."

Ida gave Jimi one of those looks that said, "You know more than I do?"

"Do they know what's wrong with Mother?"

"I heard Ms. Isenberg and the others talking about her just the other day, Jimi. They didn't seem to care I could hear them as I served their dinner. Ms. Isenberg was telling her people she had urged Mother to take her medication."

"One of Ms. Isenberg's staff said Mother looks *very* weak, 'like a walking corpse.' I think that's the reason she has not appeared in public lately."

Jimi finished dicing the carrots, put them in a giant stainless-steel pot, then started peeling potatoes.

"When did you last see Mother, Ida?"

"A few weeks ago, in one of the tunnels. I was going to the library to pick up a cookbook. She was coming from somewhere below. I bowed my head as she passed by."

"Ida, please keep this to yourself, but do Mother or Ms. Isenberg ever talk about Audrey ... or me?"

"Not whenever I've been around them. Why do you ask?"

"No reason ... Do they ever talk about Delia?"

"I'm sorry, who is Delia?"

"Never mind."

During one of Jimi's shifts a few days later, Pelligrino stepped into the kitchen to let the staff know about a town hall meeting in the square.

"All must attend," she said. "Ms. Isenberg is going to make an important announcement."

After everyone gathered in the square that evening, Isenberg and her lieutenants entered, their faces blank.

"I know we promised we would be returning to the surface soon to begin construction of our new home," said Isenberg. "Unfortunately, I have sad news."

The silence was deafening.

"The drone we launched from New Eden has returned. Two days ago, we completed our analysis of the data. The preferred location for our village is not as safe as we'd hoped. Radiation levels are too high. When the seas washed over the Earth, nuclear facilities, factories housing lethal materials used in manufacturing, and toxins we had long buried underground, were uprooted and tossed all over the planet.

"We are scouting a new location, but it will take time. I ask for your patience and ..."

Jimi stopped hearing Isenberg's words when someone whispered in his ear.

"I have news. We should talk."

It was Christo Sanchez. Jimi agreed to meet him near the tunnel by the library. He left Audrey in Ida's care.

"We will also expand the agricultural space to grow more food," Isenberg was saying as Jimi left the square.

Sanchez was popping a coca leaf into his mouth as Jimi arrived.

"Some habits never die, eh Sanchez?"

"Too bad for you, bourbon doesn't grow on trees."

"Yeah, you're still a jerk ... Isenberg said the farm is expanding. I'll bet you won't have coca leaf for much longer."

"I won't let that happen."

"Look, what do you want, Sanchez?"

"I see your skin is like mine, less blue than the others."

"I started drinking the 'Kool-Aid' much later. Like you did, apparently."

Sanchez stopped chewing on the leaf. He gave Jimi his dead serious look.

"Isenberg lies, Jimi. They had the results of the drone data analysis weeks ago."

"Well, looks like we're going to be stuck living underground for another year, so who cares if she wasn't honest about *when* they knew?"

"Another lie, Jimi. Ten generations of our people will live and die before we can survive above ground. The radiation levels are deadly, much higher than Isenberg says.

"Even Mother calls the land above us the 'Valley of Ashes.'"

"I don't believe you, Sanchez. Why would they lie to us about something that serious?"

"It was Mother who ordered Isenberg to even tell us that much. Delia also told me she was the one who convinced Mother to give Isenberg that order."

"You've spoken to Delia? ... Sanchez, *don't lie to me.*"

"I have, Jimi. I am not lying. Maybe I don't like you much, but she does."

"But how could *you* see her? Nobody sees her. I've tried."

"I am Mother's personal guard, Jimi. I watch over the tunnel that goes down to her living quarters. No one gets past me without Mother's say-so."

Jimi's mouth started talking before he knew what it was going to say.

"Take me to her."

"I can't. Mother has forbidden Delia from seeing you, or Audrey."

"But how do you know that?"

"I told you, I'm on guard at the entrance to the tunnel. When Isenberg goes down there for meetings, their voices carry up the tunnel like I'm sitting in the same room with them."

Jimi stepped right up to Sanchez, his eyes looking down at him like knives.

"Tell me what you heard. Tell me everything you know."

"Why the hell do you think I'm here? Delia sent me. I have a message for you."

Jimi took a step back. His head felt like it was going to spin off his neck. Sanchez reached out to steady him.

"Don't faint on me, Jimi. You want to hear Delia's message, don't you?"

Jimi gave him a nod; Sanchez delivered the message.

Mother found a solution to the radiation problem, he began. In her laboratory, she modified a component of the genetic brew that's added to the water supply for New Eden. Her plan is to alter human physiology, so it can neutralize the radioactive isotopes in the wasteland above.

There was only one problem, said Sanchez.

"It will take the 10 generations I mentioned earlier, before we evolve to the point where our bodies can neutralize the isotopes."

"No, Mother is a Deus. She can fix that."

"Mother is weak, Jimi. She grows weaker every day. She's severely depressed, because she cannot accept her failure. I've heard Isenberg talk to her about it. It's sad, very sad."

Jimi could see tears welling in Sanchez's eyes.

"Sanchez, don't give up hope."

"We're going to die in this grave under the ground, Jimi. We are the last humans. We are doomed."

"It's because we are the last of our kind that Mother *will* find a way to save us. I know this."

"If you saw how weak Mother is, you would not believe that, Jimi. Our god is not the real God."

Jimi put his head down. He thought about Delia. Asked Sanchez how it was he could talk to her.

"When Mother is resting, Delia emerges This is why Delia can speak with me, Jimi."

Jimi remembered a question he never got an answer to.

"If Mother dies, will Delia die with her?"

"Delia told me she doesn't know what will happen if Mother dies, Jimi. Isenberg keeps telling Mother to revive herself, claims there is some kind of energy source she can tap into. But Mother refuses, like she would rather stay weak to punish herself. They argue about it all the time."

"But, if Mother stays weak, will Delia get stronger?"

"Nobody knows … but Delia wanted me to tell you she's trying, Jimi. She wants to be with you and Audrey."

Blue humans

Jimi was helping Audrey change her clothes one day after school. Her skin was becoming so blue. Faster than his was changing.

They went for dinner in the cafeteria. Audrey had pasta with tomato sauce and a side of steamed carrots. Jimi chose the other item on the menu, chick pea stew, which he helped prepare earlier that day. Two glasses of water were dropped off at their table.

"We get water for dinner now?" Jimi asked the server.

"Breakfast *and* dinner," the server said.

"Started today. Didn't you read the memo from Ms. Isenberg?"

"Of course. Must have slipped my mind," Jimi smiled, his teeth showing.

"They give us water during lunch at school now, daddy."

"Oh? When did they start doing that, sweetie?"

"A long time ago … after the big meeting in the square."

"Why didn't you tell me?"

"You never asked."

Shortly after dinner, Jimi was walking with Audrey down the tunnel to the library. He promised Ida he would pick up a book about cooking with fresh herbs, and Audrey was excited about the game night the librarian arranged for the colony's children.

The lighting had recently been set to minimum levels in the tunnels to conserve power. Audrey said she could see "just like it was daytime," but Jimi found it difficult to see very far ahead.

"Look, it's mommy," said Audrey.

Jimi's eyes squinted. He grabbed Audrey's hand to keep her from moving forward.

Up ahead, coming straight at them, was Mother.

"It's her, daddy, it's really mommy. Come on!"

"Stop Audrey."

Jimi could feel dizziness in his head.

"We're going to stay right here, until she passes us. Don't say a word."

"But why?"

"Please, sweetie, just do as I say."

"OK, daddy."

Mother moved slowly, like walking was painful for her. She was much thinner than before. Her clothes looked creased, like she'd been sleeping in them. Her face was ghostly.

Jimi could see Sanchez now, trailing Mother like a guard dog. His skin was much bluer than when Jimi last saw him.

As Mother got close, her eyes locked with Jimi's.

Jimi turned his face away. He tugged Audrey's hand forward and began walking. When they passed Mother, his heart was one beat away from exploding.

"Wait …"

Jimi wanted to keep walking, but his feet stopped. There was an unusual softness to Mother's voice. He and Audrey turned around.

Audrey shook off Jimi's hand and ran to Mother.

Jimi wanted to yell, "Stay away from her!" But his mouth said nothing.

Mother bent over to embrace Audrey, tried to lift the little girl up to her bosom but couldn't, so she dropped to her knees instead. She kissed Audrey repeatedly on the cheek and neck. Audrey held on to her, tighter and tighter.

"Mommy, where have you been?"

"I miss you … both of you … so very much. Come closer, Jimi. *Quickly*. I don't know how much time I have."

Jimi froze.

"It's me, Delia."

Jimi moved up beside them, got on his knees and wrapped his arms around them.

"We've missed you, Delia. So much."

"I want to be with you, Jimi. Audrey, you are so beautiful."

"Tell me you are coming back to us, Delia."

"I'm trying, but it's so hard, Jimi."

"What can I do to help you? What can I do?"

"You need to be patient, Jimi. Mother is getting weaker. I am getting stronger."

Jimi heard a sniffle and turned to look. Sanchez was standing a few feet behind them. Tears trickled down his face.

Delia's eyes started glowing blue.

She stood up and took a step back from Jimi and Audrey.

"Peace be with you, my children."

She turned from them and continued down the tunnel.

Sanchez passed by Jimi and Audrey, his face tilted away from them, as he wiped away his tears.

Jimi and Audrey watched as Mother slowly walked down the tunnel, Sanchez at her heels.

Audrey wrapped her little arms around Jimi's neck and put her head against him. He could feel her eyes dropping tears on his skin.

Jimi stood up and placed Audrey back on the ground. He reached down to wipe the tears from her face. He looked at his fingers as he went to dry them on his pants. Audrey's tears were as blue as the color of her skin.

"Why are you doing this to us, Mother? Why?" Jimi cried.

Mother stopped and turned slowly to face them.

"It was necessary, my child."

"But why are you changing us? What did we do wrong?"

Mother cast her eyes to the ground. When she looked up again, she said: "We all get … what we deserve."

Mother rounded a bend in the tunnel and disappeared from view.